A Less Convenient Path

CONVENIENT RISK SERIES, BOOK 3

SARA R. TURNQUIST

MOUNTAIN
SUMMIT PRESS

If you would like to stay up-to-date on this and other series from Sara and receive a free ebook, sign up for her newsletter:

https://saraturnquist.com/list

*For Mary...
a friend who keeps me honest on my path.*

CHAPTER 1

Lost

Mariena Gu Achi gazed at the sun descending to the point where the sky met land. The purples, pinks, and orange filled her vision. It stole her breath. And firmed its claim on her heart.

Still, a sickness settled in her midsection. How would they ever make it?

Her brother stirred beside her. So young. So trusting.

He relied on her. Needed her to find a way. But that didn't mean she could.

Her heart weighed heavy, its movements becoming laborious.

The chance of her and her brother being captured by Apache and sold into slavery...or worse...lay as a yoke across her shoulders.

That was if a coyote didn't find them first.

How would she manage? It was simply too far. And everything stood against her. She bit her lip. Perhaps the pain would stave off the tears threatening to fall.

Nisto didn't need that.

No, he couldn't know that she was lost.

That *they* were lost. And hopeless.

Even if he tried, Cutie could no longer hear the sound of cattle. Noises that were the staple of his typical day would not fill this one. And he so needed a break from the drudgery of normalcy.

Oh, it wasn't that he didn't love his life on the ranch. He had become...accustomed to it. Comfortable with it. Where else would he want to be?

But today was his.

More often than not, he allowed himself to be drawn into Wharton City in his off time. But lately, he found solace in the dusty trails that lay far from the reaches of the city. Or the ranch.

Unexplored.

Untried.

Not a soul for miles.

He pushed his painted horse harder, faster. Striving for that peace he never seemed able to quite reach.

Hadn't Brandon started to trust him again? While his boss spoke of forgiveness and what that meant, it seemed impossible. Cutie had wronged the man. And the rancher had nearly lost everything: his ranch, his wife...and his very life. All because Cutie got a little restless. A little greedy.

And for what? A handful of crisp bills to gamble away?

His chest ached. He shoved the thoughts to the edge of his consciousness, but they would move no further.

A stream appeared off to the right. The horse needed little prompting to veer that direction. How long had he pressed her?

The animal slowed as they neared the clear flowing water. Still, the thundering of the hoof beats drowned out all other sound.

Even when the mare had all but stopped, just short of the cool water, the pounding remained. Did Cutie's own heart race so wildly?

Sliding from the saddle, he laid a hand to the horse's slick muscled neck. A layer of sweat betrayed just how hard she had worked for him.

Why had he pushed her so? He knew better. It would not be safe to run her like this on the way back. She would not likely survive it.

Clicking his tongue, he pulled gently on the reins and led her the short distance remaining to the stream.

While she drank, he crouched and soaked his bandana. Wiping it across his face, he relished the coolness against his overheated skin. Had he been running from the devil? Or something worse?

He frowned and gazed at the swirling water.

Something...there on the edge of his consciousness, threatened to creep forth. Was this what he worked so hard to elude?

Dare he, in this place, test this thing?

Settling back on his backside, he rested his elbows on his knees and squinted at the great rock formations in the distance—seeming to have been painted unique shades of purples and reds by God's own hand.

God.

Now there was a thought.

God.

Indeed.

He rubbed his face against his shoulder and caught sight of movement further downstream by the water's edge.

What was that?

Perhaps nothing. He focused again on the butte. Still, it nagged on the edge of his awareness. Something *was* there. Or someone. Had he been followed?

He almost laughed. Who would care to? He wasn't important enough.

Glancing to that side, though he kept his head turned forward, he sensed more than saw motion.

He jerked his head toward it.

There. In the brush. Not even a good hiding place.

He rose, keeping an eye on the bush as he did so, and moved his hand to hover over his gun. "Who's there?"

No answer.

He shot a quick glance at his horse. She grazed nearby. Should he walk her over with him?

Backing up, he grabbed for the dangling leather and secured it to a tree branch. Never once taking his eyes off the place where he had noted the movement.

"Nothing? No answer?" He took careful steps forward, a hand on his revolver.

As he came closer, he picked up on more sounds. Small movements. Whispers.

"Show yourself!"

The movements stilled.

His steps arced wide to come alongside the bush. He pulled his gun from its resting place as he came around to the back side of the obstructing bush.

When all was exposed to him, he found two sets of deep brown eyes staring wide at him.

Mariena stared at the revolver pointed at her face. She tightened her lips into a thin line and hardened her jaw.

No fear.

With steady movements, she shifted Nisto until he was behind her. Though it mattered little. If this man wanted to kill them, he would simply shoot her and then Nisto.

Still, she could not help but create a barrier between the weapon, its owner, and her young brother.

The man eyed them. What was he thinking? Why didn't he just do what he intended?

He cocked the gun then lowered it. "What the devil?"

The devil? Did he think she was a devil? Perhaps it was true that the white man thought all her people nothing but savages. And her...a she-devil.

Mariena forced her features to remain neutral. Best not give the man anything else to support his assumptions.

"You are going to get killed all sneaking around behind bushes."

She continued to watch him.

Nisto whimpered, still curled in a ball behind her.

The man ran a hand over his face. "Great. No English."

Dare she? What good would it do for her to expose her language skills? Why shouldn't she?

The best weapons are those kept secret. One of Father's wisdoms.

But this man might have food. Or may even help them. They had evaded death for too long already. They could not elude it much longer.

Not reasonably.

This man had not ended their lives when he'd had the chance. Perhaps he could help. Perhaps he would.

"Ah...just never mind. I'll forget I ever saw ya'." The man waved his hand in their direction and turned toward his horse.

"Mister Sir," she said. The words sounded strange, even to her. Heavily accented by her native tongue. Could he even understand her?

He jerked around, eyes on hers once again. "What?"

She rose with hesitancy.

Nisto put his legs under him and started to lift his body as well.

Shifting, she admonished him in their language and held a hand down. "No! Let me talk to him first."

Nisto stilled and then crouched once more.

"You speak English?"

"Yes." Best to keep her words few. Better he didn't find out how simple and limited her English was. Would it anger him?

"Who are you? Where are you from? What are you doing out here?"

Her head spun with the many words. She worked to decipher his questions. "We are of Tohono O'odnam."

"The Desert Indians."

She nodded.

"I thought what of ya' didn't go to Mexico headed to San Xavier to the Reservation."

A great ache filled her chest. She looked to the ground. It wasn't for him to see.

"So?"

She looked off to the side. "My nation is split, as you say. And my tribe started the trip to Mexico."

"You took a wrong turn." He made a snort-like laugh.

Her eyes jerked up toward his. There was indeed humor on his face. Would she ever smile again? "We were attacked."

His smile fell.

"My brother and I are all that is left of my village."

"I'm sorry."

She folded herself in her arms, shivering despite the warmth of the sun bearing down on them.

"Are you headed for the reservation now?"

Looking down at her arms, she worked to control her features. "We are lost."

"In this wilderness?" His tone betrayed his shock. "Do you realize how dangerous that can...?"

His words trailed off. Why had he not finished his question?

She turned her gaze up toward him once again.

Their eyes met for the briefest moment before he looked away.

And she understood. The man felt sorry for them. Pitied them. Her heart sank. This was far worse than the fear of the gun. The heaviness in the pit of her stomach weighed that of a thousand stones.

Must she appear so helpless?

She closed her eyes. What choice did she have? Without a home, without her parents, her family, her tribe...she *was* helpless.

CHAPTER 2
Known

What was he supposed to do?

Surely no one could expect him to do anything with this young woman and boy.

Was it even appropriate?

Would others think he was taking advantage? What would his boss think? Would Brandon let him bring these two refugees to the ranch? How could he even wonder such a thing? Of course, the man wouldn't want these two left out here.

Would Cutie then be taking advantage of the man's kindness?

But if Cutie didn't help...an animal or another Native tribe would finish them off for certain. And they wouldn't be kind or care what others thought.

He looked once more at the two Tohono O'odham. The girl, maybe five years his junior, watched him with large deep brown eyes. Fathomless. Maybe even a bit hopeful.

But her eyes narrowed. Perhaps she didn't trust him.

There was, then, another barrier to overcome.

The smaller boy huddled near his sister's skirt. What must he have seen? Have endured?

Too much for one so young, certainly. Boys his age should be concerned about what they would catch next time they went fishing. Not how they would survive. Or how they could overcome such hard memories, as he must have.

Cutie glanced in the direction of his horse. How would he get them back to the ranch? That was, *if* he decided to help.

They were miles from any semblance of civilization. And the horse could not bear the weight of all three.

His gaze wandered to the stream.

Dare he leave them behind and seek out help?

Or should they journey back at the pace of a dying snail?

The journey would take days.

He didn't have food.

They had not the hope of shelter.

He would be risking his own neck.

"You will leave us then?" Her voice was not accusing. But gentle. Expecting. Matter-of-fact.

How could she know his thoughts? Was he so transparent?

He pushed out a breath.

She looked away. "We will do what we must."

Raising her arm, she turned her face toward her brother.

He stood beside her and pressed his face into her side.

"And you will do what you must." Her dark eyes fell on his once more.

Cutie found himself unable to look away. Did she somehow bewitch him? A weight fell upon his chest. And the prospect of leaving them out here, alone in the desert, became unthinkable.

Regardless of the challenges.

Regardless of the risk to him.

He would see them to safety.

Letting his hands drop from his hips and fall by his side, he took a few steps toward her.

She pulled back, eyes wide, hugging her brother to herself.

Was she so alarmed? So fearful of him? Even more so than when he had a pistol pointed at her?

He halted and held his empty hands out. "I will not harm you."

Her brows furrowed.

He held a hand forth, waving in the direction of his horse. "Come."

Her expression of confusion deepened.

"We will find a way. Together."

Remaining as she was for several moments, he second-guessed himself. Perhaps his plan was not so simple. Maybe they would not let him assist. If so, could he ride away, knowing their lives were forfeit?

He pushed out a breath. Had he been holding it? He couldn't be so worried, could he?

The young woman continued to watch him. Her arms tightened around her brother. The movement was small, almost imperceptible.

Would she be quicker to trust him if it had just been her? Was she only now hesitant because she felt responsible for her brother's wellbeing?

Did Cutie care enough to convince her?

He let his hand fall then turned and walked toward his horse. But slowly.

"Mister sir!"

He spun.

She seemed to stretch from the waist, leaning forward.

"Yes?" He kept his voice even.

"We need your help. May you help us?"

His eyes held hers. Did she know what she asked of him?

Her gaze softened.

Somehow, he knew she did.

He nodded and extended his hand once more.

This time, the young woman stepped forward, keeping her arms around her brother. She moved toward Cutie. And, as she neared, he led them to where the horse grazed.

The journey ahead would be great. And fraught with unknown danger.

But, with any luck, they would survive to face down the challenges that awaited them in Wharton City.

Mariena distracted herself with the movement of the scenery, as slowly as it moved. The man had insisted she and Nisto ride upon the horse.

Horses made her uneasy. They had too much of their own mind. Stubborn.

Wasn't that how her mother described her?

But this was not the time to dwell on Mother.

She leaned forward and whispered to Nisto in their tongue, "I think this man will keep us safe."

He nodded but remained silent.

Should she expect anything else? He hadn't spoken much since... since the attack. How she wished she could have protected him from the images...from the memories. She could no more erase them from his mind than she could her own.

Best to let the horse's movements keep her wary than to work to fight these demons.

Nisto had always been good with horses. She could rely on that, at least. If the horse got antsy, Nisto knew what to do.

But the man had the reins. Surely, he would not let the horse be out of control.

She had placed much trust in him.

Their very lives.

Hadn't she?

Or were they already dead and he their only hope?

Either way, his fate was now intertwined with theirs.

She opened her mouth to speak, but thought better of it. What was there to say that he would not abhor?

He turned toward her. Had she, in fact, spoken?

"Maybe we switch?" It would not do for her to let him walk the entirety of the distance.

Facing the horizon once more he shook his head, his hat swaying from side to side.

Stubborn man.

Why wouldn't he let her share the burden? Did he intend to walk the whole way back to his ranch? What had he said? Perhaps three days' journey?

What would that do to his body? To his feet!

She would not allow it. Yes, she could be just as hardheaded as he.

Reaching for the nape of the horse's neck, she grabbed for the thick hair there. And pulled.

The animal let out a screech-like sound and halted. But not before Mariena's heart nearly bounded from her chest. Would the horse buck her and Nisto off? Had she made a serious mistake?

Dark blue eyes were on her in a moment. "What the...?"

She slid, somewhat wobblier than she would like, from the mare's back. But even as her feet touched the ground, she wasn't certain they would hold her.

The man was beside her in a moment. "What are you doing?"

Dare she release the stability of the horse? Shifting toward him, she kept one hand on the animal's side. "I walk now. You ride."

He forced a breath through his clenched teeth and muttered a word she did not know. A curse of some sort?

His eyes settled on hers again. They fairly flashed as he spoke. "I won't have it."

"And I will not. You walk for three days. No good."

Placing his hands on his hips, he turned his attention to the horse.

Nisto maneuvered a leg over the horse. Did he intend to drop down as well?

"No," she admonished in their language. "You remain astride."

He stilled and settled his leg back around the horse, ducking his head as if he were being punished.

She hadn't intended to speak to him harshly. Had she? Or was this, too, the effects of the images that haunted him? Her brother, barely seven winters old, had started to withdraw. If only she could help him.

Her lip quivered and she bit it. There was no reason this man needed to see. He might think her weak.

When she looked at him again, she found him staring at her. What had he seen? More than she wanted him to?

His gaze softened and he crossed his arms over his chest. "Only for a little while."

She nodded. So, the man could be reasoned with.

Good.

Perhaps this journey would not be so terrible after all.

Cutie stoked a small fire. They didn't need the warmth, but the rabbit cooking over the flames gave way to rumblings in their bellies. He had not eaten anything that day, save what he'd had for breakfast that morning and the few rations he'd dispersed between them from his pack earlier that day.

The chorus of groans and grumbles from their midsections reminded them what exactly would make this journey difficult.

But he had the pistol.

Though he hadn't had reason to bring extra bullets.

How could he tell the young woman with the dark eyes he only had two bullets remaining? And they were best saved for protection from any wild animals that may come upon them.

He gazed across the lapping light even then; the flickers on her skin highlighted high cheekbones, thin, longer features, and full lips. She was lovely.

But he shouldn't be thinking such thoughts. Their survival was of utmost importance. And here he sat gawking at her. That was almost as bad as...as selling out your friend for thirty pieces of silver.

Oh, that he could take it back.

Looking to the side, he wished away the thoughts, the memories. But they remained. Taunting him.

Her gentle voice drew his attention. She spoke soft words to her brother. Did she soothe him? Tell him a story? Or talk about the strange man attempting to help them?

Perhaps he might ask their names. That would be a good bit of information to have.

He cleared his throat as he reached forward and turned the animal on the spit. "What should I call you?"

Her eyes shot to his. "Call me?"

His face warmed. "Your name? Something other than 'young woman'?"

She gazed into the fire. Did she not remember her name? Or did she not wish him to know it? Was there some mystical belief attached to names in her tribe?

"I am Mariena."

"Mariena," he tried the name. Unfamiliar to his tongue, but it fell smoothly.

"Cutie." He pointed to himself.

"You are cute?" Her brows furrowed. "Small and pretty?"

He was suddenly thankful for the dimness around them. Could she see his face color? Running a hand along the brim of his hat, he tried to think of how to respond. "Cu-tie. It's a nickname. Like what people call me instead of my name."

"Why don't they call you what you are named?"

He licked his lips. "Because I have the same name as my father."

"This is not good?"

"No. It's fine. But it can be confusing."

"Oh."

Silence befell them for several moments. Should he speak? Would she?

"And what is this name no one calls you?"

He hesitated. What was this resistance to share his given name? Embarrassment? Shyness?

She watched him. Waiting.

Sighing, he picked up a stick and poked at the fire. "Charles."

"Ch-ar-le-s." She enunciated each sound.

He smiled despite his discomfort. "Charles."

She tried again. "Charles."

It sounded more like one syllable, made almost music-like with her accent. He liked it. Was that okay?

No. It wasn't.

Rising onto his knees, he checked their dinner. A few more minutes. He sat back on his feet.

"This Nisto." She wrapped an arm around her brother.

"Nisto."

She nodded.

"Does he speak?"

Looking at her brother, her features fell. "Yes. But no."

Cutie's brows furrowed.

She ran a hand through Nisto's hair. "He has not spoken since..." Her words trailed off, and she seemed lost to herself for a moment.

But he could guess where her mind drifted. And where Nisto's went often.

"That is over now. You are safe." What a strange thing to say. They were far from safe. Still, he could not stop the words.

She looked at him. Her eyes glazed with moisture.

Did she trust him? Or had they come with him because he was the only hope they had?

He turned away first. A weight settled in the bottom of his stomach. What a fool he was. There was no way to know what they had been through. And here he dared offer them hollow assurances.

But getting them safely to the ranch was the least he could do.

And of that, he was determined.

CHAPTER 3
Desperate

Two days. They had two days remaining to traverse this wilderness. *If* they managed to survive. Mariena shifted her brother's weight. Nisto had long since fallen asleep against her.

Her lips were dry. What she wouldn't give for a sip of cool water. But she dared not ask. They needed to ration what they had.

And food.

What would they do for food now that anything the man Cutie had was gone?

She glanced at his back. Somehow, she could not make herself associate such a name with this man who risked his life to save them. With a man whose controlled stance and broad shoulders betrayed a muscled physique that was anything but diminutive. No, to her, he would be Charles.

Would he permit such familiarity? She had only time to discover if this allowance would be made.

Nisto groaned.

Did he wake? Could she make him more comfortable and keep him at rest?

She looked this way and that. And frowned. There were precious few possibilities atop the mount.

Cutie turned. His warm eyes were on her.

She offered the best shrug she could manage.

He frowned.

Because he was upset? Or because he regretted their situation?

Shifting to guide the horse toward one of the grand desert structures, he pressed on.

Mariena sighed. *Must it be this way?* Always a reason for him to regret she and Nisto traveled alongside?

When they neared a sparse piece of shade, Cutie turned and reached out his arms.

Did he want her to pass Nisto to him?

Could she? Her heartbeat quickened. Dare she trust her brother into this man's care? Even for a moment? Hadn't she promised her mother she would look after Nisto? And now, that was all the more imperative...

But this man had offered salvation when none existed.

That did not mean trust had been secured.

Cutie pushed out a breath. Loudly. "Pass me the boy."

She put a hand to Nisto's cheek and pressed him closer. What if Cutie dropped him? Saw him injured? What if he could not, after all, be trusted?

"It is no need. I can..." She moved to dismount.

Cutie's hands landed on her legs. "Do not. You'll both end up in the dirt. Or break a bone. Then where would we be?"

Her gaze fell upon his hand, solid on her thigh, though separated by her skirts. Was it possible for her to be heated by his touch? What was this?

She looked to his gaze. Though confusion passed through the clouded blue eyes, they were clear and seemed honest enough. Why should she suspect him still? Could he not have brought harm upon them any number of times had he wished it?

Fighting a hesitation and the growing ache in her chest, she moved Nisto away from herself and leaned him toward Cutie's outstretched hands.

The man needed no further prompting. He took hold of her brother, sweeping him from her grasp with ease.

With no further regard for her, Cutie carried Nisto to the shaded piece of ground. Then, leaning his back against the rock wall of the structure, Cutie slid down until he sat upon the earth, still cradling a sleeping Nisto.

All of this took place without stirring her brother. How was that possible?

Cutie's gaze met hers once more. His brows furrowed. He need not ask the question in his mind. It seemed loud enough in his features.

Would she not join him?

Would she?

She looked at the horizon...the journey ahead. How many steps yet to cover? Still, Cutie took time that Nisto might have a rest. She glanced back at the cowboy holding her young brother. A gentle warmth poured through her chest. A pleasant warmth. It soothed the ache created from Nisto's absence from her arms.

Cutie smiled.

At her.

Was she...staring?

She was.

Jerking her head to avert her gaze, she hoped he did not see her face heat. She turned her body away from Cutie and wondered at her dismount. Cutie had assisted her each time she had gotten off the animal. And the few times she had dared ride among her people, someone assisted her down as well.

How would she do this? Did she use the thing her foot was in? The stirrup? Would that aid her enough? Or could she just slide off?

Swinging her leg over the pommel, she began to feel uneasy. The world shifted. Was the horse moving? Or was it in her head?

She gripped the saddle and pressed her weight forward, preparing to slide off.

The mare sidestepped.

And Mariena lost her already precarious balance, pitching to the ground.

The earth came up to meet her. Hard. Fighting the pain coursing through her body, she opened her eyes, but she couldn't see. Her eyes itched and burned. And she couldn't pull in air. What was this?

Rolling to her back, she fought for a breath, clawing at the front of her dress. If she loosened it, perhaps she would find relief.

Strong hands pulled her upright and then to her feet.

She coughed.

Air!

Could she stand? Her legs were as soft pine. They would not hold her.

An arm passed below her knees and another behind her back.

Another word was muttered that she did not know.

She opened her eyes again. The stinging remained, but light now made blurred shapes of the things around her.

A solid, rather warm body pressed against her. Moving forward. Did he carry her?

Then she was on the ground again, a cool surface at her back.

"Mariena?" The gentle voice was harried. Concerned perhaps?

Cutie's figure loomed before her, shadowed by the sunlight behind him.

"Y-yes?" Her voice seemed too raspy. She continued to drag in air.

"Are you crazy or something?" His words were quick and his tone harsh.

"What?" Everything around her began to take a more defined shape. Her vision cleared. But he wasn't making sense.

"You could have gotten yourself killed!" Though his voice was forceful, there was something more. Something exasperated. Did he care?

"I...I just..."

"I know what you 'just.' But you didn't."

She dropped her head. What was the point? Her lungs burned from effort.

He mumbled something then lifted his head as hers came up. And their eyes met.

"Are you injured?" His hands were on her ankles. Massaging.

What was he doing? Should she enjoy it so much? A pleasant sensation rushed from the place where his hands kneaded and filled her all the way up her limbs.

No. This wasn't right. He was...

And she was...

His hands moved up to her calves.

She struck him.

"Whoa." He put a hand out. "I'm trying to decide if you broke anything."

"I think you must keep your hands away." Could he not see? Her face warmed. Surely it had color to it. She ducked her head.

"Hey," he softened his voice. "I...I'm not one of those guys that..." His words became fractured. Was he so flustered?

"Please," she said with more force than she'd intended. "I will check."

He nodded and sat back on his heels.

She leaned forward and turned her feet this way and that. Then felt along the length of her legs. Bending them up at the knee, she tested its veracity. And let out a yelp.

"Your knee?" A warm hand landed on her arm.

She nodded.

"May I help?"

Opening an eye, she caught his kind gaze and nodded.

His hands surrounded her knees and eased them back to the ground. He rubbed the sides of first the left then the right knee.

When he put pressure to the sides of the right knee, she cried out again.

He grimaced. "I'm sorry."

She bit her lip and nodded. Must she be such a coward? So... distressed? But as she found the courage to look at him again, she did not find pity in his eyes, only concern. And perhaps regret.

Yet not as she anticipated.

He seemed angry with himself. Why?

She didn't have time to think on it before his blue eyes locked on hers once more. How was it possible for them to be so deep? And still so clear?

"I do not think it is broken."

Glancing at his hand still on her knee, she realized his touch remained.

He jerked away. Had he just noticed, too?

"It is not a good idea for you to bear weight on it. Even if you can."

So she would ride and he walk the remainder of the journey? No. It could not be so. She would not have it.

"I can..." she started in protest.

He leaned forward.

She silenced. Her breaths came in raggedly. The scent of him, the nearness of him...it made her head swim.

His eyes moved over her features. What did he search for? Did he mean to intimidate her? Or merely speak in reprimand? Had he lost all words as she had? Did he feel what she did?

Azure pools found rest on her lips.

She froze, unable even to breathe.

A groan nearby drew her attention.

Nisto.

Looking at him, she watched as he stirred. Would he wake? She then shifted her gaze back to Cutie.

He blinked and leaned away, looking off to the side. What was he thinking?

What had *she* been thinking?

She had allowed her mind to venture somewhere she could not follow.

Cutie had to get his head in the right place. What was he thinking?

Yesterday had been difficult enough—holding her so close, taking in the scent of her hair, the feel of her body...and the way his concern for her had filled him. It wasn't right.

He couldn't take advantage of this young woman. And he wouldn't. He refused to.

They were maybe a day shy of Brandon's ranch, and he didn't need to hear their bellies grumbling nor feel the ache in his own to know food had become imperative.

What would he do? Dare he trade their last couple of bullets—the only protection they had left—to hunt for food?

If he didn't, was there any other way?

He wasn't useless in the wilderness, but he'd become so reliant on his pistol, he'd not put his mind to capturing game in many years. Would his boyhood methods work?

Perhaps he should give them a try.

Turning from his solace, he moved back toward where he had left Mariena, her brother, and the horse. How much longer should he prolong his respite? Dare he push it further? Would it seem reasonable?

His turn to relieve himself had probably pressed the boundaries of believability at this point. Yes, he'd best make his way back.

To her.

And his confusing feelings.

Then he would either find a way to capture food or face them with his shortcomings.

He strode on feet that were far too sore. The reality of an all day, non-stop walk wore on him. And his steps showed it. But he much preferred it to risking Mariena's injury on foot.

Allowing his footfalls to be as light and slow as possible, he approached the place where he had left the others.

Open space greeted him.

Where were they? Had something happened?

His pulse raced. What could have become of them?

Did Mariena leave him behind?

He rejected the thought as it entered his mind. It would not take. While he didn't know her well, something within him would not accept malfeasance from her.

Then what?

Should he...?

Thud.

A soft clap pulled at him. It could be any number of things. But it was his best lead.

Lengthening his stride, he pushed past the ache and toward the sound. Not too far away, he spotted a rock, crushing an animal, with disturbed dirt around it. And his horse's lead protruded from underneath the stone.

His gaze followed the length of the rope and there, behind some shrubbery, stood a stoic Mariena, and Nisto with his arms crossed and a grin across his features.

Looking at the rock-trap and then at Mariena, Cutie wondered as he watched a smile slowly spread on her face as well.

How did she manage? What did she know of trapping animals? How had she come up with a dead fall having so little at her disposal? There was certainly more to her than one could find on the surface.

Her teeth now shown. She was breathtaking.

"Dinner!" she announced.

He nodded as he came closer. Lifting the stone, he noted the rather large rabbit that had come upon their trap. A prize, no doubt.

As he looked toward Mariena once more, she leaned on her brother's shoulder, using him as a crutch on the side of her weak knee, and came toward Cutie.

His words failed. How did this keep happening to him? What was it about her? His pulse, which had calmed, sped again.

He forced his attention to the rabbit. These moments could not continue. It was his duty to see these two to the reservation. And that's what he would do.

Anything else would be selfish.

And he would not spoil her for momentary enjoyment on his part.

He would not.

Mariena reached for her mother. "No! I can't leave you!"

"Go! Take your brother and go!"

She sniffled, gripping Nisto's hand.

"It's your only chance. Our peoples' legacy...your father and my legacy *must* live on in you." Mama touched Mariena's cheek for a moment then released her and pushed Mariena toward the back of the tent. "Now, go! They are near."

"Come with us," Mariena pled, looking back as she pressed Nisto under the flap.

"I must give you time to escape. It is the only way." Mama's eyes were full and so deep.

Mariena did not argue further. But she wanted to etch Mama into her memory. Forever. To remember her features, her love, her sacrifice.

So, she hesitated. For a moment.

Strange arms came around Mama, a large knife in hand...

No!

Mariena jerked upright. The night sky greeted her. A gentle warmth at her side.

Nisto.

He slept beside her.

Not far off, a small fire continued to burn.

She pulled her knees toward her face, wrapping her arms around them. What had she seen? Had it been only a dream?

Yes, her true memory had ended when Mama bade them go. She told them she must stay and give them time, a chance. Then Mariena had held back her tears and slipped under the flap after Nisto.

What if she *had* lingered for a few moments more? Would she have seen...?

It was too much.

Despite the warmth surrounding her, she shivered.

A hand pressed her shoulder.

The Apache!

She jerked away.

But as she turned toward the intrusion, blue eyes met hers. Concern naked in them.

And though her heart still tumbled within her chest in preparation to run for her life, she exhaled and relaxed within herself. She was safe.

Cutie withdrew his hand. "Are you all right?"

She nodded, eyes wide, not able to tear her gaze away from his.

"Bad dream?"

She ran a shaking hand over her face and through her hair. "Something as such."

"Memory?" He settled on the ground beside her. His voice was soft and so tender. It caressed her worn senses.

She didn't answer. But she didn't have to. He knew. Somehow.

Hugging her knees, she let the evening breeze wash over her and allowed herself this moment with his kindnesses so she didn't feel alone. Though it would only be for a time.

Her gaze still rested in his.

But he didn't seem to mind.

A few breaths later, his features hardened. Was he angry? She couldn't bear that.

He swallowed and grasped his fist in his other hand. "I hate what happened to you."

Could it be? His anger was for the Apache and not the burden she and Nisto heaped upon him?

Her eyes watered.

He muttered and looked off into the distance.

Oh, how she wished he hadn't broken eye contact. That had grounded her. Tears stung her eyes as they cut across her face.

Why did she let his presence draw her in so? It was dangerous. She didn't have to lean into it so much.

His gaze found hers again. And his blue eyes widened as they set upon her. The muscles in his jaw clenched. More anger for the Apache?

Her tears would serve no one. She wiped at them and worked to even her breathing. When she glanced at him again, she found his gaze was still upon her.

"It does no matter." She attempted a smile. Did it appear as awkward as it felt on her lips?

His brows furrowed.

Pulling her braid over her shoulder, she fingered the plaited hair. How could she change the subject? There was little need in so much darkness.

"Let us not speak so sad." Her smile became more genuine. "What of you? Rancher?"

One eyebrow lifted. Was he skeptical of her motives? He need not be. She only wished to think on more pleasant things. Who wanted to dwell on grief?

"I am a ranch hand, that's true." He spoke slowly, as if choosing his words with care.

"And will you dream to have a ranch one day?"

He shrugged, his gaze shifting to the fire.

"No?" Why would he not want his own ranch? "Is not this what all ranch hands want? Work for?"

"Maybe."

She held her thoughts and watched him. The dancing flames flickered in his pupils.

"Maybe that's not for me."

"Hmmm..."

That pulled his eyes back to her. A question beckoned on his features.

"I thought...all ranch hands same." Her lips would not lift. There was more behind her words. Something she had come to believe differently about Cutie. "To Indians."

His eyes darkened. "Not me. I'm not that way."

She nodded. "This...I see."

His gaze entranced her. Could she pull away? If she wanted to? For in that moment, she did not.

At length, he stood, breaking their contact once more. "I think you should get some sleep."

He moved to the other side of the fire as she stretched her legs out beside Nisto. But there was one thing she needed to ask.

"Mister sir...?"

He paused, turning, giving her his attention once more. "Please, call me Cutie."

She offered a half-smile. "I might ask...if you are okay...could I call you Charles?"

It seemed as if he became a statue. He stopped breathing even as far as she could discern.

Then his throat bobbed as he swallowed.

Was her request a step too far? Too much?

After several moments, he spoke. His voice almost uncertain. "My name...is Cutie." He gave her his back.

At least he couldn't see the fresh hurt.

Cutie settled himself across the fire from Mariena's reclined form.

Why had she asked that?

And why had he responded so harshly?

She hadn't deserved such. But he couldn't let her do that. No. That would be too far. He had already let her in too much.

They would be at the ranch by midday tomorrow. That would provide the space they needed. If his words hadn't.

Perhaps it wasn't so bad that he had spoken thusly. Maybe she should be put off. Would that create the much-needed distance between them?

Yes, it was for the best.

He allowed himself a moment to look across their small camp to where she now lay.

She had turned her back to him. Her long dark hair, much loosened by the winds that day, fell and pooled behind her. Why hadn't she bothered to tighten her braid? Was she so weary? So worn that even that task seemed overwhelming?

But the dark river that flowed down her shoulders captivated him. What would it be like to dip his fingers into its depths? Was it as smooth as it appeared?

She shook—a slight tremble, almost imperceptible.

Why? Because of his words?

His fingers ached. He stretched them out from the fists they had formed. Was he truly so disturbed by her emotion? Or by his own?

Leaning his head back, he looked toward the night sky. If only he could pray. If only God would hear. Then perhaps he could ask for guidance. For wisdom. For how to still his thundering heart.

But God would not hear him. Not after all he had done.

A burning anger filled him.

If he lived a million lifetimes, he could not pay the penance for his actions. He was doomed, hopeless.

His throat burned.

No.

There was no allowance for self-pity.

He had earned his place. Now he must accept it.

Never could he measure up. And never would he deserve the unspoiled innocence of someone who deserved every good thing in this world.

Never.

Mariena prayed they would arrive soon. The sun beat down upon them and the heat threatened to choke them, but that wasn't what drove her trepidation. Cutie couldn't walk much farther. And he would collapse before admitting it.

Her words asserting that she was well enough to walk with Nisto's assistance had fallen on deaf ears. As had her insistence that the horse might be able to bear the three of them.

Stubborn man! Had he no care for himself? Why would he punish himself so?

He looked back at her. Had he sensed her thoughts?

She met his gaze. Her heart pounded with guilt, and every part of her wanted to avert her eyes, lest he see more than she wanted him to.

"It is not far now." Sweat beaded his forehead, and his skin had reddened.

She frowned.

But he had turned away.

Had he seen her displeasure?

As she watched the horizon, she spotted a stream.

"Cutie!" She raised an arm in that direction and turned toward him. A stream! It would mean refreshment. For all of them.

He didn't respond, but continued to place one foot in front of the other.

Did he not hear her?

"Cutie." She spoke louder.

No reaction.

His shoulders heaved. How had she not seen this before?

She looked closer...his steps were no longer even.

"Cutie!" she screamed.

Still no acknowledgement.

His breathing had become so hard she could hear each inhale and exhale from her position above him.

Had he been overcome with the heat? This had happened to others in her tribe—boys playing too long in the sun without water. Her mother had warned her and Nisto about it.

But what could she do?

Cutie kept moving forward, though much slower. He drew the horse along with him.

She couldn't reach Cutie from atop the saddle. Might she risk dismounting? That hadn't gone so well before. Dare she attempt it again? If she didn't...and Cutie continued...

He may be too far into danger as it was.

"Nisto, hold tight," she commanded, pressing his hands to the pommel.

He whimpered, lifting his hands and reaching for her.

"No! You must hold here. Tight!" She put his hands to the pommel again.

He nodded.

She jerked on the horse's mane. Hard.

The horse stepped back, rearing slightly.

Mariena held firmly to Nisto. But the mare's upset was short lived. The horse calmed in a matter of moments.

Cutie paused, raising a hand to the horse, blindly reaching. Could he not see the large animal? He seemed disoriented.

Mariena acted as quickly as she could. Securing her uninjured leg in the stirrup, she brought her other leg around. Now she sat sideways on the horse. With as much care as possible, she lowered herself.

She fell to the ground. Her knee screamed at her, but the fall was not as damaging as it had been before.

Rising, she hobbled toward Cutie. She reached, grasping for his arm, soon making contact. His skin burned through the thin fabric of his shirt.

"Cutie!"

He turned toward her. His features were contorted, brows furrowed. Was he as confused as he looked?

How could she get him to the stream?

She grabbed the reins with the hand of her injured side, allowing the horse to support her weight. Then, pulling Cutie closer to her side, she hooked his arm.

And they began the arduous walk to the stream.

Every step ached and burned.

Every step was a victory.

And with every step, Cutie's breathing became more ragged. His whole body seemed to be on fire.

Some several feet short of the stream, he stumbled.

God, no. Help us.

She gritted her teeth—if only she were capable of dragging him.

And, moments later, when Cutie collapsed, he pulled her down with him.

Furious tears stung her eyes as she disentangled her limbs from his.

She rolled him to his back.

His eyes were closed, and he struggled for breath.

"Cutie!" Her hands moved over his arms, his chest. Could she wake him? Even as she tried, she knew she couldn't. This was not normal sleep.

He was dying.

"Cutie, no!"

She looked toward the stream. What could she do? Her mind was blank! What would her mother do? What had she seen her mother do?

Putting a hand to his head, she leaned over him. "I'm sorry, Cutie."

He was impossibly hot.

Cool him down.

She needed to cool him down. How was that possible?

Think, Mariena, think! Stop feeling so sorry for yourself and think!

Her gaze moved to the stream again. She tore at the hem of her skirt and rushed to the gently flowing water as much as she could while limping.

She dove her hands into its coolness with the ripped off cloth in hand. Then she rushed back to Cutie, as fast as her injured knee would allow. Leaning over him once more, she pressed the cool linen to his face, to what area of his chest she could reach, and then to his face again.

It would help. Some.

Maybe.

But he needed real help. And fast.

How?

She looked at the horse. Surely the animal knew the way to the ranch. If she trusted it. But dare she leave him alone out here? Vulnerable? He needed the cloth to be cooled again and put to his skin. Over and over.

Her gaze fell on Nisto.

No.

She could not leave him. It would be too risky. What defense would he have against a wild animal? Or an evil man?

She couldn't.

Her head dropped.

But it was the only way to save Cutie. The man who had risked everything to save them.

Could she watch him die? Would she be able to bear it? She ran a hand over his forehead and into the dark blond waves atop his head.

No. She couldn't.

She wouldn't.

"Don't worry," she whispered, too softly for Nisto to hear. "I won't let you go."

Standing, she moved to Nisto with the cloth. There was a firmness in her spirit she wasn't certain she had known before. It was good. For she had to assure Nisto all would be well.

She came to the horse and lifted her arms.

Nisto slid into them.

"I need you to be a strong brave for me."

Nisto nodded.

"You must take this cloth to the stream, dip it into the water, then bring it to Cutie and cool his face. And do it again. Over and over until I return."

His eyes widened.

"I must go for help. If I do not, Cutie will die. It is the only way."

Nisto's gaze wandered over her features for a moment. Then he nodded.

She drew him to herself, embracing her little brother. "I will be back soon. I promise."

He tightened his hold on her for a moment and then let go.

She released him.

Without anything further, he took the cloth and moved off to the stream.

Tempted to watch him, she forced herself to work her way onto the horse—not the easiest task she had undertaken, but not as difficult had she not been doing so for the last three days. With one more long look at the two she was leaving behind—the one who was cemented in her heart and the one who had found his way in somehow, she urged the horse forward.

Cutie opened his eyes to the sound of his name. Was it Mariena? Did she need him? Had he fallen asleep and left her in danger?

He struggled toward full consciousness. But his thoughts, his brain, his body, were all slow to respond. Mucking sluggishly toward the only pinprick of light in his awareness, he rose from the darkness.

"He's coming around."

Who was that? The voice sounded deeper, masculine. What had happened to Mariena? Had they been captured? He fought for the light, approaching it with painstaking slowness.

"Cutie?" Another male voice. It seemed familiar.

But still it was not Mariena.

"Hold on there, pal. All is well," the voice soothed.

Hands clamped onto his arms, stilling him. Had his body been moving?

The light seemed only somewhat closer, but still too far away. Would he ever reach it? If he did, would she be on the other side? Or had he failed her?

Coolness pressed against his skin. The sensation was sharp. It pushed his stagnant awareness, thrusting it toward the brightness.

His eyes opened.

Two figures were silhouetted over him, their outlines blurred. Were they friend or foe? How did they know his name?

He jerked from the hands on him, but others joined in securing him.

"You are safe," one of the figures said.

Where was he? His surroundings were dim, the room shadowed. Light peeked through curtains, which covered a window.

As he continued to blink, his vision began to clear. The men above him became clearer and the room's structure and holdings were more evident. He knew this place.

And these men. Their voices were familiar.

One of them released him and stepped to the head of the bed. The man's features took form—Brandon Miller.

Cutie let out a breath. He *was* safe.

But what had happened to him? To them? To Mariena? Where was she?

"Mariena...?" Cutie tried to sit up.

Brandon held up a hand, pressing Cutie back down onto the bed. "Yes, you are concerned about the woman. I understand. Don't be. She is well. Safe."

Cutie furrowed his brows. Was she? He wanted to see her. To see for himself that she and Nisto were okay. Only that might slow the pounding in his chest.

But as he looked at his boss's face, the calm he found there helped him relax. He could trust Brandon. More than anyone else in the world. Still, he could not help his questions. "Where...?"

Brandon's mouth spread into a smile. "She is with Amanda. If we're not careful, my wife will have drawn up plans to build onto the homestead in the next hour."

Cutie caught Brandon's only half joking sentiment, but he did not let that alter his stern expression. He was still disturbed, needing to confirm Mariena's wellbeing. And bothered by the reality of that need within him.

Warring emotions crashed within him. His heart ached all the more for what he could not explain. Dare he give words to it?

"We almost lost you." Brandon leaned back, nodding to the other man.

The only hands that remained on Cutie's arms vanished. Cutie focused on that figure. Could it be...Dan?

"You had us worried." Dan met Cutie's gaze.

Cutie swallowed, hard. Forcing words out that did not speak of Mariena, he said, "What happened?"

"Heat stroke." Brandon folded his arms in front of his chest. "Pretty bad, too."

"Heat stroke?" Was his voice as raspy as it sounded to him?

"I can't imagine how far you walked. If it hadn't been for that young woman riding like the devil to find help...well, I don't think you'd have had a chance."

"Mariena? She...she rode to find help?" It wasn't possible. She was too afraid of the horse to...

"Oh, yes. It was near impossible to get her off that horse." Brandon looked at Dan, who nodded along.

Had she left him out in the desert alone? Weak. Dying. Perhaps she took the chance to save herself and her brother. That she came upon Brandon's ranch was lucky for Cutie. Would she have kept riding otherwise?

But there was something else nagging at him. Did he dream it? Words spoken softly to him in his daze...her words. Yes, they must have been nothing more than wishful thinking. Still...

Knock, knock, knock.

Cutie turned his head toward the door.

Brandon called out, "Who goes?"

Dan stepped to the latch.

"Someone who is rather desperate to see Cutie." It was Amanda's voice. Was Samuel wishing to see him?

He looked down. They had opened his shirt and bared his chest, perhaps to cool him. Every part of his upper body was soaked—his hair, his skin, even his shirt. From perspiration? Or from being cooled? It mattered not.

Brandon looked to him.

What did it matter if Amanda or Samuel saw him like this?

He nodded.

Dan started to open the door.

Cutie worked to sit up and scoot back so that he leaned against the headboard.

As he did so, the door whacked the wall.

Amanda called out, "It is all right, don't be so hasty…"

Jerking his attention toward the doorway once again, Cutie found his eyes caught on Mariena's.

Hers were red-rimmed and puffy. Over him? Or for her situation?

She stood just inside the room, next to a towering Dan, eyes fixed.

His pulse thundered, and his breathing quickened. He longed to reach for her and assure himself that she was indeed unharmed.

Then he remembered. She left him. For her own salvation.

He averted his gaze and closed his eyes. But could he honestly blame her?

Still, he could not deny this thing inside him, this heat when she was near. Did she feel it, too?

She took a step closer. "I am here."

His brows furrowed.

"You called. I am here."

He could not pull his gaze from hers now. "I…what?"

"For me." She dropped to her knees by the bed, grimacing.

Why? *Her wounded knee!* Had she been bandaged? There wasn't time to think on it before she touched his hand and continued, "You called for me."

Did he? In his care for her as he sought consciousness…did he call for her?

He lifted a hand to her face but dropped it almost as soon as the thought entered his head. With her so near, he became all too aware that his shirt was open and his chest uncovered. Not only did she see what she should not, she could also see his heavy breathing, which he wished she did not.

But her eyes were set on his.

He was elated. And saddened. At the same time.

She should not...

He could not...

"I...am well," he managed. "And relieved to see that you are also."

She dipped her head slightly.

"But I should rest now." He looked to Brandon. Would his boss save him? Save Mariena's innocent eyes?

"Yes. Cutie has been through much. He needs his rest." Brandon stepped alongside Cutie, attempting to insert himself between Mariena and the bed.

Mariena's features fell, but she allowed Amanda to help her rise.

Dan stepped forward and took her arm, helping her hobble out of the room.

Something deep down heated in Cutie. He did not like the way Dan touched Mariena's arm. Or how he looked at her while offering his assistance. Cutie shook his head. There was nothing untoward in Dan's manner.

Mariena looked over her shoulder once more before she and Dan were out of sight.

It eased the fire in Cutie's belly.

Brandon joined Amanda by the door. "You are much too spent for worry. Just rest and know that Mariena and Nisto are safe with us...for now."

Cutie nodded. "Thank you."

Brandon smiled and, putting a hand on the small of Amanda's back, led her from the room before securing the door behind them.

For now? Did Brandon imply that Mariena and Nisto must eventually go elsewhere? But this, Cutie already knew. It was best, after all.

For everyone concerned.

"This will be your room for now." Amanda opened a nondescript door in the hall.

But Mariena didn't take much notice. Her heart longed for the room a bit further down. The room where Cutie lay.

It was for naught. He had made it clear he would rather rest.

Turning her focus to the room before her, she forced a smile to her lips.

Amanda remained at the doorway, her arm outstretched. Was she waiting for Mariena to enter?

But should she? Would that be rude? Did Amanda only want for Mariena to gather her bearings before being led in?

Mariena had not spent much time around the white man. She did not know, much less understand, their customs. Not enough to navigate even the simplest of things. Such as this.

Amanda jerked her head toward the interior.

Was that a sign Mariena must enter? She swallowed and took tentative steps forward, careful to glance in Amanda's direction often should one of her movements cause ire in the woman.

Amanda seemed pleased as Mariena entered the fine accommodations.

Mariena stopped just inside. There was nothing wrong with the space. In fact, it was more than she could hope for. Better even than what she would have thought to have. Her people lived in makeshift structures in the desert. A permanent building with a bed, pillows, and linens...it was a luxury.

Was it too much?

Amanda moved past her. "Will this be all right?"

Had the woman misread her? Or did Mariena's expression speak of displeasure? "I-it is most wonderful." Though she tried not to trip over her words, it was difficult.

Amanda, now standing in the middle of the fine room, faced Mariena and smiled. Her whole being warmed.

Mariena could not help but like her. Was the woman as trustworthy as she seemed? Would this Amanda see to Mariena and Nisto's betterment or would they find nothing but disappointment from these Millers?

Cutie trusted them. But was that enough? Mariena's gaze shifted to the window and the field beyond. Cattle moved about in the distance.

Cutie...

He appeared well enough. Would he recover completely? Return to his life here and forget about her?

Her chest ached. What was this? Did she think he would take on their plight beyond getting them to safety? She was a fool.

There could never be more. He was a ranch hand. His future lay here. And she...was destined to confinement on a reservation somewhere. To live and die at the whim of those who commanded the army.

"Mariena?"

A hand touched her arm.

She jerked toward the voice.

Amanda now stood beside her. The woman's features had contorted. Was she as concerned as she seemed?

Mariena brushed at a tickle below her eye. Moisture.

Had she been moved to tears by her thoughts? Nonsense. There was no real benefit in her sadness. It would be what it was. She could do nothing to stop it. Or escape it. Tears would not serve her.

Looking to Amanda, she took hold of the swirling emotion within her and pressed it down. "Excuses, please. I am well. Only tired."

Amanda's brow creased. Did she doubt Mariena's words? However, she did not give words to it. "It will be an hour before dinner. Please, do rest. You've earned it." Her smile returned.

Was she as genuine as she seemed? Or was Mariena just blindly hopeful?

Amanda squeezed Mariena's arm with gentle pressure and moved past her to the door.

Mariena let her eyes wander back to the window.

"Oh, Mariena?" Amanda said from behind her.

Mariena turned and looked over her shoulder.

"You are certainly desperate for clean clothes. I'll lay out one of my dresses. Then we can launder your garments if you'd like."

Mariena nodded. It was a kind gesture.

Amanda jerked her head down once and slipped through the door, closing it behind herself.

And Mariena was left to her solitude. As much as she longed to fold within herself, she focused on her surroundings. The outside world did not hold much interest, but it offered reprieve from her swirling thoughts.

The bed had been dressed comfortably. Marina stepped closer, running a hand over the top quilt. Soft fabric called for her to test its folds.

She looked down at her dress. Amanda had been right. The cloth had collected much of the wilderness on their journey. As she examined the entirety of her skirt, she spotted not only bits of earth, but also streaks of blood.

Closing her eyes, she wished she could shut her mind against the memories.

Yes, she was weary.

Of the physical strains of the last few days.

Of the fight within her to forget.

Of the worry for Nisto.

Of her growing regard for Cutie.

Of all of it.

This time, when tears rolled down her cheeks, she did not regret them or try to stop them. She fell upon the bed and clutched the lone pillow to her chest.

Would her life ever be okay again?

His vision seemed rather hazy when he opened his eyes. But Cutie's world took shape and form in short order. The room was dim but for the sun coming in through the dark curtains over the window. They didn't do much to staunch the bright light.

Yet it seemed less bright than when he was awake before. Was the sun setting? Had they let him sleep through dinner?

He groaned.

Why should that bother him? It wasn't like he had any driving need to be there. Still, he couldn't stop the regret that ebbed through him. What caused it?

But he knew. He just wouldn't admit it.

He missed the opportunity to see Mariena. To watch her across the table, without pretense or a reason to be near her.

Yes, arranging to have time with her would be more difficult now if he didn't want to admit to the others...and to himself...that there was more to it than concern for her safety.

And he could not make himself do that. It wouldn't be right.

Agh...this thinking would get him nowhere.

Now, in the dimness of the room, without onlookers, he could test the limits of his body. He flexed his muscles. First his hands and arms, raising his fists into the air over his head. Seemed fine. No pain. No resistance.

Further down his body, he moved his torso and lower limbs as he gained confidence that he was, indeed, well and fully capable.

He tightened his abdominal muscles and pushed up with his arms, rising into a sitting position on the edge of the bed. Then turning, he let his legs fall over the side, his feet meeting the floor.

Opening and closing his fists, he relished the strength he still had in his body. Had he truly been as close to death as Brandon said? It was difficult to believe.

The door creaked.

A slender line of light appeared before a silhouette cast a shadow into the room.

"Cutie?"

Brandon? Had his boss come to check on him?

The door opened wider. "Glad to see you're up."

Cutie offered him a half-smile. "It's good to be moving around."

"I brought you some fresh clothes."

Cutie looked down. His had taken a beating on the trail.

Brandon stepped into the room and set trousers and a shirt on the bed. "But only when you're ready."

"I imagine Cook would prefer I change before dinner. Unless y'all ate already?" Cutie began working his already unbuttoned shirt off.

He couldn't see Brandon's features well, but he heard an intake of breath.

"Dinner will be soon. Wouldn't you rather someone bring you a plate?"

Cutie paused. That would make more sense. But his desire to see Mariena tugged at him. Would it be obvious if he didn't take Brandon's advice? Did he care?

"I think I'm all right. I'd like to join everyone."

Brandon shrugged. "If you're sure you feel up to it."

"I do, boss." Cutie finished pulling his arms out of his sleeves.

"I'll let you get to it, then." Brandon nodded. "Dinner'll be on the table in about fifteen minutes. And I don't have to tell you how Cook feels about late-comers."

Cutie laughed in spite of himself. "No, you don't."

Brandon stepped out and pulled the door closed.

Getting dressed took longer than it should have. But Cutie took extra care. As much as he wanted to make it to dinner on time, he didn't want to eliminate the possibility of going because he'd strained something.

As he pulled on his own boots, still quite a sight, especially against the clean clothes, he prayed he would be on time. Cook did not suffer that kind of disrespect lightly.

And he doubted even his recent brush with death would be an acceptable excuse.

With his clothing set in place, he opened the door and peered out. No one in the hall. Which room had they put Mariena in? Uncle Owen's room? Lucy's room?

What did it matter? He had to get to dinner.

Stepping through the house, he pushed himself a bit more than he might should have to get to the table. Though the distance was not great, he had started to sweat when he entered the large room.

The chattering of voices he heard as he approached quieted when he turned the corner. All eyes on him.

Great.

He scanned the group. And could not help that his eyes were drawn to her.

Mariena sat between Amanda and Dan. She, likewise, had changed from her desert-worn garments and was now clad in a dress. Was it one of Amanda's?

It hugged what of her curves he could see above the table much better than her other garments had. The deep yellow of the dress set off the brilliance of her skin tone. And her hair had been loosened, gathered on top and only that part secured.

He drew in a slow breath and forced his exhale to be just as slow.

Her face colored and he realized that he stared. Had the others noticed?

Nodding to everyone, he smiled. "It's good to be up and about."

"Did that Cutie finally get to the table?" It was Cook. And judging from her tone, she was not happy.

He grimaced and scooted behind Slim to his seat. Sitting, he ducked his head as the door to the kitchen opened.

"Where is he?" Cook's features were colored as well. But most likely for a different reason.

"Yes, ma'am. I'm here," he croaked out. How bad would this be?

She leaned over the table, her small eyes glaring at him, piercing his weakened exterior.

What could he do? He raised his head and slapped on his finest grin. "And I am the luckiest man alive."

One of her eyebrows went up. Had he thrown her off balance? "Why would that be?"

"Well..." He forced himself to hold his smile and not swallow. "Think of all the fellas that don't get to enjoy your food tonight. I know. I was deprived for far too long. And I don't aim to be makin' that mistake again."

Her eyebrow bounced up, rising almost to her hairline. "Cutie, you are a charmer."

But was it enough? He held his breath.

"I can't stay mad at you." Her lips spread across her face. "Welcome home!"

Cutie let out the air he'd been holding.

Cook slapped the table and laughed.

Others joined in with their own amusement.

As the laughter died down, Amanda stood. "Here, Cook, let me help you bring those dishes in."

Mariena started to rise. "I can…"

Amanda held a hand up. "You are a guest. Please, sit. Enjoy."

Cook and Amanda disappeared into the kitchen and the interchange between the men picked up again.

Slim said something to Cutie, but he had a difficult time focusing.

Dan had engaged Mariena in conversation. She peered up at him with a shyness Cutie was surprised to see. Would he describe her as timid? Still, he watched as she muffled a giggle. Was she flirting with Dan?

"Cutie?" Slim leaned closer.

Cutie looked at him.

Slim had turned in the direction Cutie had been looking. Was he trying to discern what Cutie had been gawking at?

"What did you say? I'm sorry. I was lost in thought." Cutie shifted his silverware and plate before leaning back in his chair and crossing his arms.

Slim gave him a strange look. What was he thinking? "I asked how you were feeling? You seem well enough."

"I am. Better and better."

Cutie cut a look toward Mariena. Her cheeks had colored. Because of Dan? Cutie forced his attention back to Slim. He did his best to keep up the interaction with Slim, but even he could sense that his mood had darkened.

Because of Mariena?

Was there something wrong with her interchange with Dan? She had not made promises to Cutie. And he had not made any to her.

Still, he boiled just under the surface. He was not certain it could be contained. Perhaps it *would* be better if she left.

The sooner the better.

CHAPTER 5
Reaching

Mariena moved the broom across the boards on the porch. Amanda would not let her do much around the ranch, but she found things here and there. Cook seemed more understanding that Mariena wanted to help...even *needed* something to occupy her time.

For how long, she did not know. What would become of her and Nisto? It was not for her to determine. Was their fate now in the hands of the Millers? Or would Cutie decide?

Either way, what was the delay? Why did she and Nisto tarry? It gave them false hope and a sense of home they did not truly have.

The Millers were fine people. Brandon seemed capable and kind. A good man. And he clearly loved his wife. Amanda, for her part, had a strong spirit about her. It was borne of a deep consideration for others, though.

Maybe...just maybe...they would make a place for Mariena and Nisto. Was that possible? Even if the Millers wanted it to be so?

What did Cutie want?

Just thinking of him made her thoughts swirl. There was little certainty when it came to that man. Things that once seemed sure, no longer gave her reason to believe. Or hope.

It would be best she not think about it too much.

She flipped her braid over her shoulder and surveyed her work. There would probably always be dirt on this porch. Such was the way of ranch life. But it looked better.

Setting the broom back in its place, she turned toward the yard where Nisto played.

Only, he wasn't there.

Her breath caught.

Where could he be?

She took in a slow, deep breath and tried to calm her thoughts before they ran away from her. Nisto was safe on this ranch. But the ranch was a big place...with many things that intrigued a young boy. In all likelihood, this was not a matter of him being taken or running off after danger, but of being enchanted by something nearby.

Now that her breathing had evened and her thoughts were more reasonable, she stepped off the porch. It shouldn't be difficult to locate him.

She looked around the yard. What would have caught his attention? There were the pastures farther away with the cows. Not as interesting. The barn wasn't as far away. And the sounds of horses within carried even to this distance.

What else was within the barn?

She caught herself. *Did Nisto wonder the same thing?*

It was as good a place as any to start.

Moving toward the large structure, she attempted to keep her pace even and unhurried. There was no reason for alarm.

She stepped to the oversized doorway, leaning in and trying to spot her brother. The barn was lit only by the morning sun streaming in from various openings—a fair amount of light. Still, there were dark corners and shadows.

But the smell. Now *that* was rather unique. The urge to raise a finger to her nostrils became almost overwhelming. Still, she resisted. Anyone could become accustomed to a smell. She let her senses take it in and settle into the new sensations as she moved into the barn.

She opened her mouth to call for Nisto when she heard another voice. Far away at first, but she drew closer to it, inching over to the horse stalls and ducking into the first one. When she peered out, she bit her lip to muffle a gasp.

Farther in the barn, outside the opposite set of stalls, Cutie held the reins of his horse—the animal that had faithfully led them through the wilderness. As Cutie moved his arm over the horse's body, she spotted a brush in his hand. While he worked it over the mare's coat, he spoke to Nisto.

She closed her eyes and focused on his words.

"Horses are a lot like people. If you're good to them, they'll be good to you. They can sense bad in a person. And they know whom they can't trust. Dogs are that way, too."

There was silence for a moment.

"Would you like to brush her?"

What was Nisto's response? Did he nod? Whisper 'yes?' Did Cutie hand over the brush? She had to know.

Peering once more out of the stall, she watched Nisto brush the animal's side with Cutie behind him, a hand over Nisto's, guiding the young boy's movements.

Why was he spending time with Nisto? Teaching him? Showing him how to work with a horse? Maybe it wasn't much to Cutie, but it would mean something to Nisto. It would grow his trust in Cutie, a bond he had begun forming in the wilderness. And that would only make it more difficult for Nisto when they had to go.

But she couldn't be angry. Her heart was touched by Cutie's tenderness toward her brother.

Setting her back against the wall, she slid to the ground and, swallowing her sobs, let her tears come in silence.

Because, as difficult as leaving would be for Nisto, it would be that and more for her. She had already let Cutie into her heart.

And somehow, she had to get him out.

Cutie slid the stall door closed and wiped the sweat from his brow. The day had been long. Longer than he remembered they could be. And it was, as of yet, only half done.

Was his body still not recovered?

Stepping into the intensity of the sunlight, he glanced at the homestead. Lunch would be on the table in the next hour. Perhaps he should find a place to sit a piece. Rest. Let the cares of the day melt away.

The porch beckoned—a fine respite from the heat of the day. Might he find peace of mind there as well?

As he turned in the opposite direction, however, his heart spoke otherwise. The wide-open spaces, the wildness of the unkempt land beyond the pastures. It called to him.

Closing his eyes, he let the wind whip around his body and cool his skin. It brought with it the scent of this untamed earth. Intoxicating.

Dare he venture forth?

It had brought him nothing but trouble the last time.

The rustling of grass nearby drew him from his thoughts. He turned toward the sound. There, coming over the slight rise in the land between the pastures, was Mariena. Had she seen him?

Her face was turned toward the ground.

It seemed she had not spotted him.

She bore a basket filled with wildflowers, looped over one arm, and she all but glided, swaying as she walked, in his direction.

Even if she hadn't noticed him yet, she soon would.

Did he wish to speak with her? Or not? If he wanted to avoid her, he'd best hide. And quick.

But he couldn't make himself move. Not when he caught a glimpse of her carefree form once more. She was so like the wilderness he craved. Unknown, yet still a treasure to be discovered, explored, unpacked, and cherished.

Her eyes caught his.

He should avert his gaze.

But he couldn't.

She slowed. Tendrils of hair that had loosened from her braid trailed across her features.

Her movements resumed. And her feet carried her toward him. The closer she drew, the lighter her features became as her lips offered a smile.

"Hello," she said, stopping several feet short of where he stood.

He nodded.

She looked to the ground. Was she as nervous as he felt? Why must it be this way? They had spent every waking moment with each other in the desert. Hadn't they earned the right to skip these simple pleasantries?

"How are you liking the ranch?" he tried.

She peered up at him, a half smile gracing her features. "Oh, much well."

His shoulders relaxed and he released a long breath. Had he been so tense?

"And you? Is it good to be back?"

"Yeah." He glanced at the bunkhouse. Was it home? Did he view it that way? Or had his betrayal ruined that? He couldn't say for certain.

She watched him, her eyes unwavering on his. Did she see something deeper? Could she peer into his thoughts? It seemed so.

Was that so bad?

What was he thinking? Of course, it was! He couldn't let her in. Let her see...

"What is it?" Her dark eyes bored into him with such familiarity. Had he permitted too much? Given her some impression that he...that they...

It wasn't appropriate.

"It's time for lunch. Let's head in." He turned and walked toward the homestead.

Did she follow? He had not heard movement behind. Dare he turn?

Several paces away, he could stand it no longer and he looked over his shoulder.

She stood, planted in the same spot she had been. Her features unreadable.

What could he say that wouldn't encourage or offend?

Nothing.

But his tongue was quicker than his brain. "What do you want from me?"

Something flashed in her eyes. "Truth."

Ah, the one thing he could not give. Still...for a moment, he imagined himself putting voice to his thoughts, his feelings. He let himself dream her response. Dare he think she would welcome it?

It did not matter. Nothing could fix his past, or erase the wounds he had caused.

Make him whole.

He shrugged and turned. "I'll see you when you decide to come in."

As much as his heart ached, he refused to look back.

No, that might be his undoing.

Mariena stepped onto the porch. All was still. Evening was the time of day she both craved and dreaded. Nisto had gone to his room—to sleep or to calm his thoughts, she did not know. But it allowed her some time to be by herself.

Staring across the field, she mused at the stillness. As was true of this land she loved so, it was not quiet. The movement of the cattle and the calling of a multitude of insects made music of the night air.

Out in the wilds of the desert, her people made life to the rhythm of this music. Though its participants may be different. Coyote and all manner of untamed animals led the chorus.

She leaned against one of the porch posts and closed her eyes. Life seemed so perfect, so simple, so safe at the moment.

How could she have known they hinged precariously on a precipice? That every breath was a gift? And security the greatest of the illusions?

No. Her father's arms, her mother's voice singing over them was all she ever needed to bring peace to her spirit. Would she ever feel that peace again?

Moisture built behind her eyelids. Dare she let the tears loose?

She opened her eyes, a tear escaping. Her gaze settled on the single points of light around her—a lantern outside the bunkhouse, the candlelight in the homestead rooms behind. Could she let lose her tightly held control? For just a moment? Could she not?

She rubbed her hands together. They were rough and wrinkled from the dishwater. Strange to her. Pushing them down the front of her cloth skirt, she wondered at the strange feel of that as well. Had she abandoned the animal skin for good?

Almost as if she had no thought to it, she moved across the porch and stepped down onto the earth. Then her feet picked up speed. She lifted her skirt and raced across the yard, away from the barn, the bunkhouse, from all signs of this rancher's world.

How long and how far she ran, she could not be certain. But when that place drifted enough to her backside, she fell to her knees.

Hands met the ground, stinging with the impact. Would there ever be someone to catch her? Or would she always have to be strong? For Nisto. For her parents' memory. For her tribe.

Could such be asked of one person? Was she up to the task? Or would she prove too weak?

Dipping her head, she fought the tears once more. If she were to hold it together, she dared not break, not even for a moment. She must learn to swallow her tears and bury her heart. Maybe then...

What?

Searching the horizon as she searched her heart for the answer, she shied from what she feared.

Maybe then she could free herself from this man.

Lifting a hand to her head, she shook.

Hadn't she lost enough?

If the Apache had not come and all was well, her tribe would have made it to Mexico and rejoined other Tohono O'odam tribal groups. Her parents would be no doubt arranging her marriage. She would wed a strong brave who was trusted by the chief and by her father to care for her and her heart. This, too, she had lost.

That future was but a vapor, now gone.

All that was left were these hands, with their limited capability. These arms, with what strength they had. And this heart, perhaps fractured now. What good was she to Nisto?

"Mariena?" Hands fell on her shoulders.

She startled, jerking upward as the figure leaned over her. As she turned, her gaze found Cutie's eyes.

Not him. Anyone but him.

Could she pull away?

As she moved away from his hands, his grip tightened. Would he not release her?

"What troubles you?"

His eyes seemed deeper in that moment. Was he so concerned? Where just earlier this day he had been dismissive?

She turned away. "Nothing for to bother you." But her voice cracked. Her hand flew to her mouth. The tightly held control was slipping. From the evidence of his consideration?

He turned her shoulders until she faced him. For a moment, he searched her face.

Hopeless. She could do nothing to escape his censure or her own display of emotion.

One of his hands came to the side of her face. "Please, talk to me."

She swallowed, blinking. That might keep her tears at bay. But moisture slid down her face. She was losing the battle. "I..."

He tilted his head, his eyes fixed on hers. Did his gaze flit to her lips every now and then?

She flushed despite the deep loneliness, a pit hollowed within her. A glimmer of hope sparked in that moment. Was it possible...could it be maybe...that he might fill it? Dare she let herself fall on him?

His thumb caressed her cheek, and she was undone.

Her tears flowed.

She was uncertain whether she fell into him or if he pulled her into his chest, but in the next moment, she was against him, held tightly, the beat of his heart under her ear. Her body shook with sobs.

His arms pressed her firmly to himself. A hand smoothed over her hair. "It's all right. You're safe."

How could he know? Or even suspect...?

But he did.

Though the words he spoke were few and far between, his movements, his caresses spoke louder than anything she would have wished to hear.

When she let loose the collar of his shirt and turned to look up at the night sky, it was as if the stars no longer bored down, but rather smiled, upon her. As if the generations before her, maybe even her parents, watched on. Perhaps even approved.

Perhaps.

Cutie continued to hold her in a firm embrace. Had something changed here?

She leaned her face into his shoulder, breathing in the scent of him.

Was this the beginning?

Cutie urged his horse to continue walking the fence line. Was the painted mare as distracted as he? Or was his mind drifting obvious to his steed? For he could not keep his thoughts on what he was doing.

Last night had been...

Well, many things. Amazing. Terrifying. Perfect. Encouraging. Fulfilling. Impossible. Unrepeatable.

How could he have indulged himself so? Given Mariena hope where none existed? He was a cad.

What did she do to deserve the likes of him?

But when he saw her running and followed her, found her bent over and trembling, how could he help but gather her in his arms, give her comfort? How could a gentle woman such as she hold it together for so long? The memories of her tribe and parents alone must be difficult to move forward with every day. Much less caring for her brother and not falling apart.

She needed someone to lean on. If only for a moment.

But that wasn't all there was to it. And he knew it.

He wanted to be that person. For her to rest on him, take solace in him. Bottom line, he wanted to hold her.

Thank goodness, that's all it was. He at least had that much sense about himself. Would he ever forgive himself if he had taken advantage of that vulnerability in her?

No. No one should.

Still, there would be fall out. What must she think? What else could she think?

He needed to put an end to it now. There was no sense in letting her feelings grow, if she had feelings for him at all. That would lead nowhere good. It couldn't.

The horse came over the hill. Cattle moved and grazed. All looked as it should.

When would he pull Mariena to the side? He must do it soon.

He envisioned her features as she received the news. Had she a care, it would not go well.

Could he truly bring down such difficult words to her? Hurt her? When she'd had such hardship already?

He must. For her.

This was about what was best for her. Not what he wanted.

The barn came into view.

A couple figures stood at the fence just beside the structure. One was definitely a child and one a woman. As he neared, he guessed it to be Mariena, Nisto, and perhaps Brandon.

His heart flipped. Could he face her so soon? What would he say? What would she say? Still, he could not slow or stop time as he drew closer to where they stood.

Mariena held up a hand in his direction.

Brandon and Nisto also greeted him.

Cutie waved with his hat. His heart now raced. How could it betray him like this?

Moments later, he pulled his horse to a stop and hopped down. Then he walked the few feet that separated him from his boss, the youngster, and *her*.

Nisto ran to Cutie, raising a hand toward the mare's muzzle.

Cutie smiled at him, stopping the animal so she could enjoy the boy's kindnesses.

Mariena and Brandon were upon him soon after.

"Everything look good out there?" Brandon asked, adjusting his cap to give his eyes better sun coverage.

"Yes. Dan and Slim are still out in the field."

Brandon nodded, looking at Mariena.

But her eyes were on Cutie. And her face had a rosy tint to it.

Brandon's gaze went from her to Cutie and back. His mouth slid into a half smile, but he remained silent.

Cutie wanted to sink into the ground. But he couldn't keep his eyes off Mariena. The color on her cheeks was becoming. And, in spite of himself, it warmed him that he brought out such a reaction in her.

"Nisto, want to help me water Patch?" Brandon slid the reins from Cutie's hand.

Cutie jerked his head toward Brandon. "Boss, I can…"

Brandon waved him off. "Not to worry. I got it. You just make sure Mariena gets to the house for lunch."

Cutie nodded, turning his attention back to the young woman.

Her dark eyes were on him. Pulling him in. How was it she could hypnotize him so easily?

There was something he had wanted to say…*needed* to say. But he couldn't remember. Every thought had been pressed out except his awareness of her. His heart expanded and each thud sounded more certain, more solid, more sure of what he wanted.

He should pull free from her spell. Gather himself. Think.

She chewed her lower lip and looked behind herself at the barn. Did she fear an audience?

Shouldn't they?

But the others were the farthest things from his mind.

He shook his head. That wasn't right. His senses should not be so dulled.

Shifting his gaze about the area, he sought a more private place. It only took a moment before he spotted a promising prospect. There. By the far side of the barn.

He turned his attention to her, reaching for her hand.

Her brows furrowed. Was she confused? Concerned?

It gave him pause. What, after all, were his intentions for seeking solitude? Were they entirely appropriate?

He hung his head and let his hand drop. They were not. What was he thinking? His body warmed.

She stepped nearer.

He looked up.

A smile lit her features. "I trust you." She slid a hand into his.

He licked his lips. She shouldn't. But with her fingers threaded in his, something changed. His shoulders lifted, as if they became broader. And his whole demeanor became stronger.

For her?

Because of her?

What was this? Whatever it was, he liked it. Perhaps too much.

He let out a breath. And his shoulders dropped. The spell was broken. He remembered.

There was much to say. Much to make her understand. Would she hate him? She had every right to.

Reaching for her other hand, he avoided her eyes. "Mariena," he started, the word choking as he pushed it out.

"Yes?" Her voice hitched with hesitation. Could she guess what he was about to say?

"You are...everything a man could want." He chanced a glance at her eyes.

They glistened.

That stabbed at his heart. Could he go on? He had to. Turning his gaze back toward their hands, he forced himself to continue. "You... deserve so much. Much more than I..."

She gasped sharply. Might she faint?

He jerked his head up.

Her eyes were on something in the distance.

"Mariena, what...?" He looked over his shoulder.

There, over the far hill, a triplet of riders, bearing down toward the ranch as quickly as their mounts could carry them.

Who could it be? What might they want? Did it concern Mariena and Nisto? She certainly seemed to think so. But who would even know they were here?

He glanced back toward her. Skin that was naturally darkly tanned had paled.

She clung to his hand.

As much as he wished he had words of comfort, all he could offer was a gentle squeeze on her hand. Though it was unlikely this business had anything to do with her, they had certainly been spotted. Any effort to shuffle her out of view would certainly be noticed and raise suspicion.

"Stay near me." He pulled her as close as propriety would allow.

Her rapid breathing was disconcerting. If only he could calm her.

His free hand hovered near his pistol. An instinct.

The riders neared, and Cutie could now identify the lead as Sheriff McAllen.

What could the sheriff want?

Cutie closed his eyes. He wished he had risked hiding Mariena. There would be many questions. How would he answer them? Perhaps he could come up with a story. He'd best think quickly.

The horses drew to a halt just short of where Cutie and Mariena stood.

Cutie forced his body to relax and tipped his hat to the sheriff. "Good day, Sheriff. What can I do for you fellas?"

The man's eyes were hard has he glanced over Cutie and straight to Mariena. "We have come to collect the Indians. Seems they are off their Reservation."

How could he have known about them? Cutie swallowed his trepidation, taking a step that put him between the sheriff and Mariena.

"This young lady is a guest on this ranch. And under our protection." It was Brandon's voice. Had he come from the barn?

Cutie chanced a glance in that direction. He breathed relief that Nisto was not with him.

Sheriff McAllen set his gaze on Brandon. "I'm afraid that's just not possible, Mr. Miller. These Indians belong on their Reservation in San Xavier. They can't be wandering about as they please. They'll become a problem. And I won't have it. Not in my town."

Cutie clenched his teeth. The man suffered drunkenness and gambling and all manner of other ills. But a young woman and her kid brother were too much?

Sheriff McAllen motioned to the men on either side of him.

They dismounted and moved toward Mariena.

Cutie kept a tight grip on her hand and, moving his other arm back, hemmed her in. He stepped back, moving them both farther away from the sheriff.

"Now, now...there's no reason this needs to get ugly. Just surrender the girl and her brother, then we'll be on our way." The sheriff's tone grated.

"What do you intend to do with them?" Brandon stepped forward.

"Escort them to San Xavier," the sheriff said, eyeing the movement of his deputies.

Cutie's hand moved from Mariena's side and back toward his pistol.

"I wouldn't do that, son." Sheriff McAllen had his gun un-holstered and pointed at Cutie in a few seconds.

"Cutie," Brandon ground out. "Don't."

Cutie and Mariena came up against the wall of the barn.

The deputies were closing in.

Cutie's heart thundered in his ears. It became difficult to hear anything else.

But time was short. They would take Mariena. He would never see her again. She would be sent to San Xavier to live with her people, yes, but strangers no doubt, who may or may not accept her. Could he let her be ostracized her whole life? She'd already been through so much.

"Wait!" he called out.

The deputies paused, looking back toward McAllen.

"What is it?" McAllen sounded bored. His tone made that apparent.

Cutie swallowed. He shot a glance at Brandon. The man would help in any way he could. Then Cutie looked at Mariena. Her eyes were wide and set on Cutie. She had said she trusted him. He hoped that was true.

"What if...if I...married this woman?"

He sensed Mariena's gaze intensify. But he refused to look at her again, keeping his eyes on the sheriff.

McAllen shook his head and dropped his gaze.

What did that mean? What was he thinking?

The sheriff met Cutie's gaze again. "Believe me, you don't want to do that."

Heat flushed through Cutie. Not want to do that? Why? Because she was an Indian? His hand tightened.

Mariena whimpered.

He loosened his grip, regretting he had forgotten he held her hand.

"I assure you," Cutie said, narrowing his eyes into slits, "I do."

The sheriff sighed, signaling for the deputies. "Then we wish you all the best, sir."

The deputies paused, exchanging a look. One more glance at the sheriff and they made their way to their horses.

"But I expect an invitation to the happy occasion." McAllen's gaze became stony once more.

Cutie pushed his chest out. "You can expect it, Sheriff."

The men pulled on their reins, readying their horses.

The sheriff paused and turned back. "And I've got my eye on this ranch."

Why did that sound like a threat? Had Cutie once more managed to make trouble for Brandon? Still, he did not take his eyes off the departing group until they disappeared.

What had he done?

CHAPTER 6
Necessary

ariena pulled a trembling hand to the collar of her dress. But her eyes were fastened on the men and their horses as they departed. Her heart raced. Would it ever still? Despite the heat, her skin felt clammy and the strength of her knees thinned. Would they hold her? They seemed no thicker than molasses. Did her body sway even now? The world around her moved at odd angles.

Arms secured her, supporting her weight so she could remain upright.

She turned to thank Cutie for...what? Saving her? Being a steady, calm current for her to rely on.

Only...it wasn't Cutie who had offered her that strength. Brandon's arms held her upright.

She nodded her thanks and pressed her lips into the best smile she could offer.

Where...where was Cutie?

Turning in the direction where he had once stood, she had difficulty spotting him. He now knelt on the ground. Was he injured?

She reached for him.

Brandon's hand stopped her. "We need to get you inside. Someplace cooler. And perhaps find you something to drink."

His tone did not invite discussion. So, she permitted him to lead her away from Cutie and toward the homestead.

But her gaze remained on Cutie as long as possible. It seemed as if he had sunk to his knees there in the dirt. For he just sat there, hands on his thighs as he stared into the distance.

Did he regret his words? Had he spoken such without thought? In so much haste? Had he no desire to marry her?

Pinpricks behind her eyes warned of the tears that threatened. And as her body continued to war over the happenings of the last several minutes, she had nothing left to fight them off.

Brandon tightened his grip on her arms. "The steps."

"What?" Did he say something? Should she be mindful of their way?

"The steps," he said a bit louder. "Let's not have you trip." He smiled at her.

She didn't have it in her to return the gesture. Though she watched her feet, she stumbled over the first couple of stairs.

Brandon's arms kept her from calamity.

Somehow, they made it up the stairs and into the great room.

"Amanda!" he called as he settled Mariena into a chair.

"Brandon?" His wife's voice seemed distant, but her footfalls drew close in a matter of seconds. "Is something amiss?"

Mariena did not so much as raise her head. But she sensed that something unspoken passed between husband and wife. Must have, because without saying anything further, Brandon moved away as his wife's smaller form came closer.

The door creaked open and clamored shut, announcing Brandon's exit.

Amanda crouched in front of Mariena; her finer features leaned in to catch Mariena's gaze. The woman watched Mariena for a moment. Was she gathering some sort of information? What could she see from the surface? She took Mariena's hand and gave it a gentle squeeze. "Let me get you something cool to drink...and perhaps a biscuit."

Mariena couldn't imagine putting anything in her stomach, but she nodded.

When Amanda released her hand, Mariena saw that it still shook.

She drew both arms around her midsection. What was this fear? How could she show it? She *must* be stronger than this. Had to be. For Nisto.

Nisto!

Where was he? Was he safe? Had the sheriff seen him? The man had known about her brother. But how?

Had Cutie informed the sheriff about their presence here? Why? And if he had, why then would he try to protect them as he had?

What of the Millers? Did they betray her and Nisto's existence to the local law? That didn't seem any more likely given Brandon's reaction.

Her thoughts swirled; nothing made sense. It was as if she had to press through thick cloth to put thoughts together.

Amanda returned, tray in hand. She set it on a nearby side table. Meeting Mariena's eyes, she smiled once more before she picked up the glass of water and handed it over.

The glass made Mariena's trembling quite apparent as the water rippled and peaked.

Amanda placed steadier hands around Mariena's and helped her raise the cup to her lips.

The water was cool and refreshing. It grounded Mariena's thoughts.

She was at the ranch. Safe. And she wasn't going anywhere soon.

Amanda relieved her of the glass and set it down. She then sat in a nearby chair.

What was she waiting for? Weren't there questions forthcoming? Of course, there were. She would want to know what had happened. What had upset Mariena.

But Amanda remained silent. Was she waiting for Mariena to volunteer the information? She would be waiting for a long time, as Mariena had no desire to revisit the events. Not so soon. And then...not talking about it was eating her inside.

What was she to think? To feel? To do?

Shouldn't she decide that for herself?

She stole a sideways glance at Amanda.

Amanda's kind green eyes peered back. Not pushing, not pressing... just waiting.

Mariena's mother was gone. Her friends were gone. Anyone and everyone she had ever trusted was gone. Could she...might she...possibly find a trusting soul here in Amanda Miller? Was she at least willing to try?

Straightening in the chair and leaning against the back, she closed her eyes and let out a breath. Yes, it would be good to have a kindred spirit again. For how long, she did not know.

Turning to meet Amanda's eyes again, she pressed her lips into the best smile she could manage. "I know you are wondering."

Amanda, likewise, leaned back. And shrugged.

Mariena glanced toward the ceiling, licking her lips. How to start? As always...it would be best...with the beginning. "I am to tell of something about in the desert."

Amanda nodded, again, her manner all patience and kindness.

It served to put Mariena at ease. "That is where this did start."

Cutie sucked in air. But it wasn't enough. His lungs wouldn't fill.

He pushed the collected air out and tried again.

Still, he was not satiated by the next breath, though he drew in as much as he possibly could. It seemed as if his very body had become confined. Though the world spread out before him, unhindered, open.

He wanted to jerk at his collar. But he couldn't make himself move. His hands lay on his thighs where they had rested when he sank onto his knees. Was he so stunned? By his own words?

Why did he now feel chained? Was that not what marriage was? A permanent arrangement. With someone he had not known two weeks yet.

And it was not just him—had he not also consigned *her* to a fate she did not deserve?

Why?

Oh, he had meant well. Yes, he had sacrificed them both for a good cause. But would Mariena see it that way?

Footfalls stirred the dust behind him, tainting the air he breathed and pulling him from his thoughts. It could only be one person. Only one man dared disturb his commiserating. The one man he'd prefer not to face this moment. Or perhaps ever.

Brandon Miller.

He refused to turn and acknowledge his boss. Wouldn't let himself mutter any word of recognition to the man.

Coward.

Cad.

A rustle of clothes told that Brandon shifted his weight. Would he just stand there?

"What a day," he said, his voice strong and measured. Almost as if he were assessing the pastureland for grazing. "Hmm?"

Cutie nodded. What could he say? What *dare* he say?

They remained in silence for what seemed like hours. But the fact that the sun didn't make progress across the sky told Cutie it had not been quite that long.

"Dan and Slim will be coming by soon."

Cutie closed his eyes. Dan and Slim. He had forgotten about them. He couldn't delay much longer without risking the other ranch hands getting entangled in his business. Not that they wouldn't find out. But it would be best they didn't...just yet.

Brandon cleared his throat. "I assume you have a plan?"

Cutie felt Brandon's gaze upon him. Could he tell his boss the truth? What if he did? What if he didn't?

He dropped his head into a raised hand and shook it back and forth. "I've made a real mess, boss."

Brandon pushed out a breath. "Yeah. I can see that."

Slapping his thigh once more, Cutie lifted his eyes to the sky.

"What I need to know," Brandon drew his words out. "Is what your intentions are toward that young woman."

Cutie lifted his head and met Brandon's eyes. The brown-rimmed gaze was warm and kind, but held a hardness as well. Did he think so poorly of Cutie?

That stung.

But how could Cutie expect any differently after what he had done to Brandon and his wife?

"I understand." Cutie kept his tone in check. He did not possess any right to challenge anyone. Releasing a breath, he let his shoulders fall. "I intend to keep my word and marry her."

Brandon's features became placid. What was he thinking? Did he respect that in Cutie? Was he concerned about what that would mean for his own ranch?

After a moment, Brandon held a hand down toward Cutie.

When Cutie took it, Brandon helped hoist him to his feet. But he did not release Cutie's hand.

"Good." Brandon met his gaze square on.

There was more in the look he leveled upon Cutie. What was it? A threat? A warning?

Brandon let loose Cutie's hand at last and glanced over his shoulder. "Looks like rain."

What? Did Brandon just change the subject? Was he finished with this then? Cutie turned in the direction Brandon gazed. Indeed, there were darkened clouds on the horizon.

"What do you need me to do, boss?" Cutie itched for a task that did not involve this debacle.

Brandon watched the sky in the distance. "I think there's an important conversation you need have with Mariena. And soon."

Cutie resisted the urge to roll his head on his shoulders. Brandon could not be serious. The happenings on the ranch had to be more critical. "You must have *something* I need to do."

Brandon crossed his arms over his chest. "Nothing that is so pressing it should keep you from your future bride."

At those words, something thick rolled in Cutie's stomach. He feared he might lose his last meal, but swallowed hard in an attempt to disguise it.

Why was he not more warmed by that thought? Was he so terrified at the prospect of marrying Mariena?

How would he get through it?

Sheriff McAllen set his hat on the worn desk. His deputies chattered outside. When would they realize he could hear them from within the jailhouse? They were senseless to not have figured it out already.

"Why would he just walk away like that?" Barnes said.

McAllen could see the man's incredulous expression in his mind's eye. The same face he made all the time. As if he hadn't a clue. Perhaps he hadn't.

"You'd think he'd have had more to say, at least." Travers's gruff voice chimed in.

That man only *seemed* to have more faith in his sheriff. McAllen had been privy to enough of these conversations through this wall to know better.

He shook his head. These two. Clowns both.

It didn't matter what they thought.

McAllen moved toward the window and gazed out. From this vantage point, he had a direct view to the saloon doors. Whoever built the jailhouse had thought that out quite well.

As much trouble as he had from rowdy cowboys getting drunk, they were not his only concern. If he wanted to keep the peace in Wharton City, he had to mind any potential threat. That included those two law-breaking Indians. No matter how innocent they may seem.

The fact was they belonged on the Reservation. That's what the powers that be had said. It wasn't his place to question. Only to enforce.

Besides, it was time such an edict had come down. The Indians were nothing but trouble. They stirred up trouble and created chaos where none need exist. Even if they weren't necessarily the source of the issue, problems seemed to follow them.

And that was something he didn't need.

Not here. Not in his town.

Regardless of what his deputies might think, his resolve was not weak. He would see those two desert Indians out of Wharton City and on their way to San Xavier before month's end. Of that, he was determined.

Mariena pressed Amanda's handkerchief to her eyes as she concluded her tale of woe. Though her tears were hot, they had mostly dried.

She looked up at Amanda. What was she thinking? The woman's expression remained kind, but there was no disguising the surprise underneath. Or the concern.

Was this so dangerous? Did it create problems for the Millers? Mariena would never wish to do that!

Amanda leaned forward and laid a hand on Mariena's. "My dear, you have endured much."

Was that all she would say? Mariena had dared hope for encouragement, advice, and some hint that Cutie's feelings for her were real.

Amanda offered none of that. Only the gentle touch of her hand and a kind smile.

That brought another onslaught of tears. And Mariena could do nothing to stop them.

"Come now, it is not so bad." Amanda's hand remained in Mariena's lap. "All will be well."

How could she not understand? Or was it because she could offer no hope where Cutie was concerned? Had Mariena misunderstood so completely? Then why did he offer to marry her?

Mariena couldn't continue spilling out her emotion like this. There had to be a limit. Sniffling, she closed her eyes and set her determination to pulling herself together. Not much could be done about her uncertainty, but at least on the outside, she could appear held together.

She swallowed and lowered her hands back to her lap. A couple of hiccups were all that remained of her ravaging sadness. Her gaze rose to meet Amanda's once more.

Amanda's brows furrowed. Surprise? Or more concern? It was no matter.

"I thank you. For the time you have to listen."

Amanda's features softened. "I will listen anytime." She patted Mariena's hand.

Mariena nodded.

Amanda opened her mouth, but the front door opened and interrupted whatever she was about to say.

Regretting the words she didn't receive, Mariena turned her attention to the intruder.

Cutie.

Standing just inside the threshold. Staring directly at her. It was almost enough to cause her trembling to resume.

Amanda squeezed Mariena's hand as she stood. "I'd best leave you two to your privacy. I'll just be in the other room."

Mariena reached after Amanda without thinking. Would that she could stay. How Mariena wished for a buffer!

But why? She and Cutie hadn't needed anyone the other night when he had held her and comforted her.

Something within her warmed at the memory. Including her features.

She peered at him through her eyelashes, hoping he couldn't read her mind.

He slid his hat off and took careful, minded steps around the furniture, into the great room, and closer to her. At last, he stood beside the chair Amanda had just vacated. Would he be so presumptuous? After all, they would be wed.

After a moment, he tore his gaze from her and stepped back, sitting on a chair a few paces away.

She worked diligently to control her breathing. But she doubted she would be able to hide the color in her cheeks. Why did she have to think of that night now?

It would be more fitting for her to remember his reaction to his decision to marry her. How he sank to the ground. As if he'd been given the worst news of his life. As if he weren't the one that made the decision.

She looked away.

"Mariena, I..." He coughed. His words sounded dry. Was he so parched? Should she bother to get water for him?

She turned to offer just that.

But when their eyes met, she lost her words. The blue pools, once so soft and comforting, were now questioning and, did she imagine it, accusing.

She drew in a sharp breath.

He looked away, using another word she didn't know.

"What have you to say?" she challenged. Her eyes were filling. It would only be a matter of time before she lost her composure.

"I'm sorry." He didn't look at her.

"Sorry?" A tear trailed down her face.

"For putting you in such a position." He tugged and kneaded his hat brim in his hands, still seemingly unwilling to meet her gaze. "I..."

The word hung in the air between them.

He didn't want to marry her. What he'd said had been said in haste.

She closed her eyes and did not stop the tears that flowed. "It is not all your blame."

His head shot up then, his eyes on her. "What?"

It was her turn to look away, placing a hand on her lips to keep her cries from coming out.

Unwanted.

Undesired.

"Believe me, Mariena," his voice had softened. "I do not think you are at fault. The blame *is* all mine. I made you think things. I got us in this mess. *You* deserve better."

What was he saying? She deserved better? Why would he think that?

"But I *will* marry you. I will make it safe for you and Nisto to stay here." His words were resolute. Firm.

Then why did his features tell another story? His face spoke of his concern, his hesitation. So, he would marry her against his will.

She would not have it.

But did she have a choice? There was no other way for her and Nisto to remain. To not be shuffled off to the Reservation. And without their tribe, there was no way of knowing what would await them there. Was there any good answer for them?

Cutie stood and stepped closer to her.

She held her breath.

He reached toward the side of her face but paused. Then, drawing his hand back, he spun and walked out of the room, out of the homestead, into the coming storm.

And once again, she was stuck. No real say in her future. Only one path before her. The man who held her heart would begrudgingly pledge himself to her.

The door slammed behind Cutie. He had hurt Mariena. That was certain. Why had he done it? He hadn't intended to injure her.

But what control had he over her emotions? Was he the keeper of her heart? Should he be?

Somewhere in the depths of his heart, he knew the answer. He'd had no right to act as he had. Selfish.

Wasn't that proof enough that he was not ready to take a wife?

He sighed.

Such musings were in the past. This would happen. That was final. He would not abide standing by when he could protect Mariena and Nisto. That was his choice. And he had made it.

He put one foot in front of the other, not truly knowing where he was headed until he was in the barn. Was anyone else here? Where had Brandon gone?

"Hello?"

No answer.

Perhaps Brandon had gone after Dan and Slim to secure everything before the storm. Something *he* should have done.

Stepping toward his horse, he felt the urge to unlatch the stall door and ride out into the coming rain. Maybe it would wash away his worries, or cleanse him of his self-centered thoughts, or baptize him in some way. Much too lofty a thought. What he truly wanted to do was escape.

He heard a scuffling in the loft.

Was someone up there?

Peering toward the overhead section of the barn, he examined the dim area for movement.

There, in the back corner. Definitely something. An animal or a person had stowed away under some hay.

Should he call for a response? Or had his earlier call been sufficient? Perhaps he should now treat the intruder as hostile.

He grabbed for a pitchfork and made his way to the ladder. It took some effort to climb with the tool, but he dared not go up unarmed.

As he reached the top, his thoughts cleared somewhat. "Nisto?"

The boy hadn't been seen since the sheriff had been here. Maybe he chose to remain hidden?

More shuffling.

"Nisto, is that you?"

Nothing.

Awareness filled Cutie. He dropped the pitchfork and moved slowly toward the earlier movement. "Nisto, it's Cutie. I'm not going to let anyone hurt you."

The boy sat up, hay falling off him. He brushed bits of the offending substance from his clothes and hair.

Cutie crouched in front of the boy, helping him rid himself of the remaining hay. "You must have been pretty scared, huh?"

Nisto nodded. His face was drained of color. As pale as Cutie could imagine.

Cutie opened his arms, and Nisto fell against him. "It's all right. No one is going to hurt you. Or Mariena."

Nisto nodded against his shoulder. The boy embraced him with such ferocity.

Cutie held him just as close, letting the youngster lean into him and feel of his strength.

As he pulled back from Nisto, he tipped the boy's chin. "Ready to go find Samuel?"

Nisto shook his head.

"No?" Why wouldn't the boy want to be with Samuel, another youngster his age? The two boys had so much fun playing and getting into trouble together.

Nisto pointed to Cutie.

"You want to stay with me?" Cutie laughed a little.

Nisto nodded.

Cutie stopped laughing. Did the boy truly enjoy him so much?

Such that he would rather be with Cutie than Samuel? Perhaps he trusted Cutie to keep him safe and he didn't feel very safe right now.

Maybe that's how Mariena felt, too.

And he hadn't offered her any comfort at all. Only hesitation, regret, and second-guesses.

He could kick himself.

Truly, he was a cad.

CHAPTER 7

Intended

Amanda laid the fanciest pink dress Mariena had ever seen across her and Brandon's bed. The rosy fabric was a medium hue, not too light and not so dark that it would not complement Mariena's skin tone. Lace trimmings and ribbons adorned the bodice and sleeves.

"What do you think?" Amanda's eyes shone as she looked at Mariena. Was she excited? Maybe even hopeful?

Could Mariena truly wear this dress? She had never put anything so ornate on her body. Picturing it in her mind was difficult.

Amanda looked back toward the dress, pinching at it here and there. "We'll have to make a few adjustments, but I think it can be ready in time.

"Oh, no!" Mariena gasped. "I would not like you to change your dress."

Amanda waved a hand. "It is a small matter. I don't have much occasion to wear it. And I have another that is suitable enough for the kinds of gatherings we might have in Wharton City."

Was she just being kind? This dress must have been expensive. The fabric alone would have cost...

"Besides, you are a bride! You must have something beautiful to walk down the aisle in. The few plain dresses you have won't do."

Mariena frowned. Did it matter what she wore? It would be a simple ceremony. Few in attendance. And Cutie would not care how she looked. Why should she? Still...

Wouldn't it be wonderful to be in such finery for even one day? To let Amanda and Cook treat her as if she were special? Even if it lasted only a short time?

And it seemed to matter so much to Amanda.

Mariena glanced at Amanda's smile, which touched her eyes as well. "If you are sure. I will like it much."

Amanda clapped her hands and grabbed for Mariena's, which hung by her sides. "You will be just gorgeous! You'll see."

Lucy toddled to her mother and pulled on Amanda's skirt. "Hold! Hold!"

Amanda released Mariena and reached for her youngster's chubby, outstretched arms. Pressing a quick kiss to her little girl's cheek, she then turned her attention back to Mariena.

"Would you try it on now? I'll get Cook, and we'll get it pinned. We need to start the alterations as soon as possible."

Hesitating, Mariena reached for the fine dress, gingerly lifting it. She moved toward the door at the same time as Amanda.

"Oh..." Amanda started. "Did you need help?"

"Ah," Mariena noticed that the buttons were down the back of the dress. "After on me."

Amanda nodded and reached for the door latch.

Mariena waited to walk out behind her. But when she stepped out behind Amanda, the woman turned. "Did you need something right now?" Her brows furrowed.

What could she mean? Hadn't she told Mariena to change into the dress? "I go to put on the dress."

"Oh." Amanda's features opened. "You may do so in my room. No need to drag it across the house. My sewing kit is in my room. We will do the pinning in there."

Was that proper? For Mariena to be in Amanda and Brandon's room alone? It didn't seem right.

Amanda grabbed for the door latch, using her body to prod Mariena back into the room. "I'll knock when I come back. I just need to put Lucy down."

Mariena nodded and swallowed as Amanda closed the door.

Now alone in a room she didn't belong in, she glanced around. It didn't feel any more right than she had thought it would. The room was as well kept as it was warm and inviting.

There were little things, here and there, that spoke of its inhabitants and their care for one another. Fresh flowers on Amanda's vanity, which Mariena imagined had been gathered by Brandon, or perhaps one of the children, freshened the area. A wall hanging over the bed that had 'THE MILLERS' engraved on it had been given a place of honor. Even the atmosphere of the room exuded the warmth between the people that shared it. As if the walls shared secrets with Mariena.

There had been no talk of where she and Cutie would stay after the wedding. Would their room emanate such a warmth? Or would it tell a different tale?

Would they share her room in the house? Or would a room be built onto the bunkhouse? She did not know what would be more appropriate.

For certain, these were details Cutie should be charged to work out. Would he even ask her opinion?

She frowned, doubtful.

But did it truly matter? As long as she and Nisto were safe, it didn't.

Knock, knock, knock.

Amanda!

In her musings and nosiness, she hadn't taken the time to put the dress on. What could she say? She began unbuttoning the simpler dress she wore which, thankfully, was buttoned down the front. "I need more minutes."

"Of course," came the muffled reply through the door. "Just open the door when you are ready for help."

Mariena made quick work of undressing and then, careful with the delicate fabrics of the borrowed dress, she began what of the process she could do herself.

When she had the garment on, she worked to hold the bodice up.

The buttons, as it turned out, went past the waist. So, due to the weight of the dress and its adornments, the sleeves wanted to fall off her shoulders. She fought with it for a few moments, trying to keep it upright, before giving up altogether. Amanda wouldn't care if she saw Mariena's shoulders.

Holding the front of the dress up with a hand at her collarbone, she opened the door.

Only Amanda wasn't alone in the hall.

Cutie stood to her side, speaking with her. But as the door opened, his eyes latched on Mariena's and widened. And then his face warmed.

Mariena gasped and slammed the door shut.

Leaning against the solid barrier, she gathered the dress as high as she could and closed her eyes. What had he seen? Had she been overly exposed?

The door vibrated as someone knocked.

She wanted to vanish.

"It's me, Mariena. May I come in?" Amanda called.

But was it *just* her? Was Cutie still in the hall?

"Please, Mariena. Cutie's gone. Can I come in?"

Mariena's heart raced and her stomach turned. But she could not put Amanda off. This was, after all, her room.

Moving away from the door, Mariena worked the latch and stepped away, still clinging to the dress.

Amanda opened the door only wide enough to slip in then closed it behind herself.

Turning, she let out a breath. "I am so sorry. I should have warned you he was out there." Amanda's brows peaked in the center and her mouth tightened at the corners. Was she so distraught?

Mariena looked at the floor.

"He had just come by to ask me something. He'd not been there more than a minute. I promise." Amanda took a step toward Mariena.

Adjusting her hold on the neckline, Mariena fought her nerves. That's all this was, right? Nerves. What had occurred had not been so devastating. In less than a week, she and Cutie would be man and wife.

Mariena pulled in a deep breath and let it out.

Now an arm's width away from Mariena, Amanda said, "I am so

sorry he saw the dress. We can make extra alterations to it so it's not the same."

"Not the same?" Was that such a concern?

Amanda smiled. "Is it not also a bad omen among your people for the groom to see his bride's wedding clothes before the ceremony?"

Mariena shook her head.

"Well, it is quite the standard here."

"I do not want extra work for you." Mariena met Amanda's gaze.

"Nonsense." Amanda waved a hand. "It is nothing. I want to do it. That way, the dress will be special. For you."

Special. For her.

New. For her.

Mariena let her gaze wander toward the sign above the bed. 'THE MILLERS' it said.

What would her new name be?

For the first time, she realized...she did not know.

Cutie rode beside his boss, heading to Wharton City. There were things to be done. Arrangements to be made. Things he had never had to do. And things he did not relish doing.

But he would get them done nonetheless.

He was ever so thankful for Brandon's presence with him today. And his boss's willingness to assist in making sure everything that needed attending was cared for.

Apparently, Amanda did the same for Mariena.

He still couldn't get the image of Mariena in that dress out of his mind. The accidental run in had spooked her, to be sure, but it had sparked something in him, something that had long been buried.

If he were to be honest, it wasn't just the dress. Though it was becoming. It wasn't just seeing *her* in the extravagant dress, though she was lovely in it. There was more to it.

He had noticed that the dress had not been secured. The sides had dipped, revealing her perfectly structured, smooth, and nicely tanned shoulders.

This only alluded to the more that was to come.

And it caused a hunger to grow in him he had forgotten.

Yes, she was attractive. Any hot-blooded man could see that. But it was more. He had an ache that went beyond that. Yet, he wasn't sure it was more than just that—desire.

Didn't a marriage require more?

Brandon and Amanda had more. They cared for each other on a deeper level. No one could deny they loved each other. But could he say he *loved* Mariena?

He doubted it.

Oh, he cared for her, yes. Desired her, no question. But would he come to love her in that deeper way that Brandon and Amanda had? Not everyone did.

Was it even something he wanted?

Deep down in his heart, he knew. He did. So very much.

That didn't mean he deserved it.

"We'll start at the church." Brandon moved his horse closer to Cutie's. "Get things settled there."

Cutie nodded.

"Then I think to the General Store?" Brandon looked over at him.

"Sure thing, boss."

Brandon nodded. Why was he being so helpful? He was so good to Cutie. Too good. And Cutie had earned none of it. In fact, he deserved just the opposite—to have been thrown out on his keester a few years back when his betrayal had been made known. But not only had Brandon and Amanda forgiven him, they continued on as if it had not even happened. What kind of people were they? Maybe they were *too* trusting.

Wharton City loomed closer, small though it was. In moments, he and Brandon moved past the stretch of buildings that made up the simple town and on to the church.

They met with the reverend briefly. Cutie was surprised how little effort it took to set the time of the event and make the necessary arrangements. Brandon did most of the talking though. That was just fine with Cutie.

Next, they were on to the General Store. Leaving their horses tied outside, they stepped into the biggest store in Wharton City. As was fitting, it had a little bit of everything, for which the residents were thankful. Mr. Otis was even kind enough to order something from the catalogue if he didn't have it in stock.

Brandon had brought a list from Cook. Just a few things, he had promised. Few enough that their saddlebags would suffice.

That left Cutie to browse the shelves. He enjoyed such on occasion. Not often.

Today, he perused though.

There were candies and foodstuffs, fabrics and sewing accouter-ments...and then he came to a rather unique assortment of goods—a selection of figurines—birds, horses, and dogs mostly.

Mr. Otis's daughter shuffled by with a basket full of jams. Perhaps to restock the shelves.

"Excuse me," Cutie called to her.

"Yes, sir?"

"What are these?" He motioned toward the carvings.

"Oh. One of the local fellas fancies whittling figures and whatnot. He asked if we would be interested in trying to sell them. As toys and knickknacks. They are quite good, don't you think?"

Cutie looked at the intricate workmanship. "Yes, quite good."

"Do you need anything else?"

Cutie shook his head but didn't look away from the pieces of woodwork.

With the swish of her skirt, she was gone.

While they were interesting, Cutie couldn't imagine what he might have need of one for. Perhaps a toy for Nisto?

He spotted a horse figure. Mariena may not care for the creatures, but Nisto definitely had a fascination with them. Cutie reached for the statuette and his hand brushed something just out of sight on the upper shelf.

Stretching farther back for it, he grasped a hidden object. As he pulled it down, he saw that it was a carved cactus flower. The detail of the desert Saguaro flower was unimaginable. If it weren't for the wood grain, he would have believed the petals just as delicate as the actual bud.

Could he...might he...buy it and give it to Mariena? How well would she receive it?

He turned the carving over in his hand, mulling over her possible reaction. It could go many different ways. But the more he looked at it, the more he wanted her to have it.

Nisto would enjoy the horse.

His decision made, he walked to the counter and purchased them both. Now he only had to figure out when, where, and how to give them the gifts. This was all new to him.

As would be so many things coming his way.

Completely new.

Mariena sat, the grass around her flowing as if waves of water in the breeze. Not for the first time, she wished to become one with the earth. What must it be like to bend only to the will of the wind? To not have to be turned this way and that by a life not of your choosing?

For the grasses leaned and swayed but did not break. How she had come so close...too close to breaking. And too often.

Perhaps even now.

Sitting cross-legged among the fine blades, she reached out a hand to caress the tops of their shoots. The feathering of their motion beneath her palm soothed her.

She closed her eyes and laid her head back, letting her face take in the fullness of the sunlight, as the great ruler of the day prepared for the end of its daily journey. Soon, it would dip below the mountains and be gone for the night. His sister would take on the responsibility of lighting the earth for the evening. In coolness, she would reign over all.

Though Mariena's people had lived more in touch with nature than the white man, this was not all that her people knew. They had heard of the white man's God. And His benevolence. His grace.

At one time, she had believed.

Did she now?

Or did she think that all she could see was all there was?

Life had taught her hard lessons. Perhaps it was too difficult to risk flights of fancy.

Her people believed in fanciful tales. Of an Earth Medicine Man and an Elder Brother. Of Coyote and Buzzard and First Born. These tales of creation and a great flood seemed fantastical.

Then there were the stories that the missionaries brought. Of a God that created the world with words. And sent His Son to die for her darkness. Her sin.

Would she prefer this risk? To risk hope in a God that loved her? What love was this? What loving God would leave her like this? Her mother and father taken away? Ripped from her? As if that weren't enough...her whole tribe had been slaughtered.

And this almighty, all loving God wasn't even kind enough to take her, too. No, she was left to live out the grief. Bear the burden. Put on a brave face for Nisto.

Wasn't this more than any god dare ask of one person?

Didn't this one God know? How could an all-knowing God not?

She pushed out a breath and pulled her knees to her chest, settling her arms and face there.

The wind blew over her once more. Only this time, it surrounded her. Blowing first across her back, through her hair, then circling her arms and legs, and around again.

It warmed her.

Calmed her.

All but embraced her.

Wait...

Was that possible?

She lifted her head.

The breeze halted.

Looking toward the sky, her chest tightened. And she knew...a part of her very much wanted to believe. But she just couldn't.

She dropped her chin to her hands.

The wind did not return.

She closed her eyes. There. That must prove something.

"Mariena."

She jerked around, clasping a hand to her chest as her heart leapt toward her throat.

Cutie stood several feet behind her, his hat in hand, hair mused. Perhaps by being bound in his hat for so many hours in the heat of the day.

His brows rose.

She held out a hand. "I am good. Only a little scared."

"Oh. I'm sorry. I didn't mean to—"

She shook her head. "No, is okay."

Their eyes locked.

Why had he come? Did he have something to say? Should she bid him sit with her?

"I, um," he said, as he looked off toward the mountains. "I didn't know where you were." His eyes fell on hers again.

She shrugged. "I came to this place to be with my thoughts."

He nodded, jerking his hat forward.

What was that about? She turned the way he indicated with his hat. There wasn't anything unusual. Her gaze met his once more, brows meeting.

"I..." His face broke into a smile, and he let out a throaty chuckle. "I hoped I might sit."

"Sit?" Why did he ask? Of course, he could sit.

"With you," he added quickly.

Oh. He wished her to invite him. Why must this be so difficult?

She let out a breath. Was she amused or frustrated? Even she was not certain. Setting a hand to the ground beside her, she said, "Please. I would like for you to sit."

He appeared as if he would step forward, but hesitated. "Truly?"

Did she appear as if she would hurt him in some way? Was something about her causing him to disbelieve her?

She nodded.

He leaned forward and smiled, still waiting.

For what, she did not know.

After some moments of nothing, he took in a breath and let it out. Then he stepped to the spot she offered and lowered himself.

She focused on her hands, still on her knees. What had he wanted that she didn't supply? Would their marriage be this way? Was it something a white woman would understand? A thickness sank from her chest to her stomach. Perhaps she wasn't fit to be his wife. There may be too great a distance between them in their ability to know each other. They came from such different places.

Cutie continued to sit and say nothing.

She turned away, looking in the opposite direction. What were they to do? He must sense this awkwardness. Did he regret his decision even more every day?

"I...I'm not good with words." His spoke softly.

Shifting to glance back toward him, she watched the angles of his face.

He didn't look at her but faced the ground. Was there a reason? Had he come to tell her the wedding would not happen?

She wrung her hands. As anxious as she had been about the wedding, to not have his protection...to have to go to the Reservation... it was just...

"But when we were in town earlier today, I...I saw something."

This was the strangest way to go about putting her off. Why wouldn't he be straight? Unless...

He turned to meet her eyes.

There was nothing of reluctance or the kind of tension she had expected. Perhaps she had misjudged him.

His gaze pulled her in, and there was little further thought except for how warm his eyes were. How safe she felt in his presence. And how she longed for him to draw her in and...

"Well..." he said, clearing his throat. "I wanted you to have it."

There was movement off to his side.

Could she pull free from his eyes? Did she want to?

At length, however, he broke their gaze. And lifted a hand between them.

There, resting in his palm, was the most beautiful carving of a Saguaro flower.

Her breath hitched. "For...me?"

"Yes." He nodded, extending his hand forward a bit. Now it was inches over her knees, just in front of her face.

Lifting shaking hands, she took the precious piece. She turned it over and around with her fingertips, grazing the smooth wood of the petals.

"I...I don't know...what to say." Her words came out in ragged breaths. No one, besides her parents, had ever gifted her anything. And never could she have imagined receiving something so precious. What could she say?

She looked at him.

He shook his head, which was somehow closer now. "Don't say anything." His words came out as a breath.

Several emotions overcame her—joy, happiness, fear, trepidation... His nearness overwhelmed her. She couldn't help but close her eyes and take in the scent of him, which she knew all too well by now.

Fingertips, roughened and firm, touched the side of her face.

She gasped and dropped the delicate carving.

The gentle fingertips gave way to a hand, pressing against her cheek.

Almost as if without thought, she leaned against that touch. Her hands reached blindly for him.

His other hand caught hers, entangling their fingers as he came ever nearer.

Their breaths mingled.

She ached for something more. How was that possible? This was more than she had ever known. What was there of knowing more to ache for?

Still, her eyes would not open.

"Mariena." Her name was spoken as if a prayer—soft, sweet, reverent.

Could she return it? All she could form was a small whimper.

Then his lips were on hers. As soft as his earlier vocalization of her name, and just as sweet. The kiss was excruciatingly tender.

He moved his lips over hers, still gentle but promising more.

She pushed her hands forward, wresting against his hand to reach him.

Still, he held her back. Why?

But she was desperate for more. She pressed into his lips, demanding something deeper.

He pulled back.

She jerked forward, following him. But his hands, holding hers back, kept her from moving too far.

His breaths came heavy, but steady.

Her eyes slid open, gazing over his features.

His mouth remained parted, his eyes closed.

"Charles," she whispered.

Brown eyes were on her then. "Don't." The word was rough, but not spoken with volume.

Why would he still hold her at arm's length? Had this gesture, this kiss, not meant as much to him as it had to her?

He pulled back farther. "I shouldn't have done that." His eyes seemed to focus on the earth. Could he not even hold her gaze?

Her brows furrowed. Did he regret it so?

"I'm sorry, Mariena." Her name no longer fell off his lips as it had. Now, she was no more than she had been to him.

And it stung.

Her chest heaved. Not from the exertion of emotion, but from the restraint of it. For she could not contain the depth of her sorrow. Nor did she care to hide it from him. She stared into his eyes. "Sorry?"

Still, he would not look at her, but he picked up his hat and examined the brim.

"That is all?" Her voice rose, the hurt within giving it force. She stood, her knees shaking. Perhaps her skirt would hide it. "You don't know…" What was the word? "…this." Placing a hand on her heart, she glared down at him.

Why would he not so much as glance? Not even to see what she indicated.

"And…you do not care to," she seethed.

There was no sense in it. She groaned and spun, giving him her back as the sky exploded in a symphony of color. It mattered not. All that she knew was muted.

Snuffed out.

Dark.

As she neared the homestead, hot tears streamed down her face.

CHAPTER 8
Joined

Cutie watched the sun creep over the horizon.

Today. It would be today.

He would bind himself forever to Mariena. And, in the process, chain her eternally.

Sleep had eluded him for the entirety of the night. With thoughts of what had transpired the previous evening, how could it not?

Why had he acted so? First, taking liberties and pushing himself on Mariena...then acting a fool and pushing her away. Wounding her.

Would it always be so? Him, uncertain of where he should stand and injuring her in the process? Truly, she deserved better. If he weren't her and Nisto's only hope, he would ride off and save her from himself.

Who would speak for her then? Dan?

The very thought caused his skin to crawl.

It wasn't that he didn't like Dan. The man was a fine friend and a good ranch hand. For certain, he had been faithful to Brandon where Cutie had not. Perhaps Dan *would* be a better choice for Mariena.

If he so chose.

Would he want to be?

Cutie thought back. To meals shared across the dinner table, instances in the barn...glances, smiles...

Yes, Dan noticed Mariena. He saw how lovely she was. How could he not?

Cutie kicked at the dirt and crossed his arms over his chest.

If given the opportunity, would Dan be honorable or take advantage? How well did he truly know the man?

He didn't.

When Cutie closed his eyes, he saw Dan watching Mariena. Appreciating her.

Even worse, he saw Mariena smiling back at Dan.

Insufferable.

The door to the bunkhouse squeaked.

Cutie pulled himself away from the wall. Had he conjured Dan with his thoughts?

Slim came from their sleeping quarters. He glanced at Cutie and winked. "What are you up so early for?"

Cutie frowned. He wished for something to throw at Slim for his implication. "I'm not up early, if you must know. I had a difficult time sleeping."

"I bet you did." Slim snickered.

Cutie stepped toward him but made no further move as Slim hopped away and ducked.

"Aw," Slim said as he straightened. "Don't be that way."

Leaning back against the bunkhouse wall, Cutie crossed his arms again.

"C'mon, Cutie." Slim stepped toward him. "Ain't this supposed to be a happy day for ya'?"

Cutie offered him a half smile and nodded.

"Then why ain't ya happy?" Slim's voice became serious.

Turning toward him, Cutie met his eyes. Could Slim be as serious as he sounded? Did he care?

Slim took a stance similar to Cutie's beside him, hands in his pockets. "I might give ya' a hard time, but I'd like to think you and Mariena will do good for each other."

Cutie stared at the sky. What could he say? Could he share his inner struggles with Slim?

An elbow poked his side. He looked at Slim.

"You're just nervous." Slim flashed teeth with his smile. "Ain't no man ever got married without some cold feet."

If only that were all it was.

Cutie shrugged. There was no reason to concern Slim that something more plagued his thoughts.

Slim clapped Cutie on the shoulder. "Let's go hit those morning chores." Pushing off the wall, Slim stepped away from Cutie.

"Hey," Cutie called. "It's my wedding day. Don't you think I should be exempt from chores today?"

Turning, Slim leveled a cocked brow on Cutie. "And all of a sudden like, the cold feet is gone."

Cutie smiled, shook his head and held out his hands. "Just like that."

"Cold feet or not, them chores need tending." Slim jerked his head in the direction of the barn. "And I ain't heard the boss excuse your ugly mug, so let's get to it."

Shrugging, Cutie opened his mouth, but the door creaked again.

"What's all this noise out here?" Dan stepped into the early morning light.

"Just this ruffian trying to get out of his chores." Slim made a face at Cutie.

Dan glanced in Cutie's direction, too. "That so?"

Remembering his earlier thoughts about Dan, Cutie lost all his fight along with his humor. "Not at all. Let's go." He walked in Slim's direction, passing him and heading on toward the barn.

After such a rocky start, how much lower could this day descend?

But Cutie knew what was in store. He had no great hopes.

The young woman in the mirror just couldn't be her.

Mariena sighed as Amanda continued to fuss over the smooth dark hair. There was not much hope in improving it further. Already, it appeared beyond any expectation she'd had.

They sat in the boarding house room the Millers had secured for the purpose of preparing Mariena for the wedding.

Why? Why were they being so kind?

Mariena dreaded the ceremony. This day. Cutie. The marriage. Everything.

But she would be dreading it in a beautiful dress and with expertly styled hair.

So far, she'd had quite the education on wedding customs among the white man. As for the Tohono O'odam, it was much simpler. None of this flair. No fanfare. The brave would take the maiden to his tent and that would be it, for the most part.

Why did they need a preacher to tell them what they were to be to one another? Why did they not decide between themselves? Another of their government responsibilities. Everything done by law. Not by love.

This marriage would most certainly be one of law, not love. Cutie had made that quite clear.

She tilted her head down to catch her breath. How had all the air escaped her?

"Oh no! Your hair will fall!" Amanda shrieked.

Mariena jerked upright.

She watched her hair wobble in the mirror.

Amanda grabbed both sides of the carefully curled mass as she pulled in a breath through her teeth.

"My sorry," Mariena said, scrunching her features.

"No," Amanda said, letting out a long breath. "It's okay. It's all okay." Was she saying that to Mariena or herself?

Mariena's eyes widened, but as she looked at their reflections in the mirror, she couldn't help but smile. They made quite the picture —her timid, almost scared face and Amanda's wide-eyed, grasping image.

"What?" Amanda couldn't help but giggle, looking at Mariena's eyes in the mirror. "Am I so humorous?"

Mariena nodded. "Yes." More laughter shook her.

"Well, then." Amanda let loose Mariena's hair and put her hands on her hips. "I'm pleased I could put a smile on that lovely face."

Had it been so apparent? Mariena's sadness and hurt on display for everyone?

The smile fell.

"No. Please don't be so serious." Amanda leaned over her, laying a hand on Mariena's shoulder.

Mariena met Amanda's eyes in the reflection. "I..." What could she say? How could she deny her feelings?

Amanda nodded. "It's all right." Her words were gentler than Mariena expected. "I understand more than you know."

Mariena's brows furrowed. How could she understand? She was married to a man that returned her love. They were alike...in so many ways. At least in the ways that counted.

"Brandon and I didn't know each other when we got married."

What? Had they not married for love?

"We married for convenience, too. He wed me to save my son and me from starving. And...well, I wasn't keen on it at all. Not for some time. But, we grew to love each other. Once I let God work on me."

God again. Mariena frowned. What was the white man's obsession with this one God?

"I believe it can happen for you, too." Amanda squeezed Mariena's shoulder and stepped back.

Even with Amanda's encouragement, it seemed a bit much to put any hope in. Especially after Cutie had made overtures only to put up barriers. Even betrothed, he had regretted the simple contact they'd had. Why should she believe he would want anything more? Or would he seek more after their vows? Perhaps that was a line he needed to cross before such contact was permitted. Was she ready for that?

After all, for her, that was the wedding *and* the marriage—the two become one.

Had she judged Cutie unfairly?

Amanda reappeared in the mirror, all smiles. "I think it's time."

Mariena drew in a breath and let it out. Could she be open again?

Hands on her arms urged her to stand.

She did so, turning and facing Amanda.

They clasped hands.

Then Amanda leaned forward and began speaking, her eyes closed. "Lord, watch over Cutie and Mariena. I pray that Mariena would be a good wife and would know Your grace and Your blessing. May she and Cutie lean on You and build their marriage on You. Amen."

Was she praying to God? About Mariena and Cutie?

Mariena's face heated. Why? If she didn't believe in God, why should it bother her if Amanda prayed to a deity *she* believed in?

Mariena didn't know. Would she ever understand the inner workings of her mind? Or find a safe haven for her thoughts?

Or for her heart?

Cutie was awkward in a suit. That's all there was to it. It was all he could do to keep from tugging at nearly every part of the confounded thing.

It was a borrowed suit at that, another of Brandon's kindnesses. Would the man's generosity know no bounds?

Wiggling his shoulders, he had the urge to reach up and adjust the confounded jacket. There was just no focusing in this thing. So itchy.

Brandon tapped his shoulder. "She'll be here soon."

Oh. Had he misinterpreted Cutie's fidgeting as nervousness after the bride?

Cutie turned toward his boss to assure him there was no such uneasiness about him, but the smile on the man's face was too much. How could he disappoint the man?

Should he be anxious for his bride?

Looking up the aisle to the back of the church, to where she would enter, he stilled. His heartbeat quickened. Maybe there was more to his disposition than the suit's fabric.

As his gaze wandered back down the aisle, he spotted Uncle Owen. Though he was only Brandon's uncle in truth, the man had become a surrogate father to them all. The older man offered Cutie a wink and a smile. Was that supposed to encourage him? Did Uncle Owen know that whole story?

He hoped not. In truth, he hoped no one knew the whole story. Or ever would.

If only the sordid pieces of his life could remain disjointed. And no one would ever be the wiser. As long as he kept everyone at arm's length...

The piano started to play the familiar bridal tune.

Cutie shot his gaze to the back door of the church, wishing there were a window somewhere on that wall.

Amanda stepped in, carrying a simple bouquet of a few flowers. She glided down the aisle, sharing a meaningful glance with her husband, and then setting her eyes on Cutie.

What was in her small smile? Was her intent to encourage him as well? He would like to hope that he and Mariena had every chance at happiness that Brandon and Amanda did, but it just wasn't the same. Brandon wasn't like him. Didn't have his scars. His rough edges.

The door opened once more, and the congregation stood. Sheriff McAllen was perhaps the first to his feet. Though his eyes were not on the back of the building, but on Cutie. And his gaze was hard, threatening.

What did it matter? Cutie would fulfill his promise today. There was nothing the sheriff's intimidation could do to stop him. Had not Cutie's own demons done their fair share of creating challenges? More so than McAllen ever could.

Cutie knew Mariena had entered the church before she became visible. The pews full of standing people blocked his view. He fought to keep still, surprised at his longing to see her.

As she rounded the left side of the church and approached the aisle down the center, his breath caught.

Nothing could have prepared him for this. Not even the glimpse of her in the dress those few days prior.

Still, it wasn't the dress. Though it enhanced her natural beauty. It wasn't the style of her hair, though it drew his eye to her lovely features. And it wasn't the flowers she bore, though they complemented the natural tone of her skin.

It was none of it and all of it.

And he couldn't tear his gaze away.

Her lips were bowed and set into resolution. But her eyes. Had he ever seen anything like them? Twin stars, shimmering. Set on him.

Deep, soulful. And hopeful.

How could it be that she had hope after all he had done? Was this a testament to her character? Or to the fact that there was a God watching out for him?

A heaviness sifted through his core. The weight of what he took on shook his foundation. But so did his desire to have it. To be that safe place for her.

As he watched, she neared and stood beside him.

He reached out and took her hand. Was he supposed to?

Her eyes widened. Was she surprised? Had he been too bold?

Still, her fingers fit perfectly to his as he intertwined them. He would not let her go. Not now. Not ever.

The preacher began. And as he led them through promises and vows that were prescribed by the church, Cutie wanted for words that meant more. Wished for things that came from his heart. Yet, he was thankful he did not need them in this moment. There would be more time to put voice to his thoughts.

At long last, he slid a ring onto Mariena's finger and the reverend allowed that he should seal their union with a kiss.

How would Mariena receive this? As a beginning? Or as a trespass? She had let him before, but that did not mean he could again.

They faced each other and he caught her gaze.

Her features were difficult to read.

But, if he wanted to take the next step, it would need to start now. The tone of their marriage would be decided here.

He leaned toward her, tugging her hands to draw her nearer.

As her lips came closer, he turned and pressed a kiss to the side of her face.

A cheer went up from the congregation.

As he pulled back, her raised brows and widened eyes spoke of her confusion and surprise.

He lifted her hand and kissed her there as well, hoping she would discern his intent.

The reverend continued with the final words and made his presentation of them as man and wife. He leaned closer to Cutie. "This is usually when you lead her back up the aisle."

"Oh, yes." Cutie nodded. "My apologies." He took Mariena's hand and set it in the crook of his elbow. Then, turning toward the small crowd, he led her back through the church.

What would the rest of the day bring? When would they be alone?

What would he say then? Dare he move forward with the marriage? Or take time to build their relationship? What was she thinking?

Perhaps there were too many unknowns.

As if the wedding ceremony hadn't been strange enough, this idea of a dinner party afterward had truly struck Mariena as odd. What reason could they possibly have for such a thing? Why not let the newly joined couple have that time to enjoy each other?

Except in her and Cutie's case. She wasn't certain she was altogether eager to be alone with him. Not after the other night.

And why had he not truly kissed her in the church? She stole a glance at him as he led her from the modest church building toward the town cafe.

The simple contact of his lips upon her face had heated her, to be sure. And she hated her body's betrayal. Or did she? She had not yet determined how much she dared hope for a change of heart in Cutie after their vows.

But a peck upon the side of her face and once on her hand? It wasn't what she expected. Yet, would she have welcomed his lips on hers? Her face warmed even more at the memory.

She turned away from him, lest he look her way.

No, perhaps his prudence had been best.

They neared the cafe, the whole of the townsfolk behind them, it seemed.

The door to the cafe opened, and they were ushered in by the owner of the small eatery. As she stepped in, she wondered at how the space would fit everyone.

Several filed in, and one by one took their seats. Some stood, but the entirety of their guests made their way into the cafe, albeit a bit of a tight fit.

That did not seem to bother the townspeople one bit.

Mariena was not so pleased. Wide spaces and openness had been her experience of the world. Her only confinement of any sort—a room holding a handful of people. This...*this*...was a bit much.

"Breathe." Cutie's voice was near. His breath was on her ear.

She suppressed a shiver. Because of his closeness? Or because of the crowd pressing in?

Her breaths continued to come and go quicker than usual.

Cutie's larger hand covered hers and squeezed. "Breathe slowly."

She looked at him. How could he know her struggle? Had he not lived among these people his whole life?

"Like this." He inhaled with a long slow draw through his nose and then let it out through his mouth, with the same steady pace.

Her thoughts seemed hazy. Everything started to spin.

"Close your eyes and try." His words seemed more a command now than encouragement.

She obeyed, shutting her eyes and imagining the open field near the homestead where she liked to sit and take in the sun and the breeze.

"Now in...slowly." His voice was gentle again, and he intertwined their fingers.

She worked to draw in the next breath with as much agonizing slowness as he had. Her lungs burned to push it out.

"And out."

How could she control it any longer? She pressed it from her body.

"Again." His words were flat. Had she disappointed him?

She did so try to slow the intake of air once more. But this time, she fought every instinct in her and slowed its exhale.

Over and over, they did so.

The sound of liquid toppling into a container bade her open her eyes. A young lady was pouring tea into their glasses. Though her gaze was focused on her work, the pink hue to her cheeks spoke more of her thoughts. Had she thought something strange of their behavior? Was Mariena now made more of an oddity than she already was?

The girl, barely a woman, peered at Mariena. What was that in her eyes? It didn't look pleasant.

When the girl's gaze averted to Cutie, a smile broke and her color deepened. Had this girl and Cutie...?

Mariena glanced at her now husband. His eyes were for her alone. Was he still concerned after her breathing? Meeting his gaze, she offered him the best smile she could conjure, which she knew wasn't much. "Thank you."

He nodded. Something passed in his eyes that she couldn't identify. Something that sparked a reaction within her. Heat now burned between her shoulder blades. It wasn't unpleasant...not truly. What was it?

Brandon clapped Cutie on the back and said something.

Cutie turned to address him.

It gave Mariena a moment to glance about the room. One look at the tables nearby and she remembered that to be unwise. She focused on where her plate would be. What foodstuffs were appropriate for such a celebration?

It wasn't long before the girl returned with their plates. Brown meat she had come to know as roast, which came with carrots and potatoes, and green beans on the side, all of it rather soft looking, emanated wonderful smells.

But why was it soft?

These things did not come from the earth this way. But, like Cook, those preparing the meal perhaps liked the produce of the dirt this way.

Would she ever get used to it?

Brandon stood and offered a prayer for the meal.

As he finished, Cutie gave her hand a squeeze and released it.

She rubbed her now sweating palm against her skirt. It was only then that she realized he had not let her go until he had to.

utie grew weary of the celebration. Being the center of attention wasn't his preference. And it was wearing on him. He turned to Mariena. She, too, seemed rather spent.

Did she not know what to do with herself? Her head was dipped and her eyes had been on her plate since the meal arrived. Were the townsfolk not engaging her in conversation?

If not for Brandon, he wasn't certain he would have anyone to talk to either. It wasn't as if he were a favorite among the people of this small town.

How many knew of his trespass? His sin?

There was no way to know.

This wasn't the time to revisit it. His wedding day...and wedding night, required more from him than this self-focused pity.

Leaning into Mariena's space, he slid a hand over hers atop the table. "It may be time for us to make our way upstairs."

"Upstairs?" Her brows furrowed.

Perhaps she didn't know. "We'll be staying here, at the boarding house."

"Oh." Her features colored—that rosy hue he found so becoming on her tanned skin. It was endearing. "We won't go to the ranch?"

Was there a bit of brokenness in her words? Could she be so uneasy? About not returning to the ranch? Or for what she feared the night would bring?

He squeezed her hand. "All will be well."

She searched his eyes. What did she seek?

It was all he could do to remain still and not pull back from her scrutiny.

"What of Nisto?"

Whatever he had expected, it wasn't that. Was she truly so concerned after her brother? Or was this only a distraction? A way to keep her mind from delving into unknown territory?

"He will be fine. Amanda and Brandon will care for him. You must know he is safe with them."

She bit at her lip. It drew his attention to that feature, which he would rather not dwell on just yet. Her lips. He remembered how they felt beneath his, how they moved against his. Soft and...accommodating. Could she want him as much as he wanted her?

Her gaze cut to Amanda then back to him. "Must I?"

He shifted so he could clasp her smooth hand between his. "It is best." Surely, she could see that. The arrangement of the boarding house room this night had been for her sake. Otherwise they would have been in tight quarters at the homestead. With too many ears.

She nodded and released her lip.

His eyes were still focused on her full, reddened lips. Could he tear his gaze away? It would not do for him to be caught up like this. Not yet. He did not wish to intimidate or scare her.

How was this to be done, after all? He wasn't sure. But he did not think the great desire rising in him, resisting his efforts to put it down, would serve either of them.

Freeing a hand and dabbing at his mouth with a napkin, he said, "Shall we?"

Her eyes widened for a moment. But only a moment. Then it was as if she became resigned. Resigned? Is that how she would proceed?

Releasing his hand, she pushed back from the table.

He stood and reached down to assist her.

She smiled at him, but did not take his proffered hand.

Still, he slid his hand around to rest on the small of her back as he commanded the attention of the crowd by raising his other hand.

"Quiet!" Brandon called out. "The groom has something to say."

Cutie nodded at his boss and scanned the room. Too many eyes on him. He swallowed hard. They waited for him to speak. But what had he wanted to say? His grasped for the words, so readily available before, but now vanished.

Brandon cleared his throat.

Oh yes. The farewells. Pressing his free hand to the table in a fist, he hoped no one would notice his trembling. "We are so thankful for everything today. The support and encouragement shown by your presence has meant so much. Not to mention this delicious meal!"

The crowd clapped.

As the cheering died down, Cutie raised his voice again. "However... I think it is time for us to retire after such a long day."

This time, the applause was accompanied by jeers and whistles.

Cutie's face warmed at the implications. And he would not chance a glance toward Mariena. Did she understand? How could she not?

Letting his hand slide across her back and down her arm, he clasped her hand and led her around the table and through the packed room.

He paused here and there when someone would reach out to him. Otherwise, he remained set on the stairs at the opposite side of the room.

Once there, he turned to the large gathering again.

Everyone had risen and now stood watching him and Mariena with baited breath. What did they want? Details? For him to insinuate something? For him to kiss her?

Did he wish to appease them with such a gesture? What would Mariena think? Which was more important?

He gazed over the eager faces then glanced at Mariena. She seemed uncertain, hesitant, and,perhaps a little scared.

No matter what the townspeople expected, he would not use Mariena to cater to their desires. What happened between him and his... wife...was for them alone. And *that* he would honor above all.

Pulling her closer, he tucked her under his arm, wanting to protect her from the many gazes surrounding them.

He raised a hand once more, waving a final farewell to the people who had gathered in celebration of Cutie's nuptials.

With that, he led Mariena up the stairs and out of sight. His heart thundered in his ears, keeping all sounds from below no louder than a muted din.

What would come of the next several hours? What did he want? What did she want?

Time would only march forward, and what was to be, would be.

Mariena swallowed hard as Cutie closed the door. She stood several paces away from him, unable to control her breathing. Could he hear it? Each breath sounded as if a gasp, they came so deep and troubled.

She scanned the small space. There wasn't much to recommend this room. Not much larger than the bed itself, the room only accommodated a tiny stand with a washbowl and another with an oil lamp as well as a chair in the corner.

The chair held a moderate-sized bag. What could it contain? Had Amanda packed something for her?

A breeze floating in from the lone window tickled her neck. And the rumble of voices below became audible. Was the crowd making their way to their homes?

Her skin heated. She knew Cutie's gaze was upon her. Though she wanted to fight the urge to look at him, she could not. Lifting her eyes to his, her heartbeat quicken, as did her breathing.

The light was dim in the room—only a lantern remained to chase away the shadows, now that the sun was setting. A lone flame licking at the wick flickered light across Cutie's face. His features were difficult to read. Because her own emotion had clouded her so?

He glanced over her shoulder and stepped toward her with determination, his mouth set. Would he simply grab her?

Dare she step back? What good would that do?

She held her ground but could not keep her eyes from closing.

He moved past her, his shoulder grazing hers.

Her eyes opened and she jerked around. What was the matter?

His attention had been on the window.

She craned her neck to peer around him. There wasn't much visible from her vantage point.

But a small group had gathered just outside. Several from below pointed at the window.

Her face heated. How could they? Spy upon them at such a time as this?

She looked away. Was there any way to cover her shame?

Wood shifted against wood. Did he lower the window? How far? Would this room become overheated without the draft?

Coming alongside him, she placed her hands on his.

He paused, catching her eyes.

She pulled the curtains closed. "There. Maybe that is all needed."

He nodded. But he did not pull his hands back, letting them linger near hers at the thin fabric of the window coverings.

Her eyes set upon their fingers, so close, yet not quite touching. How long would they remain so? Dare she draw back? Could she not? Perhaps she should wait for him, trusting him, to reach for her? And what then?

She shivered despite her determined control and let her hands fall to her sides.

But he grasped them quickly.

A breath escaped before she could clamp her mouth shut.

Tugging her, he drew her to himself until they stood facing one another.

She stared at their hands, not willing to look at him. Not sure she had the courage to do so. Would she be lost to him if she did?

Mere inches away, he stood over her, the heat of his breath on her face, tantalizing her. His fingers worked magic upon hers—moving over her hands, dancing upon her fingers. How could such a thing mesmerize her so?

But it did. The sensation it stirred in her core softened her. Could it also melt the hardness she had built up to him? For then, she might have no defenses.

"Mariena," he whispered.

She looked up at him, daring to meet his eyes at last. A tear caressed the side of her face as she did so.

But he seemed entranced by her hands. Enough so, even, that he brought her hands to his mouth and pressed a kiss to each of her fingers.

A heat filled her that was certain to make her bend to his will. How was this possible?

More tears came. He did not seem to notice, so she ignored them.

In fact, his eyes had shut the moment his lips touched her skin. Where would this go? To the inevitable? Would he seek all she had to give? Whether or not she was ready to offer it? Was she ready?

His mouth pressed against her left wrist. The scruff of a face unshaven since that morning gently scraped the delicate skin.

She whimpered. How could she have become so weak? Succumb to such tenderness in mere moments?

Her knees softened. Would they hold her?

As if he knew, Cutie's other arm came around her waist, holding her up and pulling her against him at the same time.

Only then did he look at her.

He pressed her hand against his face and looked into her eyes.

"Do you know what you do to me?" His voice was hoarse.

Something in her stomach fluttered. She opened her mouth, but she couldn't force any words out.

The intensity of his gaze on her changed. She didn't quite understand it in the haze of emotion and sensation, but it did. He examined her features. What was he looking for?

After a few moments, he gathered her impossibly closer to his chest.

Weak and without resolve, she clung to him. He was everything in this place, in this hour.

He let out a long, ragged breath. "God, help me."

She closed her eyes and leaned into him, longing for more of these pleasures. What was to come?

In the next moment, she was in his arms. Her feet were in the air, and he carried her. She buried her head in his shoulder. Did she have the strength for what was to come?

The bed cushioned her. And his arms were gone.

Questions without answers filled her mind. All crying out at once... loud enough she couldn't separate them to hear one of them.

She searched for her husband.

He hovered over the lantern.

And then the light was out.

His silhouette was all she could make out.

"Charl—" she started.

He jerked his head in her direction.

Was he angry at her address? She quieted.

Walking around the bed, he slid onto the mattress beside her. Would he not hold her? Not...love her?

He turned on his side, facing her.

She reached a tentative hand out, touching his face.

That seemed to be all he needed. He pulled her to himself, tucking her head into the space between his neck and shoulder.

"Now, rest," he whispered.

She pulled back, opening her mouth. Would he not consummate their union?

Reaching up, he grazed the side of her face. "Rest."

She lay back down next to him, letting him arrange her tightly against him. What could be the meaning of this? Did he not want her? No, that did not seem to be so. Then why?

Searching for the answer through an examination of her memory and what she knew of him, nothing was forthcoming. Was the answer then, to be found, in her? In something she had done?

Or something she was? Or was not?

So, they had gone through with it. That ranch hand had no idea.

But that didn't mean McAllen had no recourse. No, he would stamp out any and all trouble...inasmuch as *he* deemed necessary. And it was, after all, *his* job to determine what was necessary.

Cutie's eyes opened. The heat along his left side reminded him that Mariena still slept there. How long had he waited for her to find sleep? He had wondered if she would ever rest. At least, once she did, it was peaceful.

How would he ever explain his heart to her? Make her understand?

Last night, it would have been impossible. It took all his concentration to restrain himself. That had been truly the most difficult thing he'd ever done.

He looked at his bride.

She was as beautiful at rest as she was awake. But there was something in this moment of peace he liked even more—when she was not worried, or striving, or hurting. If only he could offer her this always.

His arm had long since lost all feeling, the blood flow cut off by the weight of her head. But he didn't care. He relished bearing this small burden for her.

She stirred and shifted closer to him.

Her movements and the warmth of her body did not make it easy for him to remain still, but he looked at the ceiling and prayed God would help him.

Strange...he had not dared speak to God before. But now, here he was. Praying.

Because of her.

The evenness of her breathing shifted. She had awakened.

He pulled his head back and looked down to catch her eyes.

Her lashes flickered open and her brown eyes moved about the area, settling on him.

"Good morning." He offered a smile.

"Morning." Her words seemed hesitant. And her body stiffened.

No. Please, no.

She drew back the arm that had draped across his chest and pulled away, soon sitting up in the bed.

"What is it?" He sat, too. Was she upset? Why? Had he not done the gentlemanly thing? As much as he could? As much as anyone could possibly ask of him?

She looked away, toward the washbasin. Her hair was a mess. Much of it had come free from the elaborate design it had been styled in.

But his fingers ached to touch it. Was it as silken as it appeared?

He shook his head. *Her. Focus on her.*

"Mariena?"

She pulled her knees to her chest, wrapping her arms around them. "I...I just..." Her words fell off.

"What?" He kept his tone soft as he gently put a hand on her shoulder nearest him.

Setting her head on her crossed arms but facing away from him, she didn't speak for several moments.

The silence became thick.

What had happened? They'd had tender interactions last night. And he...well, he had done what he could to keep himself in check. How could she not understand that?

He slid his legs over the opposite side of the bed. "I don't know what you want from me."

Silence.

Standing, he moved to the water basin and grabbed the pitcher. "I'll, um, go get some water."

Nothing.

Once outside the room, he drew in a deep breath before forging ahead. He had not gone but a few paces down the hallway when he heard the latch lock on the door.

It wasn't likely she would let him back in anytime soon either.

It was quite a task for Mariena to maneuver out of the elaborate dress she had been married in. But it wasn't until she had done so and dressed in the plainer dress Amanda had packed for her, brushed out her hair, and re-braided it, that she unlocked the door. By then, she had gotten much better control of herself.

"Thank you." She smiled as Cutie brought in the pitcher of water.

His eyes widened. "What—?"

She took the pitcher from him and poured the water into the bowl. Then she went about freshening her skin. Did she care what he thought? Or if he were confused? Did he, in the end, deserve an answer after last night when he refused to...

No. He didn't.

If he didn't want to treat her as his wife, she wouldn't treat him as any more than he apparently was to her—a ranch hand.

She blotted her face dry and wrung her hands dry as well before setting the towel to the side. Turning, she found him standing where she had left him, arms crossed over his chest, watching her.

"My sorry. Did you need to...?" She indicated the water basin.

He lifted his hands in surrender. "No. Not at all."

Was it just her, or did he seem amused? No matter.

She stood straight and indicated the dress, laid across the bed, and the bag, still set on the chair. "I am ready you to take me back to ranch."

He quirked a brow. "Oh, you are, are you?"

"Yes. If you help me with these and show to the wagon, we can go."

Taking a step closer to her, he rubbed his chin. She noticed the stubble, even more grown in, and could not help but remember the feel of it against her wrist. A flush of heat passed through her.

"We will be traveling by horse, wife dearest."

"Horse?" He couldn't mean what he was implying. "I don't understand."

"You, me...one horse."

Her features drained. The heat was gone. By horse? Not by wagon? "What do you expect me do with dress? Or with bag?"

"Leave them here. I'm sure you and Mrs. Miller can come up with a plan. As it is, the way back to the ranch is *my* horse. And *only* my horse." He turned and stepped from the room.

Her hands clenched. Why would he be so infuriating? He knew of her great fear of the animal. Why be so obstinate?

She would rise above it. Prove she wasn't bothered.

Stomping off after him, she caught him halfway down the stairs.

"Did you want to breakfast here?" he called before spinning to catch her gaze.

She stopped just short of slamming into him. Her chest heaved. But it was perhaps more from emotion than exertion. "What?"

"Breakfast?" he repeated, pointing toward the dining room.

She glared at him. Could she stare a hole into him? "Best I get back to ranch. Sooner."

"All right." He shrugged.

He led the way through the cafe.

The young woman who filled their drinks the previous evening walked into the main dining area just then.

Cutie nodded at her, tipping his hat in her direction.

Did he do this to upset Mariena? She could not help that fire hit her belly and moved upward. Would it show in her eyes?

Even if so, he did not turn to look at her. She forced her eyes to hold forward, on his back, and not peer at the girl.

Out the door they went; she trailed behind him. But he didn't stop there. He moved off the boarded sidewalk and onto the dirt street.

She stumbled when she stepped down, her arms flying out from her sides as she attempted to catch her balance.

Cutie spun and took a step toward her as if he would offer assistance.

Jerking her arms back into her chest, she shot him a sharp look.

He returned her sour expression and set out in the direction he had been walking once more.

She picked up her pace again, her right ankle a bit sore. Had she turned it? *Confound these shoes!* Why couldn't she just wear her skins and moccasins? Limping and hurrying along, she followed him to the livery. By the time she arrived, he had disappeared into the small structure.

Pausing outside, she leaned against the fence and scanned the area. How safe was she here? This was just down the street from the saloon. Sometimes that place could mean trouble. She'd seen her fair share of men with drink in their bellies.

A couple of cowpokes approached, their steps sloppy.

She turned away.

The crunch of their boots on the dirt road slowed as they neared the livery. Why? Had they business here? Or did they wish to harass her?

She looked for some sign of life within. Where was the blacksmith? Was he speaking with Cutie? When would they come out?

"You look like someone who needs some help," one of the men said, his voice rough.

What should she say? Dare she speak? Would that make it worse?

The other man took a step closer, he moved around behind her. "I'll say. You seem a bit...lost."

She shifted forward, away from him.

But the first man leaned in. "We might can help you."

"Or you can keep moving." A deeper voice commanded from off to the left.

She turned.

Sheriff McAllen stood, hand on the hip where his pistol rested. He glared at the two men. "You best go on now. Don't give me any reason to think you two want trouble."

The men looked at each other and then at the sheriff. They shrugged and walked off in the direction they had been headed. But not before one of the men winked at Mariena.

She shivered but didn't say anything until they were well out of earshot.

"Thank you," she said, still watching the departing figures. "I am—"

"You shouldn't be here," the sheriff threw back at her.

Her eyes were on him in a moment.

"This is exactly why I wanted you out of my town and on the Indian Reservation. I can't be wasting my time keeping track of you."

She swallowed. Hard.

His gaze beared down on her.

"What's going on here?" a more familiar voice came from behind her. Even without turning she knew it was Cutie.

McAllen looked over her head. "Nothing that concerns you." He gave Mariena a meaningful look.

She understood. It was a warning.

The heat of Cutie's body emanated against her back. Had he stepped closer? "I would prefer you not harass my *wife*, Sheriff. Perhaps you should focus on the riffraff in the town instead of the—"

"He wasn't harassing me." Would Cutie hear her voice, it seemed so small, too small.

"See there? I was only checking in on the little lady." McAllen tipped his mouth in a half smile. "You got a problem with that?"

Cutie blew out a breath; it rushed against her ear.

She fought the urge to close her eyes.

"Nice to see you again, *ma'am*." McAllen tipped his hat and stepped off.

Why did his address sound like a swear? And why was she uncertain this was over?

Cutie's hand surrounded her upper arm. "Come on. Let's get going."

Was he frustrated with her? What had she done?

He pulled her through the livery yard. And when they stopped, it was in front of the horse she had come to know and...*suffer* as well as she could.

Turning toward her, Cutie put his hands around her waist and hoisted her up. Without anything further, he grabbed for the pommel and pulled himself up behind her.

Her back pressed against his chest; she lost her breath for a moment.

There wasn't much time for her to catch it, however, as he spurred the horse on. She was pushed further into him and could do nothing more than hold on for dear life.

CHAPTER 10
Mistaken

Cutie wished Mariena wasn't so tense sitting there in front of him. But what did he expect? She and the horse didn't get along. And, right now, neither did he and she, exactly.

Why had he let her rile him up? He had let her actions stir him to anger, and then his stubbornness refused to permit him to let it go.

But with her so near, he couldn't keep his mind from drifting to those moments the previous evening. The tender moments...when he had held her, watched her release her worries to sleep, and fallen asleep himself beside her.

Then this morning, it was as if none of that mattered. She was angry. And he still didn't understand why. He couldn't have been more understanding. More restrained...

There was only one answer: she was impossible.

They neared Brandon's ranch, and Cutie urged more speed from the horse.

She tightened muscles that he thought couldn't constrict any further.

It would only be a few more moments and he could let her off the animal and turn her loose from his presence.

He would be lying if he didn't admit that it would come with some sadness. What did he want from *her*, after all? More than this.

But if this was what she wanted, this would be what she got.

Slowing Patch as he neared the barn, Cutie imagined perhaps more than actually sensed her breathing more steadily. When he pulled the reins to halt the animal, Mariena shifted as if she would slide off herself.

He dropped off to the side and lifted his arms for her.

She slid down, more quickly than he expected, and lost her balance when her feet touched the ground.

He grasped her arms, holding her upright. Had she become light-headed from the ride? Perhaps he shouldn't have pushed the horse so much.

"Thank you." She didn't look at him.

He could have kicked himself. Why didn't he think more about this? Not just of his own emotions?

Steadier, she turned and stepped away. When she put weight on her right foot, she almost toppled.

He flew to her side in an instant, his arms around her.

She pushed against him.

"What is wrong with you? Do you want me to let you fall?" His words came out in exasperated breaths.

The struggle stopped. Her hands covered her face and she shook.

"Mariena, what—?"

The door to the homestead slammed shut and hurried footfalls fell on the ground.

"Cutie!"

He looked toward the sound as Mariena stilled.

Amanda ran toward them.

Cutie helped Mariena to a bench and turned his attention to his boss's wife, who was almost upon them.

"Cutie, Mariena, I'm so glad you are home." Amanda gulped in air. Her eyes were red and swollen.

"What's happened?" Was it Brandon? Had something terrible befallen the man while they were gone?

Amanda shook her head, drawing in air as if she were trying to catch her breath. "It's Mr. Miller."

Cutie's vision became hazy. Would that he had been here! How could he have let his boss down...again? "What's happened to him? How can I help?"

"He's dead!" Amanda's tears poured anew.

Cutie grabbed for her elbows. Was he doing so for her stability? Or for his?

"No!" He shut his eyes against the news. There were other things he wanted to say, but somehow, he managed to keep his tongue in check in front of Amanda. "How? Where is Uncle Owen? Dan? And Slim? What's being done?"

"What?" Amanda's cries cleared. "Oh, Cutie! I'm sorry. Not Brandon...his *father*, Mr. Miller, has passed."

Sensation poured back into Cutie's limbs. And hope was reborn. Brandon lived.

Mariena lay awake. The day had been heavy. Perhaps too heavy.

Brandon had returned from town, but he had been little more than a shell of himself.

Such was the way with grief. No one could expect him to be himself for many moons. Perhaps many seasons.

It was different with each person.

Many things had transpired in the hours that followed. Arrangements for Brandon and Amanda to travel eastward with Lucy and Samuel. What would it be like at the homestead without them?

This night before their departure was already quieter than it had right to be. Except for the pounding of her heart.

Would Cutie come to her tonight? Everyone expected them to bed down as man and wife. Would they?

Or would he defy their expectations and return to the bunkhouse? Would she be shamed by such a decision? Would he?

She turned to her side. It should not matter. None of it. Cutie had made his decision. There was naught left but for her to live with it. Closing her eyelids, she quieted her mind and sought the respite of sleep.

Everything stilled.

Except the cries coming from further down the hall.

She opened her eyes. Who was that? Amanda?

Had the woman been so touched by her father-in-law's passing? Even though Brandon's parents lived far away, had they become so close?

Or did Amanda's heart ache for her husband's pain? Was that possible?

Mariena listened to her newfound friend mourning in the night's stillness. Perhaps...no, that would not be welcomed. Then again...maybe Amanda needed the comfort of a kind face.

Sitting up, Mariena waited, holding her breath. Dare she chance it?

The sorrow pouring forth from the other room did not quiet.

Mariena stood and padded to her door. Soon enough, she had made her way down the hall and to the oak barrier between the small corridor and the room that Amanda and Brandon shared. Only then did Mariena wonder if Brandon was within. And if not, where was he?

The men had gone into town to make the final arrangements for the trip. Perhaps they lingered. Did Brandon not know his wife needed him?

Raising a tentative hand, Mariena tapped on the door.

Crying gave way to sniffling.

Mariena closed her eyes and knocked again.

Movement within gave her hope and brought a tightness to her midsection. Was she anxious? Why?

The door creaked open only enough for Amanda to peer out.

Feeling out of place, Mariena tugged at her nightdress. Why had she believed this a good idea?

"Mariena?" Amanda opened the door a bit wider. "Did you need something?"

"I..." What could she say? Why *had* she come? "I am to see you."

"Oh?" Amanda sniffled. Bringing a delicate laced handkerchief to her face, she blotted at her eyes. "To see me? I am afraid I am...out of sorts right now."

Why must her English be so poor? Amanda had not understood. "I mean to say...I am here to help."

"Help?" Amanda's brows furrowed.

"To…" What was the word she needed? "…offer words. Comfort."

Amanda looked to something just inside the room and sighed. Perhaps it would be better if Mariena had not come. She couldn't even put words together, for goodness' sake!

The space widened and Amanda opened her arm, indicating Mariena should enter. Did she truly wish for the company? Or did she only pander to Mariena's desire to help?

Either way, the invitation had been made. And she must take it.

Stepping into the darkened room, Mariena searched for a chair. There, in the corner. But a dress lay across it. No matter. She could stand.

Amanda seemed to notice just as she did. "Let me get that." She strode across the room and lifted the well-tailored traveling outfit. Much fancier than anything Amanda wore around the ranch.

What would it be like around here without her friend?

"Please, sit." Amanda laid the dress across the foot of the bed and lowered herself on the side nearest the window. Moonlight streamed in, casting a glow across her features. Even reddened and swollen from crying, she was lovely.

Mariena looked at the chair, so far away. Dare she move it? Would that be too bold? But she could not bring her friend comfort if she remained such a distance from her.

Taking in a breath to garner her strength, Mariena grasped the back of the simple wooden chair and dragged it to where Amanda sat.

Mariena was met by Amanda's wide-eyed gaze.

"Forgive, please. I want to speak open."

Amanda nodded, dropping her gaze to her lap.

Mariena looked out into the night, her view unhindered by the curtains, which had been drawn as far to the sides as possible. "This hurt. It is not easy. And it will hurt. For long."

Feeling Amanda's gaze on her, Mariena turned to face her. "I hurt still. I think, always."

Amanda reached for Mariena's hand. "I know."

Why was it now Amanda comforting her? This wasn't how it was supposed to go! "But you…you are strong. For Brandon?"

Amanda nodded. "Yes. I am sad for Brandon. Mr. Miller was a good man. And he was good to me."

Mariena nodded. "Pain is hard. But sadness is good. It heals. The place in your heart that loved is now what hurts. Shows that Mr. Miller matter."

"Yes." Amanda's eyes glistened. "That is true. And he did matter." She squeezed Mariena's fingers. "Thank you for your words. And for being here with me."

Mariena nodded then turned toward the night sky once more.

"And you?" Amanda said, her words a gentle probe. "Are you all right? After last night?"

Why did she have to ask? What could Mariena say? Dare she speak the truth? That Cutie didn't want her?

She shook her head.

"What is it?" Amanda's voice remained soft.

"Nothing."

"Nothing?"

Mariena looked at her friend. Would she be able to keep her tears in check? She felt well enough in control. "Nothing happened."

Amanda's brow cinched. No words came. What could she say? There wasn't anything that would make it right.

Turning back to the window, Mariena let out a breath. "So, this is marriage."

Amanda's hand took Mariena's. "No. It's not."

But Mariena could not look at Amanda. Her fight against the tears was a losing battle.

"Mariena, I don't know what Cutie was thinking or..." A heavy pause followed. "Or what his plan may be. But I know he cares for you. You must believe that."

Must she?

"Trust. God will work all this out."

God again. When would all this talk of God stop? Instead of challenging her friend, Mariena nodded. After all, she had come here tonight to help Amanda. And the woman made every effort to comfort *her*.

But tomorrow, Amanda would leave for who knew how long. And Mariena would be left with her feelings, her thoughts, and Cutie.

What would the weeks to come bring?

Cutie slipped into the house as he slid his hat from his head. He was thankful Slim had talked Brandon into taking his rest. The man had retired about an hour ago.

But Cutie didn't bend to Slim's persuasive arguments of a new wife awaiting him. No, he insisted on staying with his fellow ranch hands and doing what he could to make things ready for their boss's departure.

Brandon's grief had been evident. It hadn't been that long ago that the man and his father were estranged. Had the happenings of that Christmas a few years back made such a difference? Could a matter of days together change years of separation?

Cutie's own father's face appeared in his mind. Was it possible? His chest tightened.

He couldn't think like that...hope where none existed. That wouldn't lead to good places.

Running a hand through his hair, he shifted his thoughts to the inhabitants of the house, specifically the bedroom that was his destination. What would he find? What did he want to find?

Setting his hat on the dining table, he looked at the front of his shirt. So much of the day clung to him. More so than he would have liked. Dare he carry all of it into the bedroom? Did he have a choice?

Standing behind of one of the dining chairs, he thought for a moment. Where were his clothes? At the bunkhouse? Or had someone seen to their being moved? He doubted he should disturb the other ranch hands at this hour.

That left him no choice but to slip into the room and hope that there were clean clothes within.

Moving as soundlessly as possible through the house, he stopped outside the room Mariena had had as her own these past couple of weeks.

It would be theirs—for who knew how long.

What was most appropriate? He had made his proposal of marriage without a thought as to what it might mean for Brandon, or Mariena, or even for him and their living spaces.

Brandon and Amanda had been so kind as to move them into the homestead, but was it a permanent solution? He doubted so.

With a hand on the latch, he held his breath and opened the door. Would the creak of the hinges wake her? Or would he find her already awake, unable to sleep?

The interior was dark. Curtains drawn and the lantern unlit; there was not a source of light to aid him. He paused, allowing his eyes to adjust to the dimness. As they did so, he could discern outlines—a couple of trunks, the bed, and a form breathing upon the mattress.

Two trunks. Likely then, one was his.

Closing the door, he moved to the closest one. The lid squeaked as he opened it. Had nothing in this place been oiled?

The garments within had soft fabric trimmed with lace and ribbon. Not his.

Over to the second trunk an arm's length further away. This lid made no sound. That didn't surprise him. He made every effort to maintain his things.

Though he didn't own many items of clothing, he could ensure he would not sully the bed or Mariena's nightclothes. For he dared not slip into bed with her unclothed. And it seemed too familiar to join her in naught but his nightshirt.

He made quick work of changing into fresh clothes, piling his soiled clothes in the corner. Once he dressed, he could find no reason to delay his rest. Stepping to the bed, his vision more acute in the darkness now, he let his gaze wander over his wife's figure. The bit of moonlight, scant as it was, now offered him some assistance.

She was still, save her chest rising and falling, which was slight as she lay on her side. And her hair, though it had been braided, lay in loosened pieces around her. Could he...dare he...give in to his desire to put his fingers in it?

He turned away when the temptation became too great. That might be too far.

Sitting upon the mattress, he cringed when the springs shook. But she continued to breathe steadily, undisturbed by his movement.

He lowered his body an inch at a time, until he released his weight onto the bed. Then he counted his breaths as he lay on his back. Shutting his eyes against the bit of light, he worked to slow his breathing but could not still his mind. There were too many thoughts, too much swirling emotion. How could this be? Was he not exhausted?

Fight though he did, he turned his head toward the back of Mariena's head and drew in a deep breath. Perhaps it was the unpleasant work of his day that heightened the sweet smell of lilac emanating from her. It intoxicated him.

The next thing he knew, he was on his side, his body leaning toward hers.

Even this, however, did not satiate him. He gripped the thin blanket, but his hands itched to touch her, to hold her as he had the night before. Would she wake if he did? And if so, would she welcome it?

He promised himself he would push no further but wanted only to have her in his arms.

With this firm determination in mind, he scooted closer, and reaching out, laid an arm around her.

Nothing.

The arm around her waist pulled only enough that she moved back against his chest.

Her breathing halted.

Had he wakened her?

No sound came from her.

Dare he speak first? Did he have the courage?

"I do not...understand."

He leaned his forehead to her shoulder. Must they have this conversation now?

She turned her face toward the ceiling.

He watched her in profile. Why must she take his breath away? Why must he care for her so?

"I not know what you want from me?"

The second time she echoed his earlier words. What did he want?

Why could he not decide? She offered him the lead. Would he not take it? Why not? Did he not wish for the responsibility?

"Please..." A lone, crystal-like tear shone in the soft moonlight as it made a trail down her face.

Was he such a coward?

"Mariena, I..." His words fell. Were there no more?

"What?" Her voice broke.

He pulled her even tighter against himself. Would she accept comfort from him?

She pushed against his arm on her midsection. "Don't." The word came out in a choke. "Don't."

Shifting backward, he released her and gave her as much space as the bed allowed, which wasn't much. But it permitted them to lie side by side without touching.

She continued to sniffle, curled on her side at the edge of the bed.

And he, now on his back again, lay in the night hating himself for the cad that he was.

CHAPTER 11

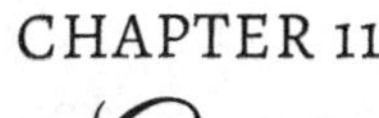

Mariena awoke with a start. Inhaling sharply, she jerked. Why should she be so disturbed?

Looking from side to side, she saw nothing but the inner walls of the bedroom she had occupied for many days now. No one hunted her. No one prepared to harm her.

Still, her heart hammered as if it would beat out of her chest. A thin layer of sweat covered her. And she couldn't shake the feeling that someone tracked her, intending to snuff her from existence.

She forced her breaths in and out evenly and told herself repeatedly that there was no such person after her. This room was tucked in the homestead of the Millers' ranch. And she was safe. Nisto was safe.

They had been plucked from certain death by Cutie and brought to this place of refuge. Only to be rescued once more by Cutie when Sheriff McAllen challenged their presence here.

Cutie.

He had come to her last night. Had held her.

Was that all he wanted?

She was uncertain. But he hadn't indicated any intentions beyond that. And she...she had thwarted him.

Dropping her head into her hands, her face burned. How soon she forgot that Cutie had given of himself not once, but twice now for her safety. Then she had let her sensitivities become wounded over his lack of action. Which, if she were honest, may be nothing more than a gentlemanly approach to his new wife and their unusual circumstances.

She peered up through fingers that covered her features. Why? Why must everything be so difficult? Did *she* make it so?

Perhaps it needed a discussion with Amanda.

Amanda!

The Millers were set to depart this morning.

Mariena glanced at the window. The sun was bright. Too bright.

Oh no!

Jerking the blanket back and sliding her legs over the side, Mariena raced toward the opening. She thrust the curtains back. The sun was indeed farther above the horizon than expected. How had she slept so long into the day?

She dressed in a hurry, hoping that something had delayed the Millers. Perhaps that was why she had been allowed to sleep.

Her hair was another matter. She ran a brush through the gentle waves created by the braid from the previous night. It wouldn't be long before they straightened.

Laying down the simple implement, she stepped from the room and quickened her pace through the house that was quieter than it should be.

Much too quiet.

Not even Cook could be found in the kitchen.

Mariena's heart beat faster.

She hurried around the dining table and toward the porch. As she stepped outside, she collided with something solid. And big.

Hands clamped onto her upper arms.

Resisting the hold, she twisted as she sought out the identity of her captor.

"Whoa! Something got you spooked?" Dan's deep voice vibrated against her chest.

She looked up at him.

His features read surprise. But his hands did not loosen. Did he think she would hurt herself? Or him?

Stilling, she let her hands rest on his arms. "No. Not spooked," she repeated the word he had used. "Just...worried."

His brow creased. "About what?"

She pushed out a breath. "Where is...the..." In that moment, their proper name eluded her memory. "Brandon? Amanda?"

"The Millers?" Dan frowned.

Mariena nodded. Why did Dan have a surprised look about his response?

"They left. At dawn."

Still enclosed by his hands on her arms, she brought hers up to catch her head as it fell.

His grip softened but did not release her. "I...I'm sorry, Mariena," he said. "Did no one wake you?"

She shook her head, her face still covered by her hands.

He let out a rough breath. His thumbs rubbed her arms.

The clip of boots on wood sounded not far away.

Dan's hands dropped.

Mariena looked toward the sound.

Cutie stood at the far end of the porch, his gaze on her and Dan, his eyes narrowed.

Dan held his hands out. "This seems like something you two need to talk about."

"Excuse me?" Cutie snipped, his words sharp and short.

Meeting Mariena's eyes once more, Dan gave her a long look. As if he wanted her to tell him if she had trouble with Cutie.

Dan turned and walked toward the porch stairs, passing Cutie.

The glare from Cutie would have seared a lesser man. But Dan kept moving, going so far as to bump Cutie's shoulder as he passed.

Cutie's gaze followed Dan's retreating form. "I said, 'Excuse me.'"

Dan paused. "And I said, 'seems like something you two need to talk about'."

Cutie's hands balled into fists.

What should Mariena do? She couldn't let these two men come to blows over a misunderstanding!

Taking a few steps forward, she entreated her husband, "It is not him."

Cutie shot her a look. Could he bore a hole through her?

The glare stung. What did he think of her? Of what she had been doing? Did he think so little of her?

She would not abide his insinuation when nothing she did had been improper. And she would not allow him to continue to treat her as if she were the enemy.

Tipping her chin up and squaring her shoulders, she put more force in her voice than she believed she had. "This for *us* to speak. Leave him be."

Cutie's brows rose. But only for a second. Then they lowered, and he turned back to Dan.

The other ranch hand tipped his hat to Cutie. "You heard the lady. Best you tend to your affairs." Dan spun and walked down the few stairs off the porch and out to the barn.

Cutie's focus fell to the floorboards. Why were his fists still clenched? Was he still so angry? At Dan? At her? What was to come?

It would not be only *his* anger forthcoming, however, she had plenty of her own to share. And it was time it had its due.

He would hear her out. And he would have to understand.

One way or the other.

Cutie held the door open for Mariena. The tightness in his throat did not ease. As she passed so close it became more difficult for him to swallow.

What had he seen, in truth?

Mariena...in Dan's arms?

And she seemed rather comfortable there. More so than she had been in Cutie's last night. How could that not injure?

Maybe it had all been one big mistake. Should he have let Dan speak for her to Sheriff McAllen? Would Dan have? Or was he only interested in what Mariena could do for him?

That thought sparked a deeper fire in Cutie...an anger that he couldn't contain. An anger Mariena didn't need to see. Or did she?

He found himself unable to speak as he let the door slam behind him.

She stopped just inside. Was she waiting on a cue from him?

He stomped into the great room. Would she follow? Scanning, he sought a place a sit. A refuge from the storm within. Nothing.

She moved into the space with slow steps. But she didn't take a chair either.

When he stopped pacing, he stood across the room from her position, as if facing off with her. Was this what he wanted?

She drew her arms up, crossing them over her chest. For protection? Out of fear?

He looked to the ground and, hands on his hips, shifted his weight from one leg to the other. Should he be the one to start? Could he break this thick silence and this…whatever it was…hanging between them if he just…started somewhere?

"Why you not wake me?" Her voice was firm, but quieter than he expected.

Jerking his head up to face her, he raised an eyebrow. "Wake you?"

"That I might make farewell?" Her gaze fell hard on him. As hard as his?

Had she wished to see the Millers off? At such an early hour? He'd thought he did her a kindness by letting her linger in sleep. But, in truth, that had been an assumption.

He let out a breath, and with it, some of his pent-up emotion. "I apologize. I thought you may be tired. It was wrong to decide for you."

Her brows arched. Surprise? At his comment? Or at his apology?

She nodded and let loose her arms. They fell by her side. Only then did she lower into a nearby chair.

What else had they to discuss but her being in Dan's embrace? It was his turn to cross his arms as he firmed his stance, planting his feet and giving them equal weight. "What was that about out there?"

"About?" She appeared confused. Was it for show?

He bit back a snappy remark. "You. With Dan. Just now…on the porch."

Her face colored. "It was nothing."

"Didn't seem like nothing." A heaviness formed in the pit of his stomach.

"I look for you. And came out of the house. Ran into Dan. He helped me. That is all."

Cutie watched her features closely. What did he believe? What did *she* believe? What part was her and what of Dan? Could it be as innocent as she said?

He wanted it to be. But the weight in his midsection indicated otherwise, warning him not to trust.

What could he say that would affirm his claim, but not offend? Would assuage his pain, but not belittle her?

In the end, he could not stop the words that pressed forth when he met her gaze. "Remember, Mariena, you are *my* wife."

She pushed her shoulders back, sitting taller. And though her eyes glistened, she opened her mouth. What was she prepared to say? Would it create further contention? Could he handle that?

"That is all." He managed, cutting her off as he stood and pressed through the tension of the room and out the front door.

What had been her reaction? As much as he wished to know it, he would not. For he had not looked at her.

No, that would have been dangerous.

Mariena set dishes out on the table. She was blessed with more chores now that Amanda had departed. Cook did not have the same hesitation about letting her help.

The smells of breakfast wafting from the kitchen were wonderful. And now that her task was completed, she could seek out Nisto. Time to ring for mealtime.

Sounding the dinner bell had been a job Samuel, Nisto, and Lucy, but mostly Lucy, divided. However, Nisto had enjoyed sole ownership of the chore since the Millers had left.

Grabbing the implements, she stepped onto the porch. Nisto had taken up with the old dog in Samuel's stead. He had risen to the responsibilities associated with the animal—feeding, watering, and even exercising the furry beast. And he took these tasks rather seriously. She looked around the yard. This was where he would usually be in the mornings, playing with the furry thing.

Neither Nisto nor the animal were in sight.

"Nisto?" she called.

Why shout for him? He would not respond even if he were in earshot.

She would have to wait for him to come. That was if he had even heard.

Nothing.

"Nisto!" She raised her volume. There wasn't time for this! Stepping off the porch, she put fists to her hips and scanned the area.

"Looking for someone?" A voice behind her spoke low.

She spun, biting back a shriek. Who had sneaked up on her?

Dan's lips spread in a smile. Was he so amused at her reaction?

Opening her mouth to chastise her friend, she was once more startled when he put a hand in front of her and with his other, a finger to his lips.

Silence? Why must she be quiet?

He then pointed up at the branches of the large tree nearby.

She followed his gesture.

And there, sitting back against the trunk, legs straddling a branch, was Nisto.

Her mouth set as her anger rose. Had he not heard her? How could he just sit there and go on as if she weren't searching for him?

She stepped to the tree's base.

Dan caught her arm. "Go easy on him. I think he misses his best friend."

Best friend?

Watching Dan's retreating form, she wondered at what he could mean.

Samuel? Had the boys become so close? Perhaps. In the time she and Nisto had been here, she had been...otherwise occupied. So much so that she hadn't expended much effort on Nisto. She'd been thankful he had taken up with Samuel. That gave her pause...did Nisto talk to him?

Pain shot into her chest. Her brother needed so much more than an absent sister and caregiver. More than the meager pieces of herself she had given him.

Yes, she must do better. For him. For Mama and Papa's legacy. They were all that remained of their tribal group; it was up to her to teach Nisto. Up to them to tell the stories, carry on the ways of their family, their kinsmen.

She looked up at her brother, though all she saw were his legs and feet. Why must he suffer so? So much taken from him.

What could she say or do to entice him to come down? She turned and leaned her back against the trunk. Having already opened that deep wound, it was only a matter of time before the grief washed over her.

Sinking to her rear, she let her head fall against her arms, which crossed over her knees. *What a mess.* Everything had become so complicated. And it need not be. Her mission was simple: care for Nisto, see him happy. She may have lost *her* chance. If she'd ever had one.

Boots stopped in front of her, stirring up dust.

Would it be Dan again? Come to pity her weak efforts?

She peered up.

Cutie stood, his working gloves in one hand. His other on his hip.

What did he want? She wiped at her tears and reined her emotions in before glancing at him again.

He had turned his attention upward.

Great. Now he, too, knew her predicament. Would he patronize her?

Crouching, his gaze dropped to be level with hers. His eyes were soft, concern shone in his features. "What can I do?"

"I not know." Her words came out but a whisper.

"I think I know where to start." He extended his free hand.

She hesitated. Was this gesture more than it seemed? Perhaps she best not look further than what was in front of her. Sliding her hand into his, she let him help her rise.

Shifting to face the tree once more, she stood beside him, looking into the branches.

Nisto had not moved. But now, he stared down at them.

"Nisto—" she started, leaning forward.

Cutie's hand clasped hers.

She halted. What was Cutie thinking? Had he a better way in mind? What did he know of Nisto that she did not?

Moving his head closer to hers, Cutie whispered, "Go back to the house. Let me speak to the boy."

She searched his eyes. What did he intend to do? To say? Should she trust him? Did she? But in that moment, she found the same warmth bathing her from his brown eyes that she remembered in the wilderness. The same that she knew well. And trusted.

Glancing at Nisto once more, she then looked at Cutie. And nodded.

He squeezed her hand and, though he held it a moment longer than necessary, released it.

When she drew away, pulling her hand back to herself, she covered it with the other, fingering the place that still felt his touch. She closed her eyes as she walked the length of the porch. Was she so taken with him? After what they had been through? She still cared. And so deeply.

The temptation to look over her shoulder before entering the house was great. If only to look upon Cutie for one more moment and fill her senses with his presence. But she dared not. What was between them still confused her. She was yet unclear of where they stood.

She had to protect her heart. Somehow.

CHAPTER 12

Difficulties

Where could Mariena be? Cutie had already been through the house. She couldn't have gone far. He hadn't seen the cart taken out today.

Moving into the kitchen, he heard Cook's music—the clutter and clanging of pots and pans.

Stepping into the rather spacious area, he jumped back just as the stout woman walked by with an armful of apples. She had almost knocked him over.

He popped his head back into the room after she had passed the doorway. "I hope you're making an apple pie!"

The woman shrieked, spinning as she threw up her arms. Apples tumbled to the floor.

"Lord have mercy, Cutie!" She put a hand to her chest. "You best thank the good Lord I wasn't holding a knife." Bending over while gripping the edge of her apron, she picked up an apple, examining it.

He rushed in and dropped to his knees, doing what he could to help pick up the apples. Although, he wasn't sure his was the keenest eye for spotting bruises. "My apologies, ma'am. I didn't mean to startle you."

"I can't imagine you thought much about it." Her tone scolded, but when he looked at her, she cracked a smile.

In moments, all the apples were off the floor and settled on a cutting board.

"Was I right?" Cutie stood straighter, wishing his back didn't disagree with him so. Lucy's bed wasn't uncomfortable. Perhaps a bit small, but it was functional. Still, as he slept there these last few nights, he hadn't gotten much in the way of rest. Too much on his mind.

"Right? About what?" Cook's brow went up.

"About the pie?" He set a hand on her shoulder. "I won't tell if you promise me the first piece."

"I ain't promisin' nothin'. *And* you ain't tellin' nothin' either." Her eyes became slits.

He knew better than to take her threat seriously. But he also knew better than to snitch about dessert.

"Now, I know you didn't come in here to spill my apples and ask about no pie." Cook stirred about the kitchen, checking this pot and those pans.

"No. I'm looking for Mariena." He evened his features out as much as he could. "Can't seem to find her."

Cook shot him a strange look. What did it mean? It almost appeared as if she had something caught in her eye. He opened his mouth to ask if something was amiss when she said, "She's out back. Hanging the laundry."

Cutie tipped his hat. "Thank you much." He turned and walked toward the dining room.

"Don't you go disturbing her chores!" Cook called.

"What?" Cutie yelled. "You want me to taste the first bite of pie?"

"Cutie—" Cook shouted as he shut the front door behind himself, cutting off any further words from her.

He stepped off the porch and around the house. It took only a few seconds to spot Mariena, just as Cook said—minding the wash.

The laundry line had been hung back here, farther away from the horses and cattle that kicked up dirt. And they weren't the only ones. This piece of land back behind the homestead didn't get much action.

Not since...

In Cutie's mind, he watched Kid Antrim's men pull him from the barn. He'd been bloodied and beaten. All for Brandon's money. His nest egg. And Cutie had been the one who betrayed the existence of it.

That skirmish had led to Amanda being shot. And this back yard was dug up. Brandon's money, a gift from his mother, or part of it anyway, had been taken.

Why had Cutie told?

Was he so jealous of Brandon and his life? Of what he had? Of what was denied Cutie?

Overcome with emotion, Cutie leaned against the back of the house. But would the structure hold him? Would anything?

He put his head in his hand. Why could *he* not answer these questions? Would he have any peace until he could?

"Cutie?" a soft voice called his name from far away, while a hand touched his shoulder.

Jerking his head up, he found Mariena staring at him. He glanced around the field. The ground was whole; the money had been moved. Kid Antrim, now Billy the Kid, was on the run, hopefully too smart to ever set foot in Wharton City again.

Cutie focused on Mariena. Her eyes were kind. Even concerned. About him? Standing straighter, he pushed off the wall. "I, um, came looking for you."

"Oh?" She glanced behind to the waiting laundry. A basket with clothing still in it sat several feet away. And several items waved on the lines.

"Yes. I had a thought...about you."

She caught his gaze, her eyes widened.

"And horses," he said, his words spilling out.

Her brows furrowed. "Horses?"

"Yes. It's not good for you to be so afraid. I think we need to fix that."

She took a step back. "I...don't know." Was she trembling?

He reached for her hand, grasping it. She *was* shaking. They weren't even near the animals and she had already become so spooked?

"I, um, need to do clothes." She spun and walked toward the basket.

But he didn't release her. Her body jerked and he tugged at her. "Mariena..."

She refused to turn and face him.

He pulled again, still gently. "Mariena, trust me. I won't let you get hurt."

She paused. Shifting, she set her gaze on him.

Why? Because he had hurt her with his actions?

Of course.

He swallowed. Hard.

What could he say?

She took a step closer to him. "Will you...help me with clothes?"

What? Did she mean for him to...?

Jerking her head in the direction of the laundry basket, she pulled at his arm.

He let out a breath. She meant help with the hanging the clothes on the lines.

Smiling, he nodded and allowed her pull to gain momentum as she drew him to where she had been previously.

When they stopped by the basket, she bent and grabbed two pieces —one for him and one for her. When she passed a blue linen garment to him, he took her hand once more.

"I have a confession."

Her eyes widened. "Yes?"

"I've never done this before."

She smiled, and her features lit up. "I can show."

With the yellow shirt she had selected for herself, she held the shoulders to the line and modeled using the clothespins to secure it.

"Now, you?"

He faced the line and, unfolding the layers of cloth, discovered he held a dress. Should he turn it sideways? Or pin the shoulders as she had? Perhaps sideways, then the garment would dry better.

Turning the dress, he secured the first pin.

She put a hand over his.

Had he done it wrong? As he looked at her, however, he couldn't be sad, for her sweet smile was compensation enough.

Together they worked until the basket was emptied. Cutie could not help but thrill at the touches and glances here and there. Did she, too, find them exciting?

Why had he avoided her for so long? Not been willing to interact with her?

And now that they were married, everything had been awkward.

No more. This would be a new start.

And whatever was between them would become what it had started to be in the wilderness.

Mariena did not try to hide her uneasiness. There was no need. Cutie knew. He understood. Somewhat.

His gaze on her seemed concerned. Not amused.

She breathed deeply. His presence gave her some level of comfort, along with the fact that he did not find her lack of ability something to laugh at.

His blue-eyed gaze held more than this, though. Underneath the concern was a heat she could not explain. Had things truly changed between them?

Perhaps not changed, but returned to the way they had been? Their interactions of late had been much easier. Less contentious.

She peered in his direction. But he wasn't looking at her. Instead, he watched the movement of her mare. The animal had been steady enough—slower in step and not apt to hurry, even when pushed to trot. Would Cutie want them to attempt a gallop?

Mariena hoped not.

His gaze lifted and caught hers.

She smiled.

He lifted one side of his mouth. Why did he not let himself relax? Be content with her?

Was he just nervous with her on the horse? Or was it an uncertainty with her?

Keeping eyes on hers, he drew Patch closer to her mare. A hint of mischief became evident on his features.

She could not be certain. But her heart fluttered all the same.

He reached a hand for hers upon the pommel of her saddle. Was that entirely safe? Did he expect her to release her tight hold and grip his hand? Dare she? Wouldn't that make her seat upon the horse more precarious?

As his horse moved beneath him, his hand tugged away. It just wasn't possible for him to keep the horse quite so close.

She would have to reach for him. Looking at her grip on the saddle, she considered just that. What would it be like to give up her fear and trust him?

When she glanced at him again, his smile widened. He offered his hand again, keeping his elbow closer to his body.

If she put her arm out, would he extend his farther? Meet her halfway?

Peeling her fingers from the pommel, she flexed them. How hard had she been gripping it?

She reached her hand out toward him with great care.

His features brightened and he stretched farther.

Her balance tipped in that direction. Worried, she jerked her hand back in. She couldn't! It wasn't safe. She turned to him again.

His blue eyes still encouraged, his hand still extended, fingers curled, waiting.

She bit her lip. How could he continue to ask this of her? Her capability on the horse was untried. This whole thing made her too unsettled, too unsteady.

But when she glanced at him, his gaze held no doubt. Only a plea. A question—would she trust him?

She did.

Must she prove it this way?

True, the horses only trotted; they weren't moving so fast. The speed only bothered her because of her unease with the animals.

She released her lip, swallowed, and let loose the pommel once more. This time, she *would* succeed.

His hand came nearer.

Ignoring the ground rushing below them, the feeling that she might tip, all of it...she sucked in a breath and stuck her arm out, grasping his waiting hand.

He squeezed her fingers, his horse drawing alongside hers.

Patch stepped unevenly on the ground. Was something wrong with the terrain? There was little time to consider it. Her mare jerked in the opposite direction.

Mariena's grip on Cutie's hand was firm...more so than it should have been. She was pulled sideways. But her hold on her husband wasn't quite strong enough to secure her to him.

He released her.

Mariena pitched to the left while her horse jerked to the right.

This seemed to intensify the animal's discomfort and fear. The mare bucked.

She screamed. Holding the saddle as tightly as she could, gripping with her hands and her thighs...she fought to retain her place. But it was no use.

One moment, she thrust about, back and forth upon the animal. The next minute, she hit the earth. Hard. And lay upon her back, fighting for air.

Cutie leaned over her, desperation in his voice. "Mariena! Can you hear me?"

She fought to draw in air. The memory of another moment like this flashing through her mind. Only now, she somehow felt both numbed and pained all over her body.

Putting a hand to the side of her face, Cutie, his face stricken, commanded, "Breathe!"

She sucked in air, gasping as she could, her hands grabbing for his arms.

"Thank God!" His proclamation seemed strange in that moment, but his eyes were sincere. He put his hands on her shoulders. "Are you hurt?"

She wanted to jerk away. How dare he! He, who asked for something she wasn't ready for. He, who pushed her into this venture on horseback in the first place.

Shoving against his chest, she worked to make words. "I...need... space."

He leaned back, his features falling.

What did he expect out of her?

She fell back to the dirt. Could she assess her injuries? She was so sore. Would she have to let him probe for broken bones?

Moving her arms and legs, she tested them as she could.

"Whoa," he said, shooting her a narrowed look. "You need to let me check you over."

She sat up and became all the more aware of the soreness in her back. But, now propped on her arms, she could better face him. "What I *need* is to get back to the ranch."

His mouth opened. Was he so shocked she was uninjured?

Perhaps she would be, too, in his boots. That had been quite the fall. And she was certain she would feel it all the more tomorrow. But she refused to let him pity her today.

"M-m-mariena, I...let me help you." He set his hands on her arms.

His voice was gentle, kind...but she would have none of it.

Pushing at him once more, she was rewarded with space again. "I *said,* I need to get back to the ranch."

"I don't underst—"

"Are you going to take me back to the ranch or must I try to wrangle one of these confounded animals myself?" Just the thought of getting astride a horse once more made her ache to the core. Not just with physical pain, but with sheer terror. But that would be the only way to return.

She hoped she would not be forced to make good on her offer and do it alone.

He held up his hands. "Please. Allow me." Rising, he turned to where his horse grazed nearby.

Pulling her feet toward her, she pushed with her hands, attempting to get her legs under her. It did not work as well as she hoped.

He turned. Why must he witness her struggle? "Did you need any help?"

For certain, her face burned she was so angry—at herself, at her body, but most of all at him. Still, she could no more deny her uselessness in that moment than she could shut his eyes to it.

"Yes," she ground out. Lifting her hands, she waited for him to assist her.

He took hold of one hand but leaned down and wrapped an arm around her waist with his other arm.

She wasn't sure she appreciated such closeness. His presence disarmed and angered her at the same time. And all in all confused her.

Turning away from him, she determined she would not let him see it.

Once she regained her feet, she slipped free of his arms and immediately regretted it, while celebrating that she could indeed hold herself up.

"Shall we?" He indicated his waiting horse.

She nodded. But as they moved toward the animal, she hesitated. Did she trust the horse? Did she trust Cutie?

Not truly.

Was there any other way? No.

Then she must do what must be done.

"What's the matter?" His face was near. Too near. His breath caressed her skin.

Stepping to the left, she said, "I wonder about other horse. How will she find ranch?"

"Don't worry. She knows the way. She'll probably follow us home." He looked her over, examining her features. What did he see? Anything she didn't wish him to?

"Then we must go." She jerked her head and stepped to his larger horse. Stopping a couple of arms' lengths away, she held her breath.

"I'll be right here," Cutie said, taking hold of the reins. "I won't let anything happen to you."

Her eyes meet his. She did not make any effort to hide the hurt or the questions there.

If he could stop these things from happening, why hadn't he?

He looked to the ground. Had he heard her silent questions?

In the next moment, his hands were around her waist and she was hoisted upon the horse. There wasn't time to be frightened before Cutie sat behind her, his body providing security and comfort.

Why? Why did she have to identify those things with him still after what had happened?

She was a trusting fool.

They neared the ranch, and Cutie breathed out his relief. They would be able to attend to any injuries Mariena had incurred.

She stiffened. Why?

With the arm he used to secure her to him, he pressed with gentle movement, encouraging her to ease back against him.

Her body resisted.

True, she had seemed angry after falling, but he assumed she had been stung more than anything. He hoped the ride would calm her ire. Apparently, it did not.

Would she let this create distance between them once more?

He slowed the horse, and she trembled. His heart sank. This excursion had only intensified her fear of the animals.

When the mare came to a halt, he paused, wanting to assure her that all was well. He leaned forward, preparing to speak soothing words to her.

"Why the wait?" Her words bit.

Should he be deterred, or fight for those more endearing interactions he knew they had—and could have?

"I only want to be sure you are comfortable." He spoke softly, his face close to her ear.

She shivered. Did he affect her even now?

Jerking her head to the side, so he saw her in profile, she said, "I am not comfortable. I am sore. And I do not like horse." Her voice broke on the last word. She turned away. What did she not wish him to see?

He released the pommel and his arm closed around her waist.

She pushed it away. "I would like down. Now."

That stung. He pulled his arms back and dropped from the saddle. Then, reaching for her, he secured her dismount. But he did not attempt to linger in the moment with her.

He stepped back and turned away. What was this anger? Why so great? The accident had not been his fault. It wasn't as if he spooked the horse.

"I will send Cook out to tend to you." He called, but he didn't look back.

She spoke no further nor did she make a sound. There was no indication she heard or cared.

Perhaps he should see her to the porch. Would she welcome his help? No, this was best.

Stepping into the house, he called for Cook.

Clanking metal coming from the kitchen was his only answer.

He stopped beside the dining table. Why would he go no further? His whole body had become deflated. There wasn't much left in him.

"Cook!" he hollered.

She stepped through the doorway between the dining room and kitchen. "Land sakes, Cutie, you look a mess!"

Glancing down at himself, he noted that he was, in fact, covered in dirt. From having Mariena's back against his chest? He shrugged. What difference did it make?

"Mariena needs...tending." He winced at the last word.

"Where is she?" Cook's wide eyes and dropped mouth asked what he already wondered himself—why wasn't *he* seeing to his wife? Why had he left her alone?

The door behind him opened.

He turned.

Dan's back was the first thing he saw.

No.

Please, God, no.

As he turned, Cutie saw Dan holding Mariena's hand, an arm around her back. The door slammed behind them and Mariena jumped, crying out in pain as she did so.

Dan's hand on her back rubbed her there.

A fire lit in Cutie's belly. But did he have a right to be angry? Did that matter?

Dan turned his head, and his gaze landed on Cutie. His eyes narrowed, and his features twisted into a dangerous expression.

Cutie wanted to return the glare, but all the fight in him was gone. He had earned that.

"Mariena!" Cook's skirt swished as she rushed through the dining room.

Cutie thanked heaven, if there was a heaven, that he was spared Cook's judgment for the moment.

Cook came alongside Mariena, relieving Dan. "Let's get you to your bed. You look like you've been through it, darlin'."

Mariena leaned on Cook and whimpered.

Cutie wished he could shrivel up and die right there. Had he pushed her to go on the horse ride? She had seemed willing. In fact, more ready than he had expected.

Mariena and Cook disappeared around the corner.

Cutie took several measured breaths, counting the number of inhales and exhales until he heard the door click. For he knew what would come. He sensed Dan's glare still on him. At least his fellow ranch hand had waited until Mariena was secured and out of earshot.

"What was that?" Dan's voice was short, his words pushed out.

Cutie shrugged. What defense could he have?

"How *dare* you leave her out there like that. And walk away." Dan put his hands on his hips. "Did you come in here for a bite to eat?"

Cutie met Dan's eyes then. He would not be bullied. "You know that's not it. I came in here to get Cook. Mariena..."

Should he let on to Dan that Mariena didn't want his help? That she rejected him? Would that only encourage Dan?

"What? Mariena what?"

"She needed Cook's attention." There. That was close enough to the truth.

"What?" Dan's words were all but spat out. "*You* are her husband. How..."

"And *you*," Cutie said, putting more force to his voice as he stood straighter. "Would do well to remember that."

Dan's eyes narrowed. "What are you implying?"

"Nothing that needs not be implied." Cutie crossed his arms over his chest.

"I think you're insulting my honor." Dan took a step closer to Cutie. "Where I come from, those are fight—"

Cutie stepped into the gap that remained between them. "Are you denying then, that you have made special efforts to step in where she is concerned? That you haven't made certain she is aware you are available if she needs someone to confide in?"

"I don't know what you're talking about," Dan shot out, then pressed his mouth into a thin line.

"No? I'm not blind, Dan. I see it. And I don't appreciate it." Cutie stuck a finger out to emphasize his point.

"You best watch your tone."

Cutie remained stoic.

"And your insinuations."

"I will not hold my tongue when things need to be said," Cutie ground out.

"Then I think we need to take this elsewhere."

Cutie let out a laugh. "Like boys in a schoolyard?"

"Like men." Dan's face darkened. He made a fist and hit his other palm. "Don't think you can insult a *man* and not face consequences."

Cutie's smile fell. "Let's do th—"

The door opened.

Neither man broke the stony gaze between them.

"What's going on here, fellas?"

Slim. Of course.

Neither responded.

"Now, I ain't aimin' to take on all these chores myself if y'all get in a tussle," he scolded.

Dan shifted his weight from one foot to the other but did not break eye contact with Cutie.

"I'm telling you two," Slim warned. "I will set Cook on you."

He stepped forward, now partially between the two men. Setting a hand on each man's shoulder, he looked from one to the other.

"I need you two to set this to the side. At least for now. We got a ranch to run. What would Brandon think?"

That broke through the angry fog in Cutie's brain. Brandon. The man deserved more than for his ranch hands to beat the tar out of each other in his absence.

He relaxed his stance.

Dan, likewise, softened his gaze. Had he the same regard for their boss?

"Now, shake on it. No fighting." Slim crossed his arms and stood straighter.

Cutie looked at Slim. Shake Dan's hand? He couldn't be serious.

"I mean it." Slim looked from one to the other. "Shake on it."

Cutie exchanged a barely amused look with Dan.

"I'll get Cook, I will." Slim lowered his arms.

Dan thrust his arm into the space between them.

Cutie took his hand and shook it. He was tempted to squeeze Dan's hand, but that would be childish. One look at Dan, and he wondered if the man had the same thought.

Releasing Dan's hand as soon as acceptable, Cutie turned to Slim. "What is this important ranch work you are alluding to?"

"Have you any idea the time?" Slim's voice was incredulous.

Cutie shook his head. He glanced outside, looking at the sun in the sky. *Shoot!* They needed to shift the herd to the south pasture today. And the day was passing awful fast. "Why didn't someone come get me?"

"I sent Dan." Slim shrugged, turning toward the door.

Dan's face colored, but he refused to meet Cutie's eyes as he followed Slim out of the house.

Cutie took up step with them but paused, taking a moment to look to the hallway where Mariena would be detailing her injuries to Cook. His chest ached.

Why couldn't she have trusted him with such? The distance between them gaped. Would they ever overcome it?

CHAPTER 13

Conflcted

Cook's hands moved over Mariena's body. Every now and again the pain would become great enough for Mariena to cry out, but for the most part, she stared at the ceiling as tears silently rolled down her face.

"I sure am sorry," Cook said as she did her work. "But I don't think you'll be needin' a doctor."

Mariena nodded. She had guessed as much.

"You'll be plenty sore, though. Them horses, no way to know what they'll do sometimes. Still, we got to live with them. No two ways about it." Cook rambled on as she continued her ministrations. She shifted to cleaning Mariena.

As much as Mariena did not want to be tended to, she kept still and let herself be cared for.

What had Cutie thought? Didn't he know she would be angry? Yet when they returned to the ranch, he acted as if she wouldn't be—whispering in her ear, pulling her closer to his chest.

Her body had fought her, wanted to react to the warmth of his breath, to his touch, but she would not have it. Not after what he had done, had allowed to happen.

Cook leaned over her once more. "You want a fresh dress or your nightgown?"

What did she want? For certain, she didn't want to leave the room in the near future. But she would have to. For Nisto.

"Dress, please." Her voice was weak. And cracked. Would she ever be whole?

Why had she hoped in something that didn't hold weight? In this thing between her and Cutie? It continued to prove too unsteady. Just like the horse.

"You'll be good as new in a few days," Cook soothed as she blotted a cool cloth on Mariena's face.

Did Cook realize the streaks were from fresh tears?

Mariena fought to keep them from coming. But the more she resisted, the more they fell.

"Oh, darlin', you hurtin'?"

What could she say? Mariena nodded. Maybe that would put Cook off. Mariena's whole being ached—sore from head to toe.

"Is it your body or your heart?"

Mariena met Cook's gaze. How did the woman know?

"I've been around for some time, dear. I've known Cutie since he was younger than he should be to be workin' a ranch hand's job."

What could that mean? Had Cutie earned sympathy in the woman's heart from his predicament in life? What exactly was that? Not that he had shared any of it with Mariena.

Dare she share with Cook what was in her heart? Or would Cook only see things from Cutie's side?

Mariena turned her head on the pillow, looking out the window.

"It can't be so bad. They say 'time heals all wounds.' That'll be true of your body. And it can be true for your heart." The woman's gentle hands helped Mariena sit to get the dress over her head.

As Cook worked the buttons, Mariena let her mind wander. Would time heal her heart? Did she want it to heal *of* Cutie? Or did she want to heal this rift so she could *be* with Cutie?

Cutie was worn out. Too many hours in the saddle. First the kerfuffle with Mariena, then the time it took to move the herd.

Not to mention the tension with Dan.

But one thing had become clear—he didn't want to let this thing with Mariena be. He couldn't. There needed to be resolution. And he wanted to move beyond that, to grow closer from it.

He had grown tired of complications and challenges. It was time they faced them together instead of being fearful of each other.

Would she accept that or push him away once more?

Was his heart prepared for that possibility?

For the moment, he needed to find Nisto. With Mariena injured, someone had to look out for the boy.

Perhaps Cook had already thought of this and the boy sat at the dinner table eating pie or cookies.

Still, it wouldn't hurt to do a sweep of the barn and around the house before going in for the evening meal.

Slim walked by in the distance. "You comin' in for grub?" he called.

"In a minute. Gotta check on something first." He pointed to the barn.

Slim nodded. "That 'something' better not be Dan."

Cutie waved him off with a half smile.

Slim laughed and turned his attention back to the homestead.

Cutie thanked the good Lord once more that Slim had intervened. What would it have done to Brandon if he discovered that Cutie and Dan had come to blows in his absence? Cutie had caused his boss enough trouble.

He'd sure done enough thanking of the good Lord for someone who wasn't even certain he believed God existed. Yet, he had found himself beseeching God and thanking heaven more often of late. Could it be that somewhere, deep down, there was a hint of belief? Or was it Cook rubbing off?

He rounded the side of the barn and came to the open field behind. The grunting of a frustrated young voice and the *thwack* of a blade hitting wood pulled his thoughts to reality.

There, just over from the barn's back door, was Nisto. He had what appeared to be a makeshift tomahawk—little more than a sharpened rock attached to a stick. And he threw it at a tree.

The tree bore the markings of having been hit multiple times.

Nisto heaved and yelled as he threw it again.

The weapon fell short of the trunk's center.

Nisto sank to his knees, bent over, and cried.

Cutie moved into the clearing, taking careful steps toward the boy. What had so overwhelmed him?

Caught in spilling out his sorrow, the boy did not seem to notice Cutie's approach. And as he neared, Cutie reached forth, touching Nisto's shoulder.

Launching himself upward, Nisto's arms came into the air, blade in hand. Where had he secured a knife?

The boy's eyes were wild and his teeth bared. He had covered his face with paint.

Cutie raised his hands, prepared to fend off the oncoming attack. Would Nisto stab at him? He seemed all too ready to do so.

Recognition lit in Nisto's eyes. He dropped the large knife.

And crumpled.

Cutie caught him. "It's all right, Nisto. It's all right."

The boy wailed. What kind of emotion had been pent up in his body? And for how long?

Nisto cried and cried, his body shook and flailed.

Cutie held him securely. "I know." What else could he say? He continued to hold the young boy and let the grief pour out of him.

"They're gone!" Broken words came from a crushed spirit.

Had Nisto spoken? They were the first words Cutie had ever heard from the boy. And they were English even. Cutie swallowed his surprise and rubbed Nisto's back. "I know."

"They're all gone!"

He held the boy ever tighter. "But I'm here. And Mariena."

The boy coughed, choking on his tears.

"We aren't going anywhere."

A stiff nod against Cutie's shoulder was Nisto's only response. But Cutie didn't mind. If it took hours, he would hold Nisto and let him work out this sadness. Though the depth of the wound may have no end, neither did his care for the boy.

Mariena pressed her hand to her mouth to suppress a whimper. Her wandering had been productive—she found Nisto. But she had not been the only one.

Had she truly heard what she'd thought? Nisto spoke!

How could she not have seen his need? His great, aching need to mourn?

But it was not her, in the end, who he turned to, but Cutie.

And the ranch hand embraced the hurt in her brother, letting the young boy break for however long he needed.

This was the man she knew.

This was the man she married.

Not that man she made him out to be—the one who let her get hurt, who wounded her with his words and actions.

That was only her fear.

This was reality.

Should she go to Nisto?

No, he kept this from her for a reason.

She best return to the house and let him grieve as he saw fit.

For she trusted Cutie to be a safe place for Nisto to land. And to help him pick himself up when all had been cried out.

Cutie stopped outside the door to Mariena's room. The room that everyone thought he shared with her. Well, he hoped everyone believed he had been. Did they?

What did it matter? If he could earn back Mariena's favor, he didn't care what went on in the inner workings of anyone else's mind.

He ran a hand through his hair, wishing it wasn't as ruffled about as it must be. Without his hat on his head hiding the mused hair, he must be a sight. It had been the hat in the first place that caused the mess.

But he couldn't worry about that either. He needed to think about Mariena.

Raising his hand, he held his breath and knocked.

Rustling within alerted him that she came to the door. Had she been abed? Sleeping even? Maybe she had been resting since their return to the ranch earlier that day.

He had missed dinner altogether, caring for Nisto. The boy's intense sadness had made Cutie realize how deeply Mariena must need comfort. Something he had offered little of.

Had she gone to the table for supper? Or had she remained in her room? Kept to her bed?

And now he disturbed her. Forced her to her feet.

Leaning against the frame, he pressed his forehead to his fist. What was he thinking?

The door latch worked and, with a creak, an opening revealed Mariena. She seemed small and helpless. But she was still dressed for the day, though changed from the dress she wore on their earlier venture on horseback. Perhaps then, she hadn't been confined.

He stood straighter, letting his arm fall by his side. "Mariena." Her name came out more as a breath than he wanted it to.

His gaze caught on her eyes, which glistened. Why? Was she upset? Would she cry? Could he handle more tears today?

He would, he decided. For her.

"I, um, wanted to...well, that is, I, um...had a question to ask you."

One of her brows quirked.

Movement in the room next to hers distracted him. Had they disturbed Nisto?

She waved him in.

He stepped inside the room without thinking. The moment she closed the door behind him, his breathing became more rapid. Should he be in here? Alone with her?

That was the height of irony. They were married. If that was not cause for them to be alone together, what was? Still, things were not... quite right...between them. Not as they should be.

She came around to stand in front of him. Closer than he expected. Did she realize how near she stood? And what that did to him?

His body warmed. He prayed it wouldn't show in his features.

"What did you need say?"

"*Ask*...actually." Though his words were soft, he kicked himself. Why did he correct her? His head swam a little. What did he need to say...*ask* again?

He set his gaze on hers. The deep dark brown, such a deep amber, pulled at him. And he wanted to be drawn in.

Pulling back, he became aware that he had, in fact, been leaning toward her.

She looked to the ground. Had she been likewise captivated? What did she feel now that their gaze, the spell, had been broken?

"I tire." She turned to the bed. "May you ask me?"

With a boldness that surprised him, he reached for her arm.

She gasped. From pain?

He winced. Why hadn't he considered she might be bruised?

Turning to him, she met his eyes once more.

He closed the gap between them, not caring that he now stood closer than he might should.

She did not back away.

Another surprise.

He kept a hand on her arm, though he loosened his grip. His other hand felt for her hand. Finding it, he intertwined their fingers. "I hoped, Mariena..." Her name fell from his lips almost as a prayer would. "That you would accompany me to the Wharton City Sweetheart's Dance."

Her brows rose. "A...dance?" The word seemed strange coming from her lips.

"Yes." His gaze moved over her features, her hair...taking it all in. "A dance."

"I have not...dance before." Her cheeks colored.

"*Danced* before?" He smiled despite the thickness of the moment. "Then perhaps we can learn together."

Her lips tugged upward. Did she like that?

The tenderness of those lips captured his attention. Would he be able to release her without tasting them again?

All between them stilled. Had she sensed his intentions?

She licked her lips.

Had that been on purpose? A product of her thoughts about what he wished to do?

Whatever the truth, in the next moment, her body was against him, his arms around her, albeit his hold gentle. At least he had enough mind about him to have a care for her injuries.

She tipped her head back and her lips parted. An invitation? Dare he take it? Should he slow down? Would taking this liberty give way to others?

It mattered not. He could no more deny himself this than he could stop the morning from coming. Both were inevitable and he felt it.

She closed her eyes, and he was undone.

His mouth pressed down on her lips.

A sound emitted from her, a pleasant sound. As if she, too, needed this contact.

Her lips moved against his. Wanting. Seeking.

He could not help but pull her against himself as he returned her fervor, giving her what she sought.

Hands clung to his shirt then began to move up his chest.

His breathing quickened. This wasn't right. It wasn't the right time. The urge to break off the kiss and push her away overwhelmed him. How else might he stop this? But he tortured himself further, softening the kiss, and, finally, with great restraint, pulled back little by little until all that remained was for him to disentangle their fingers.

She leaned forward, following his movements.

"Mariena," he breathed once more. "This is not how I want this to be."

She groaned. "But, I—"

He put his forehead to hers. "No. Trust me. You would regret it. We must be...more than we are for it to be what I want it to be."

She pushed back against him, her brows furrowed.

"I know this is not easy for you to understand. So, I need you to trust me."

Her breathing seemed as heavy as his. But she nodded.

His lips brushed against hers once more. "You must know how much I *do* want you. So much."

She laid a hand on the side of his face as her body shook. Tears followed soon after.

Had she doubted that? At any point? How was that possible?

"Yes, Mariena," he said softly, his head still angled and touching hers. "I do. With every part of my being."

Her other hand came up to his face. How could she doubt herself? Doubt how attractive she was to him? Had *he* given her cause?

He thought back and put himself in her place. His heart sank. Perhaps he had.

Rubbing her back with one hand while keeping the other secured around her waist, he kissed her forehead. "Dearest Mariena."

She shifted and let her head lay on his shoulder, her hands sliding behind his neck.

"You have captivated me from the moment you slid off my horse in the wilderness."

She sniffled, a slight laugh coming forth.

"I have *never* wanted you more than I did on our wedding night... except."

Her head lifted and she met his eyes. "Except?"

"Except right now." His eyes wanted to take her in and memorize every nuance of her face.

It was odd and encouraging that this had plagued her so. But the time had come to part. Or he would not be able to control his impulses any longer.

"That is why I must bid you good night, sweet Mariena." He pulled back.

She clung to him, resisting.

"No. Please, don't. I *must* go." He lifted her wrists from his shoulders and stepped back. "Trust me."

Though he wasn't certain she did, still she nodded and remained as she was while he backed up to the door.

"The dance. You, me, day after tomorrow."

"Day after tomorrow?" Her eyes widened.

He smiled. "Day after tomorrow." Closing the door, he stole from her presence and temptation all at once.

Day after tomorrow.
It would be a long night.

CHAPTER 14

Misunderstood

Mariena looked down at the dress that had been fitted to her body. Was the teal truly the right color for her? The fabric shimmered. What was that type of linen called? It was smooth to the touch. Seemed as if her hand moved across water.

There weren't many trimmings to the fine fabric. No lace, thank goodness. She did so tire of lace.

The gown was snug at her waist and torso. After hugging her hips, the skirt fell out with some volume, giving her the slightest bit trailing behind. Cook referred to it as a train. Strange, it looked nothing like a locomotive.

The neckline dipped lower than she would have liked, but Cook insisted it had to be so. For this was a ball gown. There was gathering and layering of the fabric below her bust. And a more delicate, off-white colored fabric came out of this bunching and crossed over her chest, creating a wide V-shape just above her bust. Straps made of this same beige material held up the dress, and ruched darker teal velvet attached to the front and back at the shoulder lay on her upper arms.

Cook had just finished tying off the laces on the dress's back. She stepped away and looked over Mariena. "My, my...that Cutie ain't gonna know what hit him."

"I'm going to hit him?" Mariena spun to face Cook. Why would she think Mariena would hit her husband?

"No, child." Cook put a hand on Mariena's shoulder. "I mean he's gonna be surprised."

"Oh." Mariena angled her neck to get a look in the mirror attached to the vanity.

"Don't hurt yourself. Go. Have a look." Cook stifled a laugh.

Mariena stepped across the room, approaching the vanity with caution. What if she were too exposed? She felt as if she showed more skin than necessary.

Her reflection stared back at her, and closer and closer, bigger and bigger she appeared. Once her visage cleared, she stopped.

She turned to the right and then to the left, pausing as she eyed her figure in each stance. What had Cook accomplished? How was this possible?

The dress had a lower neckline than any she had worn, but it wasn't vulgar. If Cook said that the other ladies would be wearing similar things, she would just have to trust.

If she didn't have a better sense of humility about her, she would think herself rather becoming. A smile spread across her face.

Cook's image appeared behind her. "You are even more beautiful when you smile, you know."

Though Mariena wished to pout, she could not stop smiling. The dress did bring out the best of her curves, her skin tone...everything. What would Cutie think?

"Now if you'll sit and be still, I'll do something with that hair." Cook put her hands on Mariena's shoulders, encouraging her to sit on the vanity's stool.

"My hair?" Mariena jerked her head toward the older woman.

"Yes. Your hair. Most married women wear their hair up." Cook began to brush the long dark strands.

Mariena frowned. Up? Must she wear it so? It seemed so... confining.

Cook worked with Mariena's silken strands, struggling even long moments later still to get it up. "Lord, help me! This hair of yours is smoother than a baby's skin."

Mariena's brows furrowed. What would Cook have to do to get it up?

She soon found out.

Pull, tease, pinch, wrap, jerk, pin, tuck, and fight.

After more pain than she'd known from anything else, save the mishaps on horseback, her hair had been tucked up.

Cook heaved, and Mariena's scalp was certain to be red should anyone have opportunity to see it. Still, she couldn't help but note how refined she appeared in the mirror.

But was it her? Or a presentation of what she might be?

"You are a vision," Cook said, wiping at her eyes.

Was it truly all so moving?

Mariena didn't take her eyes off her reflection. Would Cutie appreciate the care taken with her appearance? Would he want this look for her? Or would he, too, think it wasn't rather like her?

Knock, knock, knock.

Was he here? Was it time?

Mariena flushed. Her cheeks reddened in her visage. She admitted, though, that it did add something.

She looked to the door. Then to Cook.

The older woman shrugged. "I guess I'll get it."

How did she want to be when Cutie saw her? Sitting? Standing? Leaning against the wall? Hand on hip? Bold? Timid? How could she best present herself?

Cook reached the door before Mariena could decide.

Mariena opened her mouth to call out for Cook to stop, but the woman undid the latch and swung the door wide.

Straightening, Mariena put on her best smile and leaned one arm on the top of the vanity. It was the best she could do.

"Oh, you had us all excited for nothing," Cook said, her words more of a scold than anything. She moved back from the doorway.

"What? Makes me think you aren't happy to see me." It was Uncle Owen.

Mariena nearly collapsed onto the vanity.

Uncle Owen must have come to collect Cook. Had it become so late?

But why had Mariena gotten so worked up? Was she that nervous about what Cutie would think?

Yes. She was.

After the previous night, she hadn't had a chance to see him except at meals. Even then, they only exchanged glances and smiles, a few words. Other than that, he had been consumed with ranch work or in town.

She ached to see him, to have the chance to be alone with him. And to see what may come of the evening...of their time together. Would they continue what they started the other night? Or would this be another chance to build on their relationship, working toward something deeper?

That she did not know. But she was all too eager to find out.

Cutie secured the horse to the cart. There would be no accidents tonight. Not if he could help it. He had checked and rechecked the straps. Not only that, he had selected the safest, perhaps slowest, but most sure-footed of the horses. Nothing would ruin their outing.

Taking the reins, he walked the horse and cart to the house. He hoped he wasn't coming too soon. He'd get a tongue-lashing from Cook if he interrupted Mariena's beauty treatment. But if he was late...he didn't want to think what Cook's response would be to that. Or how that might disappoint Mariena.

He could only pray he had judged the time correctly. *Please, let it be so!*

The sun had already started its journey toward the horizon, but it had not yet begun to set. Wharton City awaited him and his bride.

Slowing the horse to a halt just beyond the porch steps, he tied the reins to a post. Then he checked that his shirt was tucked in and his vest and jacket were in place. He had abandoned his hat earlier that afternoon so his hair would not be the mess it always seemed to be.

He took a breath and let it out. Yes, he was ready.

Stepping onto the porch, he smiled as he thought of Mariena and the kiss they had shared the previous evening. Would there be an opportunity to kiss her again? He must see to it there was.

As he came to the front door, he paused. Should he knock? Or step inside and ask after her within? Perhaps it would be best to knock while still outside. Less likely he would run across her by accident.

He lifted his hand and paused.

Oh no! Something wasn't right.

Glancing down, he realized he had forgotten the most important thing.

Moving across the porch with quick steps, he made his way to the cart. He reached in and pulled out the bouquet of flowers he had gathered.

There. Now he was ready.

Back at the door in a flash, he knocked.

No answer.

Knocking again, he questioned his decision to remain on the porch.

The door creaked as it opened. He reminded himself that things around here needed some oiling.

Uncle Owen's broad smile greeted him. "What can I do for ya'?"

As if he didn't know.

Cutie bowed slightly. "I come for my wife, sir."

Opening the door wide enough for Cutie to pass through, Uncle Owen snickered. He patted Cutie's shoulder as he crossed the threshold. "I bet you have, son. I bet you have."

Stepping into the area between the dining room and great room, Cutie didn't see either of the women. Where were they? He looked at Uncle Owen, raising an eyebrow.

Uncle Owen nodded. "Cook! Got a man here says he aims to take his wife out for the evenin'."

"She's a-comin'!" Cook's voice rang out, a singsong tone to it.

Footfalls sounded in the hall.

Was this more of the production? Now Cook would come, and he must beseech her for his wife somehow? It wasn't that Cutie didn't enjoy this play, but he was ever so eager to see Mariena and get on with their evening.

He looked at Uncle Owen, who just winked.

Turning back to where the hallway opened into the great room, he waited. Even if not so patiently, he could put on a good face.

Then she appeared.

And he didn't think he would breathe again.

But he wasn't sure he cared.

Her dress...

Her hair...

Her...

He wanted to rush at her, but he dared not. Wanted to speak words that were not of his nature to speak. And certainly not in front of Uncle Owen. He wished to secret her away, yet his eagerness to show her an evening out prevented such.

"What are you waiting on, Cutie? Some sort of carved invitation?" Uncle Owen chuckled.

Cutie shot him a look. Why was he still here?

Mariena peered at Cutie through her lashes as her features turned downward. She sort of hopped forward. And then Cutie spotted Cook behind her. Perhaps Mariena had not hopped, but had been bumped.

While these two, Uncle Owen and Cook, meant well, it was wholly unnecessary and just plain messed up Cutie's flow. Ignoring any further jabbing or prodding, he closed the distance between himself and Mariena. He caught her gaze. "You are lovely this evening."

"Thank you," she said, letting her face drop again. Why did she do that? Was it from shame? Or timidity?

Either way, he longed for her gaze once more.

He reached for her hand, grasping her fingers in his. "Shall we?"

She looked up at him and nodded. "Those flowers...for me?"

How could he have forgotten them...twice?

He extended them toward her. "Yes, sweet Mariena," he said, his voice lowering so his words were for her ears alone. "Though they do not compare."

She took the bundle, brought the blooms to her face, and inhaled their perfume. "Thank you."

Cook was by her side in a moment, hands outstretched. "I'll have these in a vase for you."

Mariena nodded, shrinking back slightly from the older woman, who walked off into the dining room with the buds.

Cutie tugged Mariena closer. "Let's go."

Her eyes shone bright. "Please."

His chest expanded. Was a simple word from her so pleasing? Then what else could she do to affect him? He could not keep his features from heating at the thought. Turning, he led her to the door.

"Don't be out too late now, ya' hear?" Uncle Owen called before shutting the door.

Cutie cared not. His thoughts, his senses, were filled with Mariena. What more would this evening bring?

Mariena settled into the rhythm of the cart as it moved across the roughed out path. Rocks and bumps along the way gave her reason to scoot closer to Cutie. Which, he didn't seem to mind.

And it distracted her from the horse, the animal that from the moment she stepped from the porch had given her heart reason to quicken. Must they involve a horse? Was there no other way?

Cutie had squeezed her hand and moved close. "I'm here."

Despite the fact that this had been true before when another horse had thrown her, it still gave her a measure of comfort. His presence gave her comfort. And seemed to bring something in her to life.

Now, she couldn't help but lean into his side, breathe in the scent of him. He smelled of sun and leather. She closed her eyes and memorized it.

"You all right?" His hand pressed against her arm.

Not opening her eyes, she smiled. "Holding the moment."

He chuckled and his hand eased off her arm. Did he need to keep both on the reins? That was probably best. Control the wild animal better.

"How do you hold the moment?"

Had his voice deepened?

She breathed in. "Take in the air. Hear the nature. Feel the world at peace."

"Is it?"

Was he facing her? It seemed the heat of his breath brushed the side of her face.

Tickled and excited by the warmth of his words in the same moment, she lost her concentration. She opened her eyes and turned to him. His face was so close.

"Is it what?"

"At peace?" Why did his eyes seem so wide? Because they were so close or because she wished never to look away?

"Yes." Had she spoken out loud?

His lips caught hers. A hand touched her face.

He filled her mind, her senses.

And then he was gone.

She murmured as his touch left.

"I know." His words were simple and soft.

When her lids opened, he faced forward once more. Were his words a sad explanation for his retreat? That he must focus on the road?

She wrapped an arm around his elbow and leaned into him.

The movement of his muscles beneath her hands as he maneuvered the cart and horse intrigued her. He was rather capable. What more could those arms do to protect and care for her?

Pressing her face into his shoulder, she hid her features. Did he know what he did to her?

How much time passed as she enjoyed this closeness she allowed herself? She wasn't sure. But after some time, his arms flexed as he pulled on the reins. Did he slow the animal?

She peered out. The buildings of Wharton City surrounded them as they drew near the center of the main road. Soon enough, Cutie stopped the horse and turned to her.

She lifted her head but could not make herself disentangle from his arm.

He lifted a hand to cup the side of her face again. His thumb stroked her cheek and his eyes searched hers.

Leaning toward her, he claimed her mouth once more. This was not the same as the tender, gentle kisses they had shared. With his hand, he urged her to angle her head by tipping her chin. Then their connection deepened. His lips became hungry.

And she offered willingly what he wanted.

This, too, however, did not last. He pulled back after mere moments of bliss.

Her head spun. For a full minute, she wasn't sure where she was.

Why did he release her this time? She looked at him, though somewhat in a daze. Her brows furrowed and she parted her lips to speak.

He put a finger on them. "Believe me, I want nothing more than to continue this. But if I do, if *we* do, I won't get to show you off at the Sweethearts' Dance."

She groaned. "I don't care."

He tipped her face with a finger under her chin and pulled her closer, smiling. When had his arms come around her?

"But I do."

She snuggled into his chest, wrapping her arm around his midsection.

The horse stirred and shifted.

Her hands gripped Cutie.

He clenched his teeth as he reached for the reins.

It seemed to not matter. The animal made no further move.

Not that she cared. She wanted down. Now.

"Let's get inside, hmm?" Cutie rubbed her back with his hand that had remained around her.

She nodded against him.

He turned to drop down. Would he leave her up here alone? Could she let him?

Clinging to his arm, she tugged at him.

He looked back. Confusion filled his eyes.

How could he not understand?

"I have to get down to help you," he explained. "I don't know how else to do this."

She frowned, looking at the backside of the horse then at him.

"Trust me." He gripped her hand, bringing it to his lips. "I'm still right here."

She nodded, though her heart raced and everything in her was unsettled. Did she believe him? All the things that could go awry went through her mind.

It was but a moment after he had disengaged and dropped down before he reached for her.

She scooted across the bench, already reaching for his shoulders.

Once her fingers connected with his jacket and his hands with her waist, she could breathe again. He lifted her slightly and let her fall to the ground in front of him, guiding her descent.

Now on solid ground, she met his gaze.

A smile filled his features and his fingers touched the side of her face. "I've got you."

She let out her breath and nodded.

He let loose her hands for a moment to secure the horse and then took her hand, pulling it under his arm, into the bend of his elbow. "Ready?"

What would the evening bring? While she hadn't enjoyed being around the townsfolk for their wedding, this may be different. She had Cutie's favor now. Perhaps if she allowed herself, she could have fun. And maybe make the acquaintance of some of the women.

She became aware of the couples passing them on the wooden sidewalk, heading toward the cafe.

Cutie tipped his hat in their direction. The men would do the same and the women nodded. So, Mariena did the same, nodding in return.

More and more as they neared the cafe, they saw these pairs. A few times, it didn't seem as if the lady of the couple saw her. Perhaps they were focused on seeing friends—too attentive on where they were headed.

Although, as they approached the cafe opening, Cutie's demeanor had changed. Was he unhappy? Had she done something to upset him?

She looked at him in profile.

Yes, his mouth had become a thin line. He might appear stoic and thoughtful to others, but she had seen this look. It meant he was displeased. Why?

They entered the well-lit cafe, all the brighter due to the darkening sky outside.

The music had started and couples filled the floor, twirling across the wooden boards. But the people near the door stopped their conversations when she and Cutie entered.

Yes, something was amiss for certain.

A couple of the pairs moved off, further into the room.

What was it?

Many eyes in the room fell upon them and stared. Or did she imagine it?

She gripped her husband's arm tighter. "Why are they—?"

He turned to catch her gaze. "Because they have never seen anything like you."

What? They hadn't seen Tohono O'odham? But that couldn't be. Many came to her wedding. Other tribes of her nation lived in these parts. That wasn't possible—

"You are breathtaking." He leaned closer.

She lowered her brows. Did he speak true? That didn't seem likely.

"Let us have that dance," he said, extending his opposite arm toward the area filled with twirling couples.

She looked around. All the eyes, the glares...

He tugged her toward the dance floor.

Not willing to fight him, she followed his lead.

Pausing, he pulled her around to face him. He set a hand on her waist and, with the other he lifted her hand in the air. "Ready?"

She wasn't. The dance of the white man was foreign. Never had she danced with someone's arms around her. Did her eyes show her fear? Her limbs felt heavy and her stomach flipped with a level of discomfort. "I don't—"

His head came near hers and he whispered, "Hold onto me."

Clinging to the places where her hands met him, she did so as he began to move. His body paced and turned to the rhythm of the music, and she followed him as best she could.

Her foot caught his and she stumbled.

His arm around her waist held her to him and she did not fall.

But there were snickers.

Snickers? Why would others laugh?

She paused and looked around.

He grabbed for her hand. "Mariena—"

There were more stares, more eyes, hands covering mouths.

Warmth covered her shoulder. Was it another attempt from Cutie to continue this charade?

"May I?" Slim's voice cut in.

She looked in his direction, thankful for a friendly face among the crowd. "I..." Her voice trailed off. What did she want? Shouldn't she just ask Cutie to take her to the homestead?

"Let's take a turn about the room, shall we?" Slim said, reaching for her hand.

Cutie's chest heaved. What was he thinking? Would he insist on forcing this issue? Perhaps if she and Slim could step outside it might take some of this attention off her.

She glanced at her husband, hoping she could communicate her desire for his assent.

He glared at Slim. Did he doubt his friend's intentions? Why would he? At length, he nodded, releasing Mariena and allowing Slim to walk her off the dance floor.

"Thank you," she said as Slim continued until they were outside.

Once they stepped beyond the prying eyes of those within, she all but doubled over, arms across her midsection. Would she lose her last meal? She became uncertain.

Slim's hands were on her arms. "Are you all right? Should I get Cutie?"

"No." She put a hand on his shoulder. "I am well. Just need moment."

He nodded.

Several deep breaths later, she felt better. The air seemed clearer. Her head seemed clearer.

She leaned back against the wall. Perhaps it would be better if they departed. This town wasn't ready. And now was not the time to push the issue.

"I remember when my dad first brought us out here."

Turning toward him, she found that he, too, leaned against the wall. His arms were crossed in front of his chest and he gazed into the night sky.

She remained silent. What could Slim wish to say that could offer her solace? Did the boys at the schoolhouse not like his lunch pail?

"The town wasn't too keen on us. I got beat every day at school."

Her eyes widened. What was he talking about?

"They used all the names. Every last one of 'em." He stared off into the night, almost in a trance.

The names? For what?

"My mother, God bless her, regretted it...every day I came home busted up."

"Regretted it?"

"That she passed the devil hair to me."

"Devil hair?"

Slim turned to her, an incredulous expression on his face. As if her lack of understanding confounded him.

She looked at him then. Really looked at his hair in the moonlight. The red strands, mixed with the bits that had probably darkened over time into the almost chestnut she usually saw under his hat. Was this the first time she saw him without his hat?

No. She couldn't let herself off that easily. Meals. The wedding. Had she been looking at him and just not seeing him?

His mother likely bore the fire red of her Irish descent. A red that, on Slim, had probably been lighter and brighter in his youth.

Her stomach sank and her chest tightened. She had just done to Slim in her heart as much, if not worse, than those people in there had done to her. Dismissed him. Decided he didn't have anything to offer before hearing him out. Focused only on her own story, her own pain.

"I'm sorry, Slim." A tear slid down her face. He would think her apology was for the trials of his youth, for what he had endured. But it was truly for her judgment of him.

He shrugged. "It's in the past."

If only it were.

CHAPTER 15
Unexpected

Cutie eyed the folks around him as he made his way to the punch bowl. He was parched. More so than he ever remembered being.

With his attention on that, maybe he wouldn't be so inclined to hit anyone. And he ached to do just that. Quite badly.

A couple ladies stood around the refreshment table, whispering.

He peered at them as he grabbed the ladle.

They quieted.

One of the women grabbed the other's elbow and tugged her away from the table.

No matter. He didn't need them leering anyway.

His cup now filled, he sipped at the liquid. It slaked his thirst and, perhaps, calmed him. If only slightly.

Maybe he should take a cup to Mariena. Wherever it was Slim had walked her.

He scanned the room.

No sign of them.

But he didn't worry. Slim might have slipped outside with Mariena. That may be best. She seemed to relish fresh air in moments of stress.

"Isn't it terrible?" a voice to his left said.

He turned. The girl who worked in the cafe...Lily...leaned over the bowl, filling her own glass.

"Isn't what terrible?" he ground out, his breath coming faster than he cared for it to. Would this woman insult his wife to his face? He set his cup down lest his spill it.

"Why, the way this town is treating your lovely wife." The girl's green eyes were wide. Sincere.

His shoulders relaxed and his breathing evened. "I don't understand it."

Lily moved a step closer. "Do you not?"

He jerked his head in her direction. "Of course not." Had she not approached as friend? But foe?

"These folks are set in their ways." She looked out at the crowd. "Old ways."

He calmed once more and nodded. His thoughts darkened. What would it take for the townsfolk to accept his wife? If they ever did? Did it matter? Would it matter to Mariena?

"I do so hate to see it." Lily set eyes on him again. He felt her gaze.

"What?" He glanced at her.

"The people's scorn. You don't deserve it." Her voice seemed to quiet.

He was tempted to lean in to hear better. "*She* doesn't deserve it."

"Hmmm." Lilly murmured.

Did she have more to say? Did he?

He picked up his cup and drained it. Setting it back down, he turned to Lily and said, "I best be—"

"You and I were good friends once." Lily turned fully toward him; her eyes glistened in the lantern light.

His face warmed as he remembered what they had been. He paused. "Lily, I—"

"I think folks around here had half a mind to think you and I would end up together, you know?" Her eyes met his. There was moisture pooled there.

Something in his mind screamed for him to get out of there. To find Mariena and just go home. But he couldn't. He had done Lily wrong, and he needed to make it right.

"Lily, I'm sorry, I…" What could he say? It was true he had enjoyed her company on many occasions. Even stole a kiss or two. Thank God, he had not let it go further. But that didn't make it all right…

"Cutie," she said, her voice breaking as she stepped closer.

He took a step back as he looked around. Weren't others watching?

No one seemed to care what he or she did; they were tucked behind the refreshment table in the corner.

His hip hit the edge of the stairs. Pain shot through his leg. He held up his hands to halt her continuing advance.

Her shoulders connected with his hands. "Didn't you ever care for me?" she pled. "Even a little?"

"Lily, I…" What did he wish to say? Would either answer bring her peace?

Hands reached forth and clung to his jacket, pulling at him. Dare he let go of her shoulders to unclench her hands?

"Tell me!" she cried, tears now making themselves evident.

"I…can't." An anchor hit his stomach. What had he become?

Her head fell, her forehead pressing to his chest.

He stopped pushing her shoulders and instead rubbed her arms. "I'm sorry. I truly am."

"Are you?" The words came not from Lily, but from somewhere off to his right.

He jerked his head around to gaze upon his Mariena. She stood not five feet away, holding to Slim's arm, her expression a picture of distress.

Releasing Lily, he stepped toward his wife. "Mariena, I—"

"No!" She backed away, pulling Slim with her.

"This isn't…" What did it, in fact, look like to her? Probably what it was—him comforting another woman. "I would like to speak with you." He stepped closer to Mariena.

She bit her lip and shook her head.

People were starting to notice something was amiss, and onlookers were gathering.

Slim slid between Cutie and Mariena, setting a hand on his friend's chest. "I think you need to give her a minute."

Cutie continued to gaze at his wife over Slim's shoulder.

"Trust me." Slim's voice lowered. "This is best."

An opening ripped within Cutie. His heart tore. "Mariena..." Would she listen?

She shook her head, lowering her face.

Would she not even look at him?

"My horse is outside. I'll take her home in the cart." Slim patted Cutie's chest and moved away, taking Mariena's arm and leading her from the building.

Cutie wished he could say Mariena had seen something wrong. Or that he didn't deserve this. But it was a product of his own bad choices. The effect...the trail of a broken life.

How would Cutie put these pieces back together?

Mariena's face burned. She had known the blonde woman meant something to Cutie in the past. Why, then, had she let this situation disturb her? It was not as if he were kissing her.

The woman was upset, that much had been apparent. But it could be that it was because Cutie rejected her advances. Maybe he consoled her after having thwarted her declaration of feelings for him.

Or was there, in fact, something more? Something beyond an innocent early courtship in their past?

Why hadn't Mariena let Cutie speak? Tell her what this thing was? For now, she had been left to her own worries and imaginings, which were far worse in all likelihood.

But Slim had spoken wisely. She did need some time. The evening had been difficult—the reaction of the townsfolk, the chance to peer into her own judgmental behavior, and now *this*. Perhaps she did just need to sleep on this all.

The cart rocked to the side.

She gripped the bench with one hand and Slim's arm with the other.

"It's all right, Mariena. Just a dip in the path."

Her eyes were still sealed tight. How much longer must she remain at the mercy of this animal?

"Mind easing up?" Slim's voice squeaked a little. "I don't mean to be un-gentleman-like, but yer hurtin' me."

She loosened her grip on his arm. "Sorry." Unclenching her hold on the bench as well, she flexed her aching fingers. "I not good with horses."

"Aw, shoot. This here ain't a horse."

Her brow shot up. What? She looked at the animal leading the cart. It appeared as a horse—four legs, long neck, mane. What was it if not a horse?

She peered at Slim, ready to ask.

Slim glanced at her. "I mean, not really. We don't think of ole' Slow Poke that way."

Furrowing her brows, she turned her focus back to the horse. Slow Poke? The animal did move quite timidly. And it was true she hadn't the chance to see this particular horse at a speed any faster than this on any occasion. Could it be true? That Cutie had chosen a horse of sluggish foot for their journey? Why? For her peace of mind?

"Not so nervous now, are ya'?" Slim said, smiling.

She looked at him.

"No reason to be. Ole' Slow Poke is the most sure-footed and careful of the horses, even if it is going to take twice as long for us to get back to the ranch." He sighed. "Twice as long."

Slim turned toward the horse and leaned against the back of the bench.

Despite everything that had happened that evening, Mariena looked at the animal...and smiled.

Cutie wandered outside the cafe. He kicked at a random rock on the wooden sidewalk.

What a mess.

Looking out into the night sky, he wondered if he was worth it to Mariena. Should he even bother attempting to fix it?

She was worth it to him, for certain, but would he continue to hurt her in the long run? Maybe it was time to cut *her* losses and let her move on.

The saloon stood just across the way from where he was at the doors to the cafe. It called to him.

Dare he? Or would that be just one more sin to add on to a heap?

Sticking his hands into his pockets, he thought of Nisto and leaned against one of the posts. That life wasn't for him. Not anymore.

"You sure know how to get in a fix," a deeper voice said nearby.

He didn't want to look. So, he didn't. "Did you come here to poke at me? Kick me while I'm down? Hmmm? Dan?"

The man stepped nearer. "I won't do any such thing."

Cutie peered at him, narrowing his eyes. Then he relaxed his brows and eyelids. He had no cause to be upset with Dan. This mess was of his own making. No one else's.

As the larger ranch hand came to stand by Cutie, Dan crossed his arms. "I never thought you deserved her."

Cutie jerked his head toward Dan. "I thought you said you weren't here to kick me while I'm down."

Dan held up a hand. "Hear me out."

Settling into his stance at the post, Cutie shrugged.

"This isn't your first mess."

Cutie shook his head. Dan wasn't holding up his end of the bargain very well.

"I've watched you play on women's emotions, betray us all, most of all the boss, and then treat Mariena like she was any one of the girls you've left in your wake of heartache. Toying with her heart like you do."

"Dan, I don't need your help here. I know what I've—"

"But then I got to thinking," Dan continued as if Cutie hadn't spoken. "If there is a God...and after what you've done and you're standing here still with a job and a wife that loves you like that woman does, there must be...He must have a special plan for you."

There were no words. Nothing.

Never, in all the time he could ever have been given on earth, could Cutie imagine Dan talking about God. Not that Dan *didn't* believe in God. They just never talked about it.

But to think that he, Cutie, was the focus of a special plan? That had to be the most ridiculous thing he had ever...

What if it were true?

What if that's why Brandon had forgiven him so completely when he shouldn't have? If that's why Mariena still cared for him after all their challenges? If he had been so blessed with such a woman after the heartbreak *he* had caused...so that he could be a part of something bigger?

He looked at Dan.

But Dan was gazing up at the stars.

Cutie's heart thumped hard in his chest. So, it did still exist in there. Turning his eyes toward the heavens, he wondered...*could it be?*

But would he ever be able to please God? He'd never been able to gain his earthly father's acceptance. How could he be sure that God would bestow His?

Or was his own experience evidence enough? The grace he'd already been given? The mercy he'd already been shown?

He sensed Dan's gaze. And he swallowed. Hard.

"My father was a great man, a loving man."

Dan remained silent.

"I'm named after him, you know. My real name...Charles."

Dan jerked his head once.

"He expected great things out of me." Cutie's heart ached as he saw his father's face before him in his mind's eye—hopeful, encouraging.

"Yeah?" Dan's voice was even. Did he know there was more?

"But these things he wanted for me. I..." Cutie dropped his hands. "I wasn't enough. I never could be."

"What do you mean?" The words were quiet, almost as if from his own heart and not from Dan.

Did he truly need to be sharing all of this? Did Dan need to hear it?

"I wasn't, um, smart enough to pass the exams. I couldn't...get into the right school."

Dan shuffled, probably shifting his weight. Cutie couldn't be sure, he didn't look, just rubbed his hands together at waist level.

"I remember the way he looked at me when I got my scores. And he knew I'd never make it to the next level." Cutie nearly choked on the words as his father's pained expression filled his vision.

"What did you do?" The question didn't push, just encouraged.

"I came out here." Cutie shrugged. "Started ranching."

Dan let out a long sigh.

Cutie looked to the ground. What was Dan thinking?

"That isn't the end of the story, though." Dan's words penetrated Cutie's introspection. "It never was going to be."

Cutie glanced at his friend, brow quirked. Not the end of the story? Meeting Dan's gaze, he turned away after a moment. Of course, it wasn't the end of his story. There was more to his life.

But he knew what Dan meant—there was *more* to be from his life than just hours and days. More meaning.

Because of an Almighty God's design?

He questioned again, the possibility of a deep belief within him of God's existence. Was it there? Had it always been?

Turning to Dan once more, he opened his mouth to ask a question.

Only to find that Dan had left.

Cutie spun, scanning the area. Where had Dan slipped off to? And so quietly?

But there was, in fact, no sign of the other ranch hand.

Surely, he hadn't imagined it.

The night was still. Everyone had gone to bed long ago. Hadn't they? Did Cutie come home? Or had he stayed out with the blonde at the saloon?

Why hadn't Mariena stayed with him? Let him talk to her? Made sure he got back to the ranch safely?

How many hours had she lain here, lost in thought? How many more would she be unable to sleep? Worried. About him.

There was no use in it. She had to know.

Slipping from beneath the covers, she padded across the floorboards and next door to Lucy's room.

Tapping on the door, she held her breath.

No response.

Dare she enter without invite?

She had to know if he were within, sleeping. Pressing the latch, it moved and the door opened easily. But when she peered into the room, she found it vacant.

Where could he be? Was he, in fact, still in town? What good could possibly come from that scenario?

Maybe she could check and see if his horse was back.

Just the thought of entering the barn and counting the horses, even from afar, made her shiver.

Still, she could think of no other way. If she wanted to know, she must.

Closing her eyes, she called upon all the courage within herself. She would do this. She had to.

Stepping through the house with light footfalls, she made her way out the door and off the porch. The barn stood, a looming outline in the not-so-far distance.

Swallowing against the fear rising in her throat, she pushed on.

A breeze came from the meadow downhill just below the homestead.

She paused, relishing the refreshment from nature in the midst of her distress. The smells of the earth always did ease her mind—the grass, the fragrant blooms, the leather...

The leather?

Yes, there was a hint of leather on the breeze. She gazed down the hill.

There on the grassy downslope knelt a lone figure.

Her heart leapt.

It was him!

She knew it.

Clutching her shawl, she strode in that direction, neither caring that he may hear or sense her coming.

Though she made no attempt to disguise her movements, he did not turn. Did he not hear her? Or not care?

As she came to him, not an arms' length away, her breaths heaving, her heart aching, tears threatening, she stopped.

He released a deep sigh and dropped his head.

She fell to her knees behind him, laying her head on his shoulder blades.

As she pressed her face to his back, she listened to his heartbeat and his breaths come and go, counting them.

Only a handful of moments passed before he turned, gathering her in his embrace.

She clung to him and he pressed kisses to her hair, her face, and, at last, to her lips. They were soft and fleeting—those of restoration.

"Mariena," he said, his words soft. "I'm sorry. I'm so sorry."

She shook her head. "I am. I not trust. I should." Putting her hands on either side of his face. "You are husband."

He nodded, dipping his head. "But I have much to say. Much to tell you."

"I know." She rubbed at the scruff on his cheek. "But I know it not change me. Not change this."

He closed his eyes.

"What?" she whispered.

He put a hand on her wrist. "I am holding the moment."

She chuckled. "Yes. Please." Pressing her forehead to his, she closed her eyes, too.

After some stillness between them, he moved. Taking her hands from his face to hold in his. "There *is* much to say. I have done much I am not proud of."

She nodded.

"And I want only truth between us."

Her fingers intertwined with his, lifting to fit their joined hands to their chests. "I will hear."

They lowered themselves until they were seated on the ground.

He shared. About his father. Of his broken relationship with Lily. And others.

Though her heart hurt for him as he spoke, she did not interrupt or intervene to discount his pain or his sin, but let him pour it out. When he was finished, he set his gaze on hers with purpose. "I want to tell you, sweet Mariena, that if you wish to seek an undoing to our marriage, an annulment, I will not fight it."

Her eyes widened. "Undoing?" Did he wish not to be joined with her any longer?

"Yes." He reached out to touch the side of her face. "Though you are dear to me."

Was it true?

He leaned closer. "And dearly loved."

She sniffled, ducking her head, placing hands on his arms.

"What is it, my love?" he whispered.

"Do you not know? How those words...?" She touched her chest.

He watched her features. Did his heart swell as hers did?

"I...love *you*...Charles," she said, her voice breaking.

As he gathered her close to himself, somehow his lips found hers. And though the path to this moment had been less than smooth, they had found one another. At last.

CHAPTER 16
Connection

Perhaps now the ranch hand understood. How could he not? McAllen rode through the town, scanning the area for any hint of something awry. Though he kept his features drawn, stern, this was probably his favorite part of the job.

Did the reaction of the townsfolk last night give Cutie a fair reading on how difficult it would be to live with the Indian girl in the real world? He hoped so. If not him, then maybe *she* would be reasonable.

Perhaps.

He slowed his horse as he approached the jailhouse. Nothing had seemed out of place in Wharton City this morning. Just as he liked it: everyone minded their own business and kept their noses clean.

After sliding from the saddle, he stepped to the door. And heard voices within. One of his deputies, yes. But another man spoke as well. Not a stranger...

Someone he had made every effort to avoid in these last months.

He let out a long breath. Guess his mother was right—you can't hide forever.

Bracing himself, he pulled the latch and opened the door.

There was no delaying the inevitable...he had to face his brother.

Cutie slowly came awake. The first thing he became aware of was Mariena curled up next to him. He smiled, pressing a kiss to her hair and pulling her impossibly closer.

She stirred.

He might should feel guilty that he disturbed her rest, but he didn't. Not even a little.

Turning over, her face came around to his. She murmured and snuggled to his chest.

Bliss.

How was it he had gained such goodness? He stroked the cascading waterfall of her hair. It was every bit as silken and soft as he ever imagined. The sultriness tantalized his skin and filled his senses.

He pressed his lips against her forehead. Could he live with this need of her? How had it not been satiated? A fire still burned within him.

But he dared not overwhelm her. That would only serve him. Not honor her.

He settled against his pillow, closing his eyes. Still, the brightness of the sun prevented him from closing out all light. What was the hour?

Shifting slightly so as not to bother Mariena's return to sleep, he turned toward the window, attempting to discern the angle of the sun.

Ah, noon. At least.

How had they slept so late?

He smiled to himself. They had been awake late into the evening...or rather into the early morning. Had he been mistaken or had the sun started to peek over the horizon when he at last surrendered to his body's need for respite?

Were the others curious? Or would they have guessed?

What else could they think? They must have known after he and Mariena didn't show up for breakfast.

His face heated at the thought of the looks that must have crossed over the table at his expense.

Did he truly care though? If this were his prize?

He nuzzled his bride's neck, wishing once more for her to be awake.

Thinking over the conversations of the previous evening, he

wondered on the burden he had released. Not simply by sharing his heart and soul, but by accepting that grace was his only way to find peace.

That heaviness he had carried, that reality of not being enough, had left him. He was now free. What would he do with such a gift?

He looked at his Mariena, snuggled close to him. What would *they* do with it? With their lives—now unhindered by his past?

Leaning toward her again, he left a trail of kisses on her face and neck. Did he veer close to a line he may not want to cross yet? Finding that his wife might be angry if awakened from peaceful sleep?

Perhaps he didn't care.

Sheriff McAllen stepped into the jailhouse with all the confidence he could muster. Travers leaned against the corner of McAllen's desk and faced the sheriff's brother, who had taken the only chair available to guests.

"Don't you have work to do?" McAllen said, giving his voice a grating tone.

Travers straightened. Why did he have such a guilty look on his face? Like a kid caught with a cookie before dinner. What had he told Ralph?

Ralph's eyes were on him in a second, his features unreadable. Why had his brother come? McAllen might fool himself into thinking he didn't know, but he did.

"Y-yes, sir," Travers stammered. He nodded to Ralph and moved toward the door, side-stepping to avoid contact with McAllen. Once the deputy was out the door and it shut behind him, McAllen strode to his seat behind the desk.

A thick silence fell in the room.

"Aren't you glad to see me?" Ralph said, breaking into the tension.

McAllen caught and held his brother's gaze. "You know that's not what this is about. Say your peace. What does Pa want?"

Ralph looked down and shook his head. When he glanced up, he smiled. "You sure do shoot straight from the hip."

"Don't reckon I see any other way fittin'." McAllen did not so much as let his lips twitch.

His brother shifted. Was he so uncomfortable? This couldn't be good news. His heart beat harder. But he worked to keep his features stoic.

Ralph turned toward the window; silence filled the space once more for several moments.

And when McAllen began to lose his resolve, his brother spoke.

"Pa's time is limited. The doctor says he has only days now."

A brick wall slammed into McAllen's chest. He couldn't breathe for a handful of moments. But as he drew air in, he was thankful his brother hadn't seen.

McAllen leaned forward, resting his forearms on the desk.

Ralph's focus shifted back to the sheriff when the chair creaked. "You have nothing to say?"

Everything in McAllen screamed. But he bit back his words, not trusting his tongue. And shrugged.

"You can't be so heartless, Walter. I know better."

It was McAllen's turn to look away, pinned as he was by Ralph's glare. "What did you hope to accomplish here?"

"I thought you might want to make amends with Pa before it's too late." Emotion leeched into Ralph's words. Even without it, McAllen knew his brother cared. Maybe more than he should.

He set eyes on his brother again, a hardness now in his gut. "I think you misunderstand."

Ralph's brows drooped, meeting each other.

"I've done everything I can," McAllen stated flatly. They had been through this before.

"Can't you just make another effort? If not for Pa's sake, for your own?" Ralph's words were now laced with concern.

McAllen was touched by his brother's sadness, but he refused to look away...or let it affect him. "You don't understand."

"Don't I?"

Shaking his head, McAllen stood. "I'm sorry, Ralph, I have a lot of work to—"

"You weren't alone that night." Ralph rose. "And you aren't the only one who carries the scars."

McAllen looked at his desk, setting his fingertips on the few papers needing his attention. How could he be what his brother needed? He had failed at being what his father needed. "I really need to—"

"I know, I know," Ralph held up his hands. "I'll be on my way."

The sheriff stared out the window as he listened for the door to close behind his brother. What was the right answer here?

Mariena scrubbed at some manner of meat grease, which clung to a pot. What had the others had for lunch? She did not get to enjoy the food, which she now labored to clean up.

Not that she minded. Those hours abed had been wonderful.

She peered at Cook across the kitchen, hoping the woman did not look her way, certain her face had reddened.

Turning back to the tub of soapy water, she shoved the pot under once more and allowed herself to revel in the memory of being in her husband's arms.

What would this evening bring? Another...late night?

How could they dare allow themselves another morning missing breakfast? Could she stand the looks? The winks?

"Your fingers gonna get all pruney in there," Cook said from just behind her.

Mariena jumped.

Water sloshed onto her, the counter, and the floor.

"Oh, Cook! I'm sorry!"

Cook laughed. "I'm not." The woman grabbed for a towel and passed it to Mariena. "You'll come back around to us. One of these days."

Mariena furrowed her brows. What did she mean? Realization hit her just as soon as the thought did.

If possible, her cheeks burned hotter.

"Now, look at ya'." Cook shook and laughed even more.

Mariena couldn't help but join her. But she did hope that Cook was wrong in one thing: she never wanted this to end.

How many days had passed since life had become perfect? Cutie did not know. But things had been well. The days were a juggle of chores, smiles, touches, and stolen kisses. While the evenings were given to fire and passion.

Would it always be like this?

Cutie pushed his horse along the fence line. A storm last night, which he and his sweet bride had been too...tired to be aware of, had swept the ranch. Nothing seemed to be amiss in the pasture's barrier. No repairs needed.

For that, he was thankful. Adding to their normal chores would only pull him away from Mariena unnecessarily.

Approaching the barn, he spotted Nisto exiting.

He waved at the boy.

After the youngster saw him, Nisto paused.

Cutie pulled his horse to a halt beside Nisto and nodded.

"I finished putting out fresh hay."

Cutie tipped his hat to Nisto. "Thank you much."

Once the boy had started talking, they found his English to improve faster than Mariena's. Younger children did seem to learn with less trouble.

Then the lad insisted he be allowed to help out where possible. And, unlike Mariena, he had an affinity for horses. Samuel's chores seemed like a great place for Nisto to start.

Cutie hopped down out of his saddle. "Care to water her?"

"Sure!" Nisto's eyes lit. He did enjoy any opportunity to interact with the animals.

Sometime, Cutie would have to remember to ask Mariena what caused her to be so fearful and yet her brother be so drawn to the creatures.

As it was, he didn't usually have room for such thoughts when he was with her.

Handing the reins to Nisto, Cutie turned his attention to the homestead.

This had been a good home for him. First the bunkhouse, and now the homestead. But that needed to change. Sooner rather than later.

The time had come for him to have a serious conversation with Mariena about it. How would she feel? Had she become too attached to this place? To Cook? And even Amanda? Would she not wish to leave?

It would be best if they had the discussion soon.

He stepped onto the porch where Mariena sat in one of the rocking chairs. Was she waiting for him?

"Taking a break?" He leaned against one of the posts near her.

She inclined her head and smiled. "Something as such."

"May I?" He indicated the chair beside hers.

"I would like it."

Sitting, he looked out on the property. What would it be like to have his own house? His own land?

What exactly *was* this 'special plan' God had for him? Did it involve this ranch? Or would they leave? How would he know this plan?

"You are quiet." Mariena's voice was soft.

"I am thinking." He did not meet her gaze, but smiled nonetheless.

"About?"

Reaching for her hand, he took hold of her with firmness. "Our future."

"Oh?" The lilt of her voice alluded to her intrigue.

"I wonder what God has planned. And how I will know that plan."

"Oh." This time her tone fell. Was she not pleased with his mention of God?

He shifted to look at her. "Yes. I believe God has a plan for us."

She turned away.

Squeezing her hand, he tugged at her. "What is it?"

Nothing.

"Tell me," he insisted gently. Would she now start holding back? Fear crept in at the edge of his consciousness.

No. He would not give in to that.

God, help me see through this.

"It is only that..." Her voice trailed off.

"What? Only that what?"

"Nothing." She shook her head. Leaning forward, she attempted to disentangle her hand. "I must help Cook with—"

"Mariena," he said, with more firmness in his tone. "Don't do this. Let's be honest with each other."

She settled back into the chair and met his gaze.

For some moments, she said nothing. Then she let out a deep sigh.

"I not wish to dismiss your belief. But I cannot—" She stopped herself. "I don't think to God."

"Don't think to God?" His brows furrowed. True, they had never discussed things of God before. Why was he, then, surprised by this?

"No."

"But—" he started.

She stood. "I not try to tell you no. You not tell me yes."

Her reaction concerned him. Why the repulsion to the idea? Could they live like this? Live in close, intimate union with differing thoughts about something so big?

He stood, stepping in front of her. "I'm sorry, Mariena. I cannot accept that."

She stared up at him, her eyes widening. "And *I* do not accept this." Pushing past him, she swept across the porch and into the house.

Mariena stepped into the house. Her room. That's where she would go. And Cutie better not follow her.

How *dare* he force his beliefs on her? He may be her husband, but he was not...was *not*...

What? Her father? Her spiritual guide? How did she intend to finish that thought?

She moved through the great room, longing for the solitude the bedroom would offer.

Cook stepped from the kitchen.

Mariena grabbed her chest. Must Cook insist on startling her?

"Did I scare you again, dear?" Cook clutched at her own chest. Had she been spooked by Mariena being startled?

Mariena nodded, reaching for the back of a chair, steadying herself.

Cook pulled a paper out from behind her skirt. "We got word. From town."

"Oh?" Mariena still wasn't certain her heart would return to its normal pace.

"Mr. Brandon and Mrs. Amanda are on the way home!"

The Millers? Home? It had been so long...too long since she had seen Amanda. "When?" she managed.

"Oh, where's my mind?" Cook pulled the telegram up toward her face. Did she need to verify the date? As if she didn't have it memorized. "A week from yesterday."

Six days? That was so soon! They wouldn't have much time to prepare everything. Of course, the homestead and ranch had to be in top condition for the Millers' return.

Was Mariena truly so anxious or did this offer her an acceptable distraction from this whole God issue with Cutie?

Either way, the Millers would be home soon, and they had much to do. No matter her motivation.

"Ain't ya' gonna tell that husband of yours?" Cook tilted her head and gave Mariena a wink.

Did she think Mariena would jump at any excuse to speak with him?

"I...am not well." She put a hand on her stomach. "Breakfast not so well in stomach."

Cook raised a brow. "You need the doctor? You might be sick. I can't imagine *my* food not settling well."

Mariena could have kicked herself. Why had she insulted Cook? She held up a hand. "No doctor. I am only a little unwell. Maybe I need to lay down only."

Looking her up and down, Cook's gaze rested on her belly the longest. Something glimmered in Cook's eyes. A...spark of some sort.

"If you need rest, you need rest." Cook moved toward Mariena, waving her arms as if to shoo Mariena. "Let's get you to bed. Feet up. I don't want to hear two words from you otherwise."

Why was Cook so concerned? At least it would get Mariena out of the way for a while. Maybe even get Cook to bring her food to the bedroom. Then she wouldn't have to face Cutie at lunch.

Putting both hands over her stomach, she leaned slightly forward and allowed Cook to usher her down the hall. "I am so tired. Maybe I not well enough to leave room for lunch."

"Now I won't have you starve." Cook shook her head. "I'll make sure you get a plate. You'll have the first cut of brisket."

Mariena smiled. This wasn't bad at all. Why had she not feigned sickness sooner?

CHAPTER 17

Secrecy

Cutie closed the barn. He was becoming truly concerned about Mariena. She had not been at lunch or supper. Why? Even if she hadn't wanted to be there, would Cook have let her off so easily?

What was going on? With night closing in and his chores done, he would go to her. He refused to let whatever this was intimidate him to take Lucy's room again. She was his wife. They were surely past these misunderstandings and miscommunications.

Walking toward the homestead, he took in the evening air. It had been a beautiful day and a pleasant evening. He only wished it had not been overshadowed by whatever was between him and Mariena.

As he stepped to the front door, he did his best to stomp the dirt off his boots. Cook always appreciated it.

Then he stepped inside. The sounds of the kitchen had fallen silent. That was typical. Cook's long day had to come to a close, too. But where was she?

He didn't see or hear her anywhere. Perhaps Uncle Owen had come and gotten her already. Strange, he hadn't seen the man or his cart. And it seemed a bit early for that.

Stepping to the dining table, he set his hat down. The news of

Brandon and Amanda's return had reached him at lunch. He should stay up and make an accounting of the preparations to come. But he was tired. And he did not know what he had yet to face when he saw Mariena.

"You rest now and have a good night," Cook's voice bounced off the walls in the great room.

Where was she? Had she tucked Nisto in? That wasn't like her. He was old enough that he preferred to say his goodnights outside his room and put himself to bed.

Cook soon appeared from around the corner. She stepped through the great room. Lifting her head, she spotted Cutie. Her face showed some amount of surprise, but she seemed to have expected him. And why not? It was time for him to quit and come in.

She signaled him to come nearer, but she moved toward the dining room at the same time.

He stepped in that direction, drawing closer as she indicated.

Looking around him as if she suspected someone to be listening to their conversation, she seemed pleased to find no one there.

He resisted the urge to put her off. While he did love and appreciate Cook, he tired of her antics on occasion. And he wasn't sure he had time for it tonight.

Not with what he had forthcoming.

"Cutie, I have something to tell ya'." She strained as if trying to attain his height.

That was obvious. He almost cracked a grin despite himself.

"I'm listening," he said, making every attempt to keep the tiredness from his voice.

"That wife of yours has a secret." Cook's eyes shone.

"A secret?" Did Cook know about his and Mariena's discussion earlier? No. It seemed as if this were a good secret.

"So, she hasn't told you?" Her eyes widened.

Cutie shook his head, not sure if he should be concerned or not.

"I probably shouldn't have said anything." Cook put her hands on her hips and looked to the floor. "Me and my big yapper."

"Cook, what is this secret?" His level of concern rose.

Her head was turned to the side, but she peered at him. "I don't know if I should tell."

He crossed his arms and closed his eyes, raising one hand to pinch the bridge of his nose. "And why not?"

"Don't know that it's my news to tell."

Opening his eyes, he let out a breath. One more thing for him to settle with Mariena. "All right." He relaxed his arms, letting them drop by his side. "Night, Cook."

Cook touched his arm. "I just want to say, 'congratulations' is all."

He turned. What could she mean? Congratulations?

A knock at the door disrupted his thoughts.

"That'll be Owen," Cook said, moving past him to the door. "You have a good night now. And Lord bless ya'."

With that, she opened the door and spoke quietly to Uncle Owen. Would he come in?

Soon enough, she disappeared through the door, shutting it soundly behind herself.

Congratulations?

People only said that kind of thing when you did something like got married or had a baby or...

Wait.

Could it be? Was Mariena...pregnant?

A rush of excitement went through him. How would it be to welcome a baby into their lives? A bit of both of them in one person?

What kind of father would he be?

That thought hung in the moment.

But he set it to the side. There were important matters at hand.

Like seeing his wife.

Settling deeper into the bed, Mariena wondered at what was to come when Cutie entered in a matter of moments. Wasn't it past time for him to return?

She would have to face his questions. There had been enough hiding today. Hadn't there?

Or might she feign sleep? Would *he* allow her the rest Cook believed she was due? She thought on it for a few moments and dismissed it. Such a childish game she played.

Footsteps outside the door gave her pause. She held her breath. Perhaps he would move on to Lucy's room for the night.

Did she want that? To be without him? Even for a night? No matter what the circumstances, she so wished to be with him.

If only he found himself weary and unwilling to press through the issue this evening. Now *that* would be a blessing. Dare she hope?

The latch moved and the door opened.

She stilled.

His movement as he crossed the doorframe to enter caused her to close her eyes.

Would she do this? Seek escape this way? How could this work?

His steps paused. Did he watch her?

Would her façade hold? How did one appear when asleep? Of course, her eyes should be closed and her body still, with slow breaths. What else might she be missing?

He began to move again; she sensed it as much as heard the gentle clomp of his boots on the floorboards.

Warmth from his body now emanated to hers. Was he leaning over her?

Her breaths quickened. There was little she could do about it. How was she to stop her body's reaction to him?

Too much of her concentration went to fighting the ache in her arms, which sought to envelop him, to not speak apologies to him and press kisses to his face. Was she so hopeless?

"Mariena?" His face was near hers.

Dare she open her eyes? Did he know this was all an act? She groaned inwardly. He would have to be daft if he didn't.

She lifted her eyelids.

He crouched beside the bed near the headboard. When he noticed her gaze on him, he grazed the back of his hand against her cheek.

How was she to fight such a battle? Would he break down her defenses bit by bit?

But instead of pulling back, she took his hand in hers, intertwining their fingers.

He pressed a kiss to her captive wrist.

Their gazes locked and held. What truly was the heaviness of this thing between them? Couldn't it just be dismissed? Was he prepared to do that?

"Yes, Charles?" she answered, remembering he had actually beseeched her.

He smiled. "I find I am not so abhorrent to you calling me that." Turning her hand in his, he worked his fingers against hers. "In fact, I like it."

She let the corners of her mouth lift despite her trepidations. "Good. I like also."

His smile drooped a little. "I wanted to finish what we started earlier. We *need* to finish what we started earlier. But I know you need your rest."

How was it that everyone catered to her so quickly after her little lie? Shouldn't she feel guiltier? She didn't. For it had supplied her what she needed today—respite from this issue.

She nodded. "I do."

"Did you want to...talk?" His words were soft, reverent almost.

Why did he ask if she wanted to engage in this discussion after he declared they didn't need to have it right now? Strange indeed.

"No. I only wish to have you beside me, holding me." Her eyes held his. Would he be able to put their differences to the side enough to give her that?

He ran their clasped hands across his lips. "Then you shall have it."

Was she mistaken, or was there a touch of sadness in his eyes, his affect? As if he expected something more? Had he anticipated she would push into the discourse though he had offered an out?

Did it matter what he thought? As for her, she turned to her side and bathed in his warm presence when he slid into the bed behind her and gathered her to himself.

This was not everything that she hoped would come of this evening, but it did exceed her expectations of what might.

Putting a hand on his arm, which surrounded her waist, she rubbed the skin there.

She turned her face toward the ceiling, giving him a profile view of her. "I do love you, Charles." Her voice became quieter.

He kissed the side of her face and pressed a trail to her shoulder. "I know. And I love you, too, my desert flower. Now, let's get some sleep."

Bringing down the axe, Cutie split another piece of wood. He then pulled at the heavy instrument and it released from its target. After putting another piece of trunk on the chopping block, he raised the axe, heaved, and dropped it upon the unassuming chunk.

He took a moment to grab for his bandana and wipe his forehead. This was one of the heftier chores at the ranch. And one of the more despised. But today he had volunteered. He needed the time to think. Or perhaps just clear his mind. That couldn't hurt.

Everyday had been a rush of too many focuses—the many preparations for the Millers' return. And, while he was the first to agree it needed to be done, he wasn't sure Brandon or Amanda would. He couldn't imagine them encouraging or even wanting anyone to go out of their way, add extra chores to their plate, make special efforts for them. The arrangements Amanda had made before they left would be fine enough, to be sure.

That didn't mean it would be enough for Cook. Or the ranch hands. This was Brandon, after all. And Amanda. Two of the most giving people on earth. So they all wanted everything to be just perfect for the Millers.

But hadn't Cutie already learned the dangers of trying to make a perfect mark? The worries of hoping to attain, only to fall short? Maybe he should take that perspective into this process. What they accomplished, as loved and well-intentioned as their motives were, would be enough. It would have to be.

Mariena had kept mostly to the room, but he believed she helped around the homestead when he was out doing chores. Then returned to the room during mealtime.

As long as she insisted on needing her rest, Cook would continue to cater to her and the baby. But was that such a good thing? For her to isolate herself?

Perhaps he made too much of it. Only a few days had passed. It would be different once Amanda returned.

Each night, he went to her. They had not had their discussion. Nor had they had any further intimacies.

She would ask him to hold her and let her rest. He would oblige. How could he not?

But she hadn't told him of the child. When would she? Why had she not already? Was there some reason she shouldn't? Something he wasn't aware of? A custom of her people perhaps?

Uncertainty of the circumstances left him a bit lost as to his actions from here. Dare he broach the subject and prod her to announce it to him? Or should he let it be and trust her to tell him in her own time?

How he wished Cook hadn't flapped her yap. When would the woman learn to keep her secrets to herself?

Setting the towel out to dry, Mariena took a last look over the kitchen. There was much to be done.

Cook busied herself with the preparations of the noon meal, but she would not let Mariena assist her. She only allowed Mariena to dry the already washed plates so they'd have dishes to eat upon.

Even then, Mariena felt Cook's gaze on her. "You goin' to sit down?"

Mariena shook her head. How she regretted her untruth now. For Cook did not let her exert herself in the least and was forever ushering her to her room.

"You best sit or lay down. Yes, that's probably a good idea. Put your feet up." Cook stirred something on the stovetop that steamed. Some vegetable? It smelled wonderful.

"I think I'm better," Mariena said, her voice smaller than she'd like. But she couldn't seem to put more force in it. Not after her lie. These were the consequences she must live with.

Cook shot her a look. "What does that mean? Better? You're not better. Look at ya'. You're dark under your eyes. And swelling. Goodness. I know when someone ain't well. Get off your feet, child." She turned her attention back to the meat in the oven.

Mariena didn't move. Dark under her eyes? Swelling? Did she truly look so terrible?

When Cook closed the oven and stood up again, arching her back, she craned her neck, spotting Mariena. "You still here?" Cook shook her spoon at Mariena. "Don't make me get Cutie in here to put you to bed."

That was all she needed. Holding up a hand, Mariena bowed her head. "Not need Cutie. I go."

"I don't understand you women these days. Thinking you can do whatever you want. Even fight against the laws of nature itself..."

Mariena stepped through the door between the kitchen and the hallway, letting it swing closed behind her. And with it, Cook's rant faded into the background noises of the meal preparation.

She walked to her room. But when she took hold of the latch, she rejected the notion. This was enough. There had been enough hiding. Too much hiding.

No matter what Cook said, Mariena was no invalid.

She peered back at the door to the kitchen, as if Cook might hear her thoughts and storm through the door and force the issue.

When nothing happened, she breathed deeply. Was she then free? What did she wish to do with this newfound freedom?

Outside.

She hadn't been in nature for several days. Cooped up in her room, she'd been barred from any manner of exercising her legs.

Gazing at the front door from the place where the hall joined the great room, she dreamed. Could she? Dare she?

What would Cook do when she found out?

If she found out?

No...*when.*

Imagining the breeze beyond and the smell of the blooms, the light of the sun on her face...

Her decision was made.

Tiptoeing across the great room with greater speed than she might should dare, she slipped opened the front door only enough for her to fit through. It did not creak. Strange. Had someone oiled it?

She did not think on it long, however, as she knew she was so close to realizing her liberty.

Lifting her skirt, she kept her footfalls as light as possible across the porch and down the few steps. But when her foot touched the ground, something overcame her.

She was home.

She was alive.

Nothing confined her.

And she ran.

Where to or what for, she did not know.

But she stopped when her lungs burned and her legs ached. She fell upon the thinning grass at the small stream she had happened upon.

The water, too, called to her.

Pulling at her shoes, another remnant of her restraints, she fairly shoved her feet, paler than she had ever seen them, into the cool moisture.

It startled—the chill of the water. How was it that in such an arid place the water could remain so cold?

She closed her eyes and lay back upon the thin bed provided for her. Staring up at the clear blue, she marveled at the cloudless day. Even though she looked far into the distance in every direction, there was not a puff in sight. Only the azure of the sky and the warmth of the sun.

A smile took hold of her features and filled her heart. Here, she was only Mariena. Nothing more, nothing less. No one pressed expectations on her. There were no decisions demanding to be made. Her beliefs were not questioned.

Could it not stay this way?

She had thought Cutie was this kind of safe place for her. Had that been nothing more than an illusion? A dream *she* had conjured?

Yes, the fault was hers and hers alone.

Something deep in her chest hurt. Like a pang. As if there were a war within her. From these torn thoughts?

There was no need for her to dwell, then, on these things. She had come here seeking peace. And peace she would have.

Clearing her mind as much as possible, she closed her eyes and thought on the balance of nature. Focusing on it. Could she make this balance exist in herself?

How long did she remain thusly? Lain out in the sun? Did she drift into sleep?

For she soon became aware of a presence over her.

Not just anyone, her husband.

And he spoke.

"Mariena. Mariena!" His hands set upon her shoulders then moved to her face. "Are you all right?"

She opened her eyes.

His figure was silhouetted against the sunlight.

Setting a hand in front of her eyes, she attempted to clear her vision and see him better. It did not help. "Charles?"

"Yes." He sighed. "It is me."

"What...?" She looked from side to side. Where was she? Oh yes, the stream. The run from the homestead. Her gaze searched for his, shadowed among the darkened figure.

"Bless all!" He ground out.

Better, perhaps, than some of the words he had used. Those she had not known.

"I've looked everywhere for you." He seemed angry, yes, but there was concern there, too.

"What?" She tried to sit up. Her body protested. How long had she lain here on the hard ground?

His hands were on her arm and around her back, helping her to sit as straight as possible.

Then her ability to see him became much better. His features took shape and form. But it gave her reason to ache within. The hurt, the pain in his eyes, stabbed at her.

"Cook found you were gone and sent me looking. She was so worried. *I* was so worried. You can't do that, Mariena."

She dropped her head. "I am sorry. I needed...wanted peace." Her eyes pricked. Could she fight the tears? This was not the time to make this about her.

He nodded, lowering himself from a crouched position to a knee. "I understand. But this," he said, extending his arms out, "is a wild place. A dangerous place."

She couldn't meet his eyes, but nodded.

A hand cupped her chin and lifted her face. He found her eyes himself. "I can't begin to imagine what I would do if something happened to you...or the baby."

"Baby?" She jerked back. "What baby?"

Cutie's features dropped. "Our baby." His hand fell from her face.

"What do you mean?"

She pulled her feet from the creek. They were stiff and cold. So cold. Could she stand? Pushing against the ground, she worked to get up. But her feet would not hold her. Had they lost feeling? Staggering, she shot her arms out for balance.

Cutie, now standing, caught her arms and held her, jerking her to himself. He looked down into her face, now rather close to his. "I was made to understand you are with child." His voice held hope and pain. How was that possible?

She couldn't affirm both.

Setting her head upon his shoulder, she shook it.

He gripped her tighter. For her sake, or his?

Tipping her head back, she met his gaze. "I'm sorry. I'm not with child."

Nodding, two quick, slight movements, he swallowed.

She had done something to him in that moment. Something she couldn't undo.

"That doesn't mean we won't...have a child. Perhaps soon." His voice was deep, meaningful. And his eyes on hers were heartfelt.

How could she tell him? Why had she not? He deserved to know. And now.

"No." Her voice was clearer than she would have thought.

"No?" His brows furrowed. "Is something wrong with—?"

She shook her head. That would make all of this much easier. Pumping her ankle and wiggling her toes, pain shot through her feet as feeling returned. Setting one, then the other on the ground, she found she could now stand on her own.

Taking advantage of her newfound balance, she pressed back from his arms.

"Talk to me, Mariena. Why won't we have children?"

Was that an undercurrent of anger or impatience in his voice? She liked neither.

"I..." Her heart twisted. Hadn't she put this decision, too, behind her? "I will not."

"What?" Eyes widening, he reached for her.

She stepped farther away.

"Do you think I wish to leave them in this world? In pain? In grief? Without..." Her words trailed off. What more was there to say? Perhaps she had said enough. Maybe too much.

"Left?" Cutie's features contorted. "In grief?"

She turned her body away. He didn't need to see.

"You mean the way you were left." His voice was gruff, full of emotion.

Shutting her eyes, she discovered, did not shut out the tears.

His hands were on her shoulders once more.

She attempted to shrug them off, but his hold on her was firm.

"Mariena," he said. His breath moved her hair. "We cannot plan or prepare for all pain in life. The fact that there is death is no reason to stop living."

Sniffling, she wanted to scream at him, to scold him, to bite back at him that he couldn't possibly understand what she had been through.

Then she remembered her conversation with Slim. Would she dismiss Cutie so easily? Not truly knowing the entirety of his story?

"Do you...know what it is, husband? This sorrow?" Her words were hoarse.

"I know pain. I know what it is to run from the demons of your past. To want to stop living. And I know what it is to find purpose again. To want to live for something."

She opened her mouth to ask what that was, but she stopped herself.

God.

He lived for what he found in God.

Could she?

Turning her head to the side, she struggled against a tightness in her chest. She couldn't tell herself to just believe, couldn't make herself forget the pain and devastation. If there were a God, why would He allow that?

No, that wasn't a God she would follow.

"I...can't."

"Yes. You can. We can. Together." Cutie tugged her to himself. Pressing her back against him in an embrace.

She wanted nothing more than to give herself to his love, to the comfort of his arms. But she could not make believe in some mystical being. Not now. Not ever.

Jerking from his arms, she said, "No. I can't."

Without looking back, she stretched out her legs and headed back the way she had come.

CHAPTER 18

Frustration

Cutie awoke in Lucy's room. Again.

Today he would go with Slim to collect Brandon, Amanda, and their children.

What would he do then? With Lucy returned, he couldn't very well continue sleeping in this room. Would he make his bed back in the bunkhouse? Or would he return to Mariena's bed? That seemed less likely.

She had not allowed him but two minutes alone with her since their argument by the stream. And even in those stolen moments, she wouldn't listen. What kind of marriage was this? What would become of them?

He rubbed a hand down his face as he sat up. A short beard, several days old, scrubbed his palm. Should he shave to greet his boss and the others? Did it matter?

Sliding from the bed, he prepared himself for the day. Sounds through the thin wall alerted him that his wife did the same.

Images of her washing her face, dressing for the day, and braiding her hair did nothing good for his disposition. Rather, it made him ache for her all the more. The sting did not lessen as time passed. What was it they said? Time heals all wounds? That didn't seem to be true. Not for him.

He hurried himself through the remainder of his morning routine. What could he think on to block out Mariena? Would anything work? Except perhaps his work to memorize the books of the Bible.

"Genesis, Exodus, Leviticus, Deuteronomy, Joshua, Judges…"

Wait. Had he missed one?

Yes. There were five books in that first set. What had he missed?

Come on, Cutie. Uncle Owen was so insistent this was the right place to start—knowing where the books of the Bible were and their order.

Numbers! Yes…

"Genesis, Exodus, Leviticus, *Numbers*, Deuteronomy!" he shouted, rather pleased.

A crash next door drew his attention.

Mariena!

Rushing from his room, he pushed against her door, banging against it. "Mariena!"

The door opened, giving way to the room.

She stood just within, her eyes wide as she pressed a cloth to her hand.

"What happened?" His words came out in gulped breaths.

"Nothing." Her gaze was soft, but had an edge.

He shouldered his way into the room. "I *heard* something. Don't tell me it was nothing."

The pitcher, the companion to the washbowl, lay on the floor in pieces.

Relief washed through him. What had he feared so?

Turning back toward her, he looked her over from head to toe. He homed in on her hand, covered by a wash towel. It was splotched with red.

Stepping to her, he lifted her hand. "You're hurt."

She shook her head. "It is nothing. Only scratch."

He opened the cloth and found her skin was open. It was much more than a scratch. The cut was deep. His eyes met hers. "This is bad."

She looked away.

"Mariena," he said, pressing the cloth back over the wound. "You need a doctor."

"No."

He stepped closer. "Yes," he said firmly. His eyes settled on hers. Pressing both hands over her wounded one, he said firmly, "It's important."

She looked at the center of his chest. Her body wavered. Would she faint? Then she turned her gaze up to him. And nodded.

Relief filled him. His trip into town would happen a bit earlier than expected.

Mariena winced as the doctor turned her hand again.

"I think you've got a pretty bad cut there. You'll need stitches."

"Stitches?"

"He'll have to sew the wound closed." Cutie offered.

How was that possible? She had seen the medicine man in her village do such, but only with special medicine. And usually only for the braves.

Sucking in a breath, she nodded. Even if there were pain, she would manage. This kind of pain would pass. It would be for but a moment.

"I've got something to help with the discomfort." The doctor moved to a cabinet. And, opening it, moved around bottles and vials within. They clanged as he maneuvered them. He extracted a clear container filled with white cream.

"This salve is made from herbs I've found to be helpful in easing some of the feeling around the area I'm working on." He looked at Mariena. "It won't take away all the pain, but it will help."

She nodded. Then turned to meet Cutie's eyes. "You will stay?"

He nodded.

The tension in her eased, and she let her lips turn up slightly. She put her uninjured hand on Cutie's and shifted her focus back to the doctor. "I am ready."

"It will take a moment to get everything set up." The doctor shot Cutie a glance.

Was it her imagination or was the doctor less than thrilled to have him stay? It seemed the man would prefer to do his work without an audience. Perhaps it was just safer that way. One look at Cutie and she knew nothing could separate him from her side.

He squeezed her hand that still lay in his and crouched near her as the doctor moved about the room.

"Are you angry?" Mariena's voice cracked. Moisture stung her eyes.

"Angry?"

She bit at her lip. How could he be confused? "For such a mess with us."

"That is between us. It is a matter for us both to take blame."

Did he truly feel that way? It seemed every time they made any progress, she shut him down.

He set a hand to the side of her face, stroking the hair framing her features. "We don't have to talk about it right now."

She swallowed then nodded. Should she be so thankful for him putting off the discussion?

The doctor came back to the cot, a tray of implements in hand. "Still ready?"

Her eyes widened. What did the doctor intend to do with all those tools? She had never seen such.

Cutie, however, only watched on. Was he not concerned? If he trusted this man, so could she.

"Yes, doctor. Do it." She turned her gaze to the ceiling, setting her features to a more stoic, flat expression.

She wished she were braver.

Cutie brought her hand to his lips and pressed a kiss to her knuckles.

"If you are to stay," the doctor said, glaring at Cutie. "You must do as I say and keep your hands clear of my patient."

What? Why was he not allowed to offer her comfort?

"Those are my rules. Take them." The doctor's voice invited no discussion. "Or leave." He then directed his attention to cleaning his hands.

Mariena closed her eyes. Must the doctor make this so much harder? She needed Cutie's touch, his strength.

Cutie brought her fingers to his lips once more. Kissing them again, he spoke against her skin. "I'm right here."

She nodded, a slight a movement. Her body was nearly paralyzed in fear.

With hesitation, Cutie released her hand, setting it by her side and moving his chair to the wall. She hated that he had to do so, but she knew he did not wish to give the doctor cause to put him out.

The good doctor returned, at her side in the next moment, glaring down at her. "And now, we begin."

Cutie looked for Slim. He should be out here waiting for the stagecoach. Had it not already arrived? If not, it was late.

Mariena rested now. After the doctor finished stitching her hand, he insisted she remain in the clinic for a couple of hours before being moved.

The last thing Cutie wanted was for her wound to reopen. She seemed to fall asleep as soon as they got her to a recovery room, and he slipped out to check on Slim and Nisto.

Besides, he was sure Nisto would be anxious to hear his sister was well. The youngster had wanted to stay in the clinic, but everyone thought it best he go with Slim.

But...where were they now?

Cutie scanned the area outside the telegram office. Had the stagecoach come and gone? The empty platform made him doubtful.

He didn't have to search for much longer before spotting Slim coming down the main stretch. Where had he been? The handful of licorice was the only clue necessary—the General Store.

But where was Nisto? Had Slim lost him? Forgotten he had been charged with watching the boy?

"Slim!" Cutie called, waving.

Slim looked around, as if searching for the source of the call. At last, his gaze landed on Cutie and he waved.

He picked up his pace until he stood with Cutie. "I thought it would take a stampede or raging fire to convince you to leave Mariena."

Cutie poked Slim's hat brim up. "I didn't leave her."

"Oh, so you're with her right now?" Slim looked from side to side. "Strange, I don't *see* her."

Why must Slim be so impossible? Cutie elbowed him in the ribs. "You know what I mean! I slipped out after the stitches. When she was resting."

"I see." Slim shoved another licorice in his mouth.

"What about Nisto? Where is he?" Cutie's voice rose. He didn't often get exasperated, but Slim couldn't just be forgetting Nisto.

"Calm down. I gave him a penny and left him in the General Store to spend it."

"Left him in the General Store?" What might the not-so-well-meaning townsfolk do to a desert Indian boy if they treated Mariena so callously at the dance?

Slim waved him off. "He knows where to find me when he's done. 'Sides, didn't yer pa ever leave you to buy candy at the store when you were Nisto's age?"

Cutie couldn't believe Slim was so shortsighted. "Yeah. But in a town I knew. Full of people who knew me. And my pa."

It became clear from Slim's drooping expression that this had not occurred to him. "I think I might better..." He motioned toward the General Store.

"I think you should." Cutie nodded.

Slim stepped off the wooden platform.

And a crack sounded. Followed by the creak of wooden wheels.

The stagecoach.

It had arrived.

Slim paused. Then shot Cutie a look.

Go, Cutie mouthed.

The stagecoach came into view, pulling around the final turn and onto the end of the main thoroughfare. Nothing could stop its rush into the small town. And Cutie would not have anyone do so.

He was thankful beyond measure.

The Millers were home.

Mariena watched from the window in her room as the stagecoach flew past. She looked down at the bandage on her hand. It was sore for certain. But the pain had not been what she feared it could be.

She continued to look down onto the street below. Should she go out and follow the trail of dust? Greet Amanda and her family now that they had arrived? Would the doctor dismiss her from his care?

Standing, she did her best to adjust her dress here and there, smooth out the wrinkles. Then she turned.

And realized she was not alone.

Someone sat in the shadowed corner of the room.

But who?

Why?

She shivered but pressed her most firm expression onto her face while forcing her shoulders to square. "Who's there?"

The figure leaned forward. And his features came into the light.

Sheriff McAllen.

She worked to suppress all evidence of her surprise. At least her fear had evaporated. The man did not mean her harm.

Closing her eyes, she swallowed before opening them to meet his gaze. "How long you sit there?"

"Does it matter?" He set his elbows on his knees, clasping his hands together. As if they were here for a comfortable chat.

That was not so. And she would not pander to whatever game he played.

"I thank you for concern over me." She dipped her head. "As you see, I am well now."

He nodded and watched his hands as if he examined his fingernails.

What did he want?

She held her breath.

After a moment, she pushed it out. There was nothing keeping her in this room. Nothing to make her be subject to him.

"If you excuse me, Sheriff, I must go." She moved around the bed and toward the door, her steps as quick as she dared make them.

Her hand reached for the latch; she was almost there.

"Leave my town."

She froze. The breaths, which had been managed until now, came rapidly. And her heart thudded as if it would come through her chest.

Dare she turn and face him?

The wooden chair legs scuffled on the floor. Had he risen?

She couldn't fight it any longer. Peering in his direction, she confirmed what she had already guessed—he stood a few paces in front of the chair. That brought him dangerously close.

"What you want from me?" Her voice was not as strong as she wished. She turned, but only far enough that her body was sideways to him and to the door. If she needed to, she could still escape.

He reached up and rubbed his badge. "As I said...I want you to leave my town."

She turned her face toward him. Why was he so against her presence here? As she opened her mouth, he continued.

"You...your people are a troublesome bunch. Have you not seen with your own eyes the kind of problems your presence has created?"

Her breaths came increasingly harder. Was he right?

"First, the near-miss at the livery." He held out a single finger as emphasis. "Then the fiasco at the Sweethearts' Dance." Another finger joined the first. "Will you not see it? Will you not understand?"

She bit her lip.

"You are bad for this town." The sheriff took a step toward her.

Everything in her was ready to flee, to run as fast as she could as far as she could. But she remained planted to the spot, her eyes narrowing as they set on him.

"You're bad for *him*." McAllen's voice softened.

For Cutie?

She shifted to stare out the window once more. Cutie was out there. Waiting for the Millers. And for her.

"How long will you only look to yourself and not see how much strife you have brought down on him?"

Her hands came to her midsection, clutching there. Was that true? She had made things complicated for Cutie. Their relationship had been wrought with hardship. Was it because of her? Would there never be peace for him as long as she remained?

"But...I have nowhere..." Her eyes stung.

"There's always San Xavier."

Her eyes shot to his again.

He appeared innocent enough, but she wasn't fooled. She was well aware of his attempt at manipulation. What he had not counted on, however, was the truth behind his words.

"What..." Was she truly about to say this? To consider his words? "What about my brother? He d-does not belong on r-reservation."

The sheriff became quiet. Did he think on it? Would he concede?

She hoped he would.

"Very well. The boy might make it in the town, as he is rather young. He can forget your ways and be raised proper, I suppose."

Biting back the gasp that filled her being at his words, she trembled. Nisto forget their ways? Was that not her very mission? That she and Nisto carry on the legacy of their people? Their tribe? Their parents?

But, if this was the only way...

She met McAllen's stare and with a fire in her own gaze, nodded. "It is done."

"And you will go from this place and never return?" His eyes bored into hers.

"Yes." She shut her eyes against the wave of nausea but opened them to challenge him. "And you not try to push on brother. But let him be."

The sheriff nodded.

They stood then, staring at each other.

"What keeps you?" McAllen frowned.

She glanced at the window once more. Her heart ached to see Cutie again, to explain, or perhaps feel his arms one more time. But that could not be. Not if this was to work. McAllen was right—if she were to go, she must do so now.

Turning to the door, she gripped the latch.

A hand landed on hers.

She shot a look at McAllen.

"Do not cross me, girl. I am not to be trifled with." His brows lifted and then lowered. "Do we understand each other?"

Lifting her chin, she shoved her shoulders back. And nodded.

Then, without any sense of urgency, but keeping eye contact with

McAllen, she swung the door open, and took the first steps into her darkened future.

CHAPTER 19

Cutie had finished helping Brandon load the Millers' things onto the first cart and sent them on their way. He, Slim, Mariena, and Nisto would travel back in the other.

If they could track everyone down. Now it seemed Nisto *and* Slim were missing. Perhaps Slim had simply gone looking in other places for Nisto. Had the boy become lost?

Either way, they could use another set of eyes for the search. And he didn't like the idea of Mariena being alone in the clinic.

He greeted the doctor at the door. "Anything—?"

The doctor shook his head and pointed toward the stairs before burying himself back in his book. Something involving sketches of bones.

Cutie sighed and took the steps two at a time. The upstairs gave way to a single room. In it, he knew would be the one bed. That was where he had left Mariena resting.

When he reached the top of the stairway, he noticed that the door was ajar. An uneasy feeling settled in his stomach—a twisting heaviness.

Shoving the door the rest of the way open, he found the room vacant. How was this possible?

"Doctor!" he called.

The sound of footfalls rushing up the steps did not assuage his fears. In seconds, the dark-haired physician came into the room.

"Where is she?" He stared at Cutie wide-eyed, as if Cutie had done something with her.

"You tell me," Cutie ground out. "I left her here in *your* care."

The doctor sputtered, "I-I had to eat." He ran a hand through his curly hair. "I only went to the cafe two doors down. I couldn't have been gone for more than a half hour."

With that, the heaviness in Cutie's stomach sank, becoming an anchor, the barbs of which pierced him within.

Where could she be? Had someone taken her? For what reason? How was he to go about finding her?

He walked to the window, a fury building inside his chest. Watching the movement of people below, he could stand it no longer. Slamming his fists against the window's frame, he let out a cry from the depths of his being.

Was she lost to him forever?

Mariena's legs tired. How far had she walked? How long? The sun had started to make its descent. It would set soon. Then dark would come.

Perhaps her final night.

For dangerous things lurked in the dark. Things that did not care of body or person. Only of wildness and hunger.

And there were worse things.

Those who would take her and do much, much more to her.

No, she would never make it to San Xavier. And she doubted McAllen was deluded enough to believe she would either.

A stream to her left drew her attention. She did so wish for a drink.

Her bandaged hand stung and throbbed. There was blood soaking through to the outermost wrappings. That would only help make her a better target for those animals with the keenest of scent.

Yes, for certain, this sunset would be her last.

Leaning over the stream, she cupped water and brought it to her lips. As she considered the direness of her situation, she wondered if she should even bother with the journey.

What did it matter if she made it another stretch of wilderness or not? If she couldn't make it to San Xavier, why weary herself with it?

She sat then, by the water, and watched the rippling of tiny waves in a current that could not be stopped. Much like her life. It had been moving in a direction and at a pace, neither of which she could control, since her parents and tribe were killed.

At last, she had been able to make a choice for herself. Had she made the right one? It was not possible to live a life with Cutie, knowing that her very presence created hardship for him.

Yes, this *was* right.

She breathed in the freshness of the air, closing her eyes. There was something about the scent, however, that gave her pause. Something that did not smell altogether pleasant. Could it be…?

Turning, she saw movement in the brush.

Her heart fell.

No.

Not here.

Not now.

Not after everything they had gone through.

She stood and walked toward the shrubs, praying that if there were a God, it would not be so.

"Who is there?" she half asked, half cried as she approached.

Nothing.

"Show yourself. Now!" She bit back her tears.

More shuffling as the figure stood.

Nisto.

She sank to her knees.

And sobbed.

Cutie paced the floor in the great room.

Neither he nor Slim had been able to find Nisto. Had he gone with Mariena?

Dan, Uncle Owen, Brandon, and Amanda sat around the room, silent. Cook had taken it upon herself to put Lucy to bed.

"I just don't know what we can do," Dan said, shrugging.

"Don't know what we can do?" Cutie stopped his anxious movements and glared at Dan. "We have to go after them, of course! You know what it's like out—"

"I think," Brandon interjected, "what Dan means is that we don't have any clue where to start. How do we go after her?"

Cutie set his gaze on his boss. How could he deny Brandon's assertion? The wilderness *was* a big place. They didn't even know where she was headed, much less if she even knew how to get there.

"I understand how upsetting this must be." Amanda's tone was gentle. "We all do. This is hard on us, too. We are just as angry. Just as heartbroken. And just as ready to ride out after her."

Cutie ran hands through his hair and clenched his fingers together behind his neck. Was that true? He could not claim he had sole ownership of loss in this room.

"You know we will all do what we can," Slim said, clearing his throat.

Slim hadn't dared speak since coming back to the ranch. Cutie hadn't been pleased with him for losing track of Nisto. But Slim wasn't the only person in the room to make a mistake. And his wasn't so egregious at that.

Cutie nodded, still resting his hands on his neck. "What if..."

Brandon shook his head. "We can ask 'what if' all night and all day. It won't get us any closer to finding her."

"No." Cutie released his hands and held one in front of himself. "Hear me out."

Brandon folded his arms over his chest and nodded.

"What if she is headed for the reservation in San Xavier?" Cutie looked from one person to the other.

"Why would she do that?" Dan countered. "I thought she married you so she wouldn't have to go there."

Was that some kind of ill-timed joke?

Brandon caught Dan's eye and shook his head.

The others exchanged looks, most shrugged.

"The thing is," Uncle Owen finally spoke, "we can't know for sure. And even if we went off in that direction looking for her, how do we know which way she went? Where did she leave from? Which path will she take? Will she stay on a straight path?"

Cutie heard his earlier thoughts in the older man's words. And he knew Uncle Owen was right. They all were.

But how could they expect him to sit by and do nothing? It would be sunset soon...and then nightfall. Their chances of finding her would diminish. And the likelihood of her survival...it...

He leaned against a wall, pressing the back of his wrist to his nose and mouth. Would he lose his meal? Or would he lose his battle with the tears pricking the back of his eyes?

There was shuffling in the room. What did the others do? Though tempted to turn, he dared not. He didn't want them to see...what this situation had reduced him to.

His shoulders shook.

No, he would not be able to hold back the torrent.

A firm hand fell on his shoulder. Whose?

"It's okay to let it out."

Brandon.

Did he trust the man with this display of emotion?

He turned, meeting Brandon's gaze.

Brandon was a good man. Like Cutie's father. A loving man. He cared about those around him. Not just his family, well, his blood family. The man had made his ranch hands and Cook part of his family.

If there were anyone Cutie could trust, it was Brandon.

"I just...don't know what to do. I can't...lose her." Cutie gasped in breaths as his tears overcame him.

Brandon embraced Cutie.

It seemed strange for his boss to let him spill his emotion like this. But it didn't at the same time.

The man was as a brother to him. In so many ways. An older brother—the kind one trusted, and leaned on, and forgave back and forth.

And the kind of brother who would have his back. No matter what.

Sheriff McAllen slowed his horse as he approached the worn down house.

Why was he here?

He pulled on the reins and stopped the animal's forward progress. Maybe he should turn around and go back to the jail. After all, it was late. And this was a bad idea.

But there was light within.

That meant the inhabitants were awake. Probably.

He paused. Torn as to his next move.

The door to the cabin opened. His heart pounded.

Ralph's stocky frame became visible in the soft light of the evening.

McAllen should urge the horse behind the trees. He didn't want to be seen. Then his choices would vanish.

As he jerked the reins to the right and the horse shifted, a stick cracked.

How thoughtless could he be?

Ralph jerked his head in that direction. Surprise gave way to recognition. And the man waved at his brother.

Could McAllen now turn and walk away? After being spotted? It was doubtful.

Still, he remained in indecision. Dare he join his brother? Or keep his ignorance and guard his wounds?

Ralph's motions became bigger. Did he fear McAllen didn't see him?

Then, suddenly, he stopped. Was he suspicious of the truth? That at any moment McAllen might lose all resolve and bolt? Would that make him a coward?

Did he have it in him to live with that?

Squaring his shoulders, he made up his mind. He would face his fate. For no one, not even his brother would accuse him of such.

"Nisto!" Mariena cried in their language between sobs. "Why? Why did you follow me?"

His brows came together. "You are my sister. Should I not go with you?"

She shook her head, still gripping her stomach and rocking.

"Why, Mariena? Where are you going?"

Looking at him once more, she searched his features. So sincere. And so innocent. Did he have no idea what he had done?

Shifting her gaze to the ground, she wailed again. Would this immense sadness know no end?

The stirring of the dust made her aware that he stepped toward her. His small hand touched her shoulder. "What is it? Why are you sad? Did I do something wrong?"

She shook her head. "No. It's not that." Working to control herself, she settled her weight to the side of her hip and one leg. Then bade Nisto come closer.

He did so.

Reaching out, she took his hands in hers. "I have to go."

"Go? Where?"

She swallowed. "Away."

His features scrunched. "Away? Why?"

"I can't explain right now. You have to trust me. But your place is with Samuel. And Cutie. At the ranch. That is your home now."

"But I want to be with you." His voice shook. There would be tears soon. Why must he suffer so much in his short life?

"That isn't possible." She fought to remove all traces of emotion from her voice. "You have to go back to Wharton City. To the church. Tell the reverend you need to get to the Millers' ranch."

Twin tears rolled down his face. "I can't. I'll forget."

"No, you won't." She squeezed his hands. Then lifted a hand to wipe the moisture from his face. "I love you."

He fell to her chest.

She held him to her. The last of their village. He alone would carry their memories into the world.

The earth vibrated under them. What was this?

Pulling back slightly, she scanned the horizon. There, in the distance, a band of riders. Had Cutie and the others come after her?

As much as her heart thrilled at the thought of seeing him, she was sad. How would she tell him? How could she insist that this must be so?

"Mariena..." Nisto paled and stiffened. He clung to the fabric of her dress, his fingers capturing the cloth. Would he actually tear it?

What could cause such a reaction in him?

Her gaze moved from him to the riders once more.

And everything in her fell.

Apache.

What would they do?

She grabbed Nisto and shoved him into the brush.

His body shivered next to hers. But she couldn't worry about that now. She had to keep a level head. If she were to save Nisto.

Keeping him behind her, she peered through scant openings in the tiny branches.

The small band of Apache aimed their horses toward the stream. Perhaps they would cross and all would be well. Please, let that be all.

But they slowed.

Her stomach twisted. Had she and Nisto been spotted? Or were they only stopping to water their horses?

The group of five, all men, halted just short of the stream. They let the animals move toward it. A couple of the braves hopped down and quenched their own thirst, but three remained astride.

Many words flew between them. And laughter. What were they doing out here? Where was their village? Nearby? Mariena's legs ached to run, to remove herself from danger. But any movement would only increase her risk.

One of the men wandered farther downstream, closer to where she had been.

No.

Her breaths came unevenly.

The man paused, looking at the ground. Then knelt, setting a hand to the earth.

Why hadn't she thought to...?

He called to the others.

The bare-chested man who had also dismounted came up behind him, looking over his shoulder. Their gazes followed the tracks she had left. Straight to where they hid.

It was hopeless.

They were caught.

But...

Her fear of the Apache was great. After watching what they could do, seeing the aftermath, being told numerous stories about what they were capable of, the thought of being captured by this band terrified her more than any horse ever could.

But Nisto.

She had to do what she must to save Nisto. To give him his best chance.

The other men slid from their horses, hands on weapons. They glared at the collection of bushes.

It was only a matter of time now.

Setting a hand on Nisto's leg, she whispered. "No matter what happens, you must stay as still as possible. Don't move. Not until they have gone. Understand?"

He nodded, eyes wide. Would he obey? No matter what? She could only hope.

Pressing a kiss to his forehead, she pulled a leg out from underneath herself. And, setting her foot before her, she took a breath and pushed it out. She was as ready as ever.

Watching the Apache bands' movements, she waited. They needed to be closer, but not so much that they suspected another was hidden here.

Just another couple of steps.

Give me speed. And strength. She prayed. To whom she did not know.

Pressing her weight into her forward facing foot, she launched herself. And ran with all she had, letting out a scream.

How far could she go?

Pounding feet behind her both scared and relieved her. Dare she look back to ensure all five followed?

No, that would cost her.

Not that this wasn't an exercise in futility.

The time dragged on, the muscles in her legs were invigorated by the fright coursing through her body. But it was over too quickly.

Something hard hit the back of her shoulder, propelling her forward, off balance. Pain shot through her body, stealing her breath.

She went down, thrust to the ground by the force of the blow.

But she had to try. There was still fight in her.

Pushing up on her arms, she cried out when searing pain tore through her shoulder. The arm would not bear her weight. All her strength had gone.

What happened?

In a moment, hands jerked her upright. And something was pulled from the back of her shoulder.

She cried at the force of the ache.

Heat poured out.

Pulled this way and that, she was half-led, half-dragged to where the others still stood.

Now surrounded by these men, she tried to see them, wanted to stare at them with all the defiance she could muster. To prove her courage. But her vision became blurry.

She wasn't even certain there were only five men. Couldn't she count more? Their figures split into more and then coalesced again. What was this?

When the man came around to face her, she spotted a knife. Had she been hit with that? What would they do for her wound? Just let her bleed out? Her knees weakened.

She started to fall, but one of the men caught her. He held her while the larger of the men started what became a discussion.

Their language was mostly unknown to her; she only picked out a few words here and there. What she discerned, she did not like.

They attempted to decide whether to do as they wished with her here and discard her body or take her back to their village.

Again, she prayed they would do the latter. Perhaps that would be worse, but she did not wish Nisto to see what these men were capable of.

The strongest voice in the group had apparently committed some sort of grievance against their chief. He convinced the others that she would make a good offering to the chief.

Her world started to spin. The man's arms came around her, lifting her.

A dark rim surrounded everything she saw.

No.

Now was not the time to lose consciousness. She must fight for every chance. Mustn't she? Or would it be all right to let go?

The darkness seemed so soothing. It felt warm and offered escape.

I'm sorry, Charles. She sent out into the air. Would he receive it?

Then she slipped into the sweet night.

CHAPTER 20

Demanding

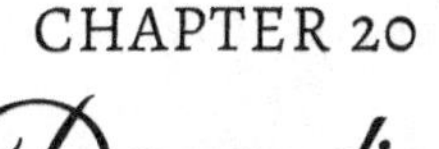

"Don't look at me like that," McAllen muttered.

"Like what?" Ralph moved to the side as his brother stepped onto the small porch.

"You know...like a cat...who just got a mouse."

Ralph bit his lip, but McAllen thought he saw the corners of his mouth turn upward.

McAllen looked away. There was no sense in this. Nothing would be different. Nothing.

"Where is he?" McAllen had to push the words out. His heart seemed to stop in the few seconds it took Ralph to answer.

"In his bedroom." All amusement disappeared from Ralph's features. He reached for the door's latch, but McAllen beat him to it. Perhaps the sheriff in him could provide strength and courage where his brother lacked it.

McAllen didn't wait for him, but stepped into the house.

And was confronted with a myriad of memories.

The place smelled the same. Even if dust had taken over. What did Ralph do when he came? Only the bare essentials?

He turned toward the stove. Ma should be there. And it seemed as if she were...for a moment. But then she was gone again. His heart squeezed.

Ralph came in behind him. "Been a while, Walt."

McAllen continued to scan the portion of the house that served as the kitchen. It seemed...wrong for Ma to not be there. But all the wishing in the world wouldn't bring her back. She had been a rock. The one who understood. Who...

"Not much has changed though."

Did he really have to be here?

McAllen drew in a deep breath. "I'm ready."

Ralph brushed past him and moved toward the back room.

Was he ready? Or would he crumble at the first cross word?

No...he was not that boy from years ago. He had grown a thicker skin. And had learned more about the hardness of the world.

Ralph opened the door to the bedroom McAllen had once thought a haven from the storms of life. Now he dreaded it.

He watched as Ralph stepped in and moved to the bed, leaning over the figure reclining within. But, for whatever reason, McAllen could not make himself enter the sanctuary of the man who had cut him so deeply.

Ralph stood and waved for him to come closer.

Could he? Dare he?

"What's the matter, boy?" the weakened voice called from the bed.

McAllen froze.

"Did you come to just stand at the doorway all night?"

Yes, nothing had changed. Pa was still the same gruff man he had been—a man who couldn't release a grudge. Or forgive a young boy's sin.

McAllen turned away and moved back to the front door.

Footfalls chased him. Pa?

No, they couldn't be.

A hand clamped on his shoulder. His heart jumped as if it would fling from his chest.

"Walt, wait!" Ralph beseeched him.

McAllen refused to slow, but in the next second, Ralph had managed to wedge himself between the sheriff and the door.

"Out of my way." He wanted to put a hard edge in his tone, but there was too much emotion; his voice wavered.

"Not until you tell me what happened. Hasn't this gone on long enough?"

McAllen looked to the side. Ralph wouldn't understand. Couldn't.

"What would Ma say? What would she want?"

Looking his brother in the eyes, McAllen swallowed. That was not fair.

"Please, Walter. Let me help you fix this."

McAllen continued to stare his brother down. What could he say? He had learned long ago that trust brought hurt. And when he attempted to reconcile with Pa, it only led to more pain. What could Ralph do?

But had he earned the right to know?

McAllen let out a breath. "Pa can't forgive me."

Ralph jerked his head back. Was he so disbelieving?

Moving back into the only area that had any space in his tiny house, McAllen faced the fireplace. "It's true."

"What could you have possibly done?"

McAllen snorted. "Something I shouldn't have—I broke the rules."

"Broke the rules? I don't understand." Ralph's voice seemed closer. But McAllen didn't care to turn. He continued to examine the stonework surrounding the chimney.

"Rules...they may not seem important at the time...you may not even agree with them. But that's not for the average person to decide. It is the citizens' responsibility to follow them. Regardless. I learned that the hard way. And I paid for it. Dearly."

"What rule did you break?" Ralph's voice became softer.

"I stayed out too late. Thought it was okay to wander for another hour."

"That doesn't seem so bad. All boys are rowdy from time to time."

If only that was all there was to it.

"But the rules are there for a reason."

"Yeah, but every now and then, you have to—"

"The rules...are there for a reason," McAllen said more harshly than he'd meant to. But he had to make Ralph understand. This was important.

Ralph's eyes widened.

"A simple rule may not seem like much, but when I broke that rule, it almost cost a life."

Furrowed brows, confusion about his face, Ralph shot out, "Whose?"

"Yours."

Cutie stared at the night sky. Would he sleep again? He did not know.

How long could he sit idly by and wait for news of Mariena? Wait for a signal as to where to start the search?

Even if he had to comb the entire wilderness, would that not be better than *this*? Most assuredly so.

He looked up once more at the stars, placed so well in the sky. At one time, he didn't think much about it. But now...

Now he could not deny God's hand in it.

Could he allow God's hand to be in this, too? If so, why would He allow Cutie to face such obstacles? For Mariena and Nisto to be out there, unprotected?

But if he were truly to believe in God, he had to take it all, he supposed. No sense in being a fair-weather friend to an almighty being. Either he believed or he didn't.

And he did.

God, I need direction. I need help. The kind that only You can offer. Will you help me?

His prayer seemed so simple. But Uncle Owen said that all God wanted was to hear his heart.

He dropped his head. This patch of grass right here, on this hill, had been their place—his and Mariena's. They'd had some intense moments here.

Letting his gaze wander over the surrounding area, he spotted something among the greenery. Something that didn't look like it belonged.

It was probably nothing.

He returned to his thoughts of Mariena and the trouble she was in.

But though this reality of Mariena's situation was truly dire, he couldn't stop thinking about whatever that was just a few feet away. Was he mad?

After some moments, he gave up and stood, walking toward the strange light-colored object. Even when he stood over it he still couldn't quite make it out in the dimness. He moved it with his foot. It flipped.

It couldn't be...

He crouched and picked it up, his fingers shaky.

It was. The saguaro flower carving he had given to Mariena as a wedding gift.

Sinking back onto his rear once more, he turned the delicate carving in his hand. How had the thing survived? Its petals were slightly misshapen, warped perhaps because of the elements, moisture most likely to blame.

Still, the flower was every bit as delicate and lovely. It earned its place on display somewhere. Not out here in the field.

A light thundering in the distance drew his attention from the carving and back to the homestead.

There, just passing onto the main path, was a rider. Someone riding in at this hour could only mean one thing—urgent news.

Mariena.

Cutie gripped the flower and ran for the homestead.

"I don't understand." Ralph finally spoke after some moments of thick silence. "I think I would remember almost dying."

McAllen held his brother's gaze. If only he could be as forgetful as Ralph. What would he give to erase his memory of the event, of the words his father spoke to him, of...

Ralph crossed his arms. "You're making this up."

"It was the night you broke your arm." Maybe that would help spark Ralph's memory of the event.

His drooped brows slowly rose. He knew.

"Yes. I had been out late, playing along a creek bank. Then I got lost.

I didn't mean to—it was dark and nothing looked the same." Why was he saying such things? These were excuses. And there couldn't be. He broke a rule. He needed to own the consequences.

"When Pa came looking for me, you followed. And...well, didn't mange any better than I in this wilderness, and we found you on our way back home. All busted up. You were lucky we found you before the coyotes did." McAllen hung his head.

"But you did find me. And I'm fine. I healed." Ralph, at least, was ready to let it go.

McAllen glanced back up to meet Ralph's eyes. "Except Pa wasn't eager to forgive my transgression. And he never did. From that moment on, I was a troublemaker in his eyes, a rule-breaker. But I never broke another rule."

"And you never forgave yourself."

Why would Ralph say that? How could McAllen hold a grudge against himself? That didn't make sense. "I don't know what you mean."

"Maybe Pa does still blame you. Maybe he won't *ever* forgive you. But that doesn't mean you have to keep yourself in this prison you've created."

McAllen furrowed his brows. Prison? He thinned his mouth into a line. Ralph didn't know what he was saying.

"Now it makes sense. Why you wanted so badly to be a sheriff. Why you won't let anyone off the hook."

"That's not true!" A fire lit in McAllen's stomach. "I only ask others to do as I do—uphold the law. And I've seen for myself—laws are there for a reason, even if I don't always agree with them."

"But not every law is just *or* right. What about slavery? It was the law. But that didn't make it right."

McAllen seethed. Ralph couldn't be right. It wasn't up to just anyone to question a law. Then everyone could question every law. Where would the order be? It would be chaos.

"Sorry, Ralph." He shook his head. "I can't live that way. Rules and laws exist for a reason." McAllen turned and walked to the front door. Ralph did not follow.

"You won't be back, will you?"

McAllen reached for the latch. What was the point in lying? In giving Ralph reason to hope? "No, I won't."

"Go do what you do best—enforce the rules. Pour your hurt into that. Maybe then this rift just won't exist. At least not in your mind."

How dare he...

McAllen wanted to turn around and show his brother what he thought of that assertion.

Breathe, just breathe.

Instead, he pulled the door open, and left.

Mariena rolled her head to one side. Why did it ache so? Why did *she* ache so?

She was on her back in some sort of tent. Was it a tent? The air was thick and smelled heavily of animal skin.

Her mind cleared. And she remembered—the Apache. She must be in their village's temporary location. But where was that? How far from Wharton City? From the Millers' ranch?

What did it matter? No one would find her. Not here. She only hoped Nisto had remained concealed. And made it safely back.

Shifting her body, she searched for wounds.

Her shoulder hurt. Bad. And her stitched hand was still quite sore.

But these were the least of her concerns. She was in an Apache camp and would face any number of tortures before they decided to end her life.

What she wouldn't give for a knife to cut her misery short.

Was there any hope of escape?

She pushed up to a sitting position. However, not quickly. Her body protested but obeyed.

Scanning the small area around her did not yield much—only a few blankets. At least she wasn't bound.

They would be senseless if they didn't post someone outside the opening of the makeshift structure. But what about the other sides?

She pulled herself to the back and tested the bottom of the thick skin. It was too tightly stretched. There was no way she could lift it enough to slide underneath. If she had a knife, she could slice it open or cut the lacing holding the skins together.

Wishing would get her nowhere.

Voices just outside pulled her focus from the seam. Who was it? What did they want?

The flap opened and a woman, several years older than her, stepped in. She had a bowl and cloth in her hand and a bag slung over her arm.

What was her intention? She didn't appear to have a weapon. Was that to prevent Mariena from taking it?

Sitting in the center of the tent, the woman indicated for Mariena to come.

Should she resist? What would come of that? Perhaps if she complied, she might make an ally of this woman.

Sliding across the small distance, she stopped just short of the Apache woman.

The woman twirled her finger. Did she wish Mariena to turn?

She did so.

What would the woman do while her back was turned? Something was torn from the back of her shoulder.

Mariena bit her lip to keep from crying out.

Had her shoulder wound been bandaged? Maybe the woman came to clean and redress it.

Trying to sit still while the woman worked, Mariena wondered when and how to take advantage of this opportunity. There wasn't likely much time.

"You know this is wrong," she said in her native tongue. Would the woman even understand her?

No response.

She tried in English.

Silence.

The woman continued to work. Her treatment of the wound stung, but it wasn't too bad.

After several moments, she came around and looked at Mariena's hand. It surprised Mariena to see fresh wrappings on it. No longer was blood coming through. Their medicine man must have visited while she slept.

Dipping her head, Mariena attempted to catch the woman's eyes. "Do you know what they intend to do to me?"

The woman flinched but continued her work. Yes, she understood Mariena. At least well enough.

"What would you do if this were your sister? Or your daughter?"

Pausing, the woman seemed to consider that.

"I have a mother, a father, a brother. They will grieve," Mariena pressed. No need to mention her parents were dead. That wasn't relevant.

The woman went back to her work, and a fresh bandage was soon on Mariena's hand.

"Please," Mariena gripped the older woman's hand as she started to stand. "Don't let them do this."

Though she didn't move, the woman's eyes locked on Mariena's hand on her wrist. She would not look into Mariena's eyes.

"If you have a heart, help me."

The woman jerked free and stood. Stepping around, she opened the flap and spoke to the guard.

He came into the small area. There was barely enough room for him to stand upright. Glaring down at Mariena, he raised his arm and back-handed her.

The force of the blow flung her to the side, and she hit the ground.

When she rose up on her arms, she looked at the woman, still standing just inside the tent.

"Why?" Mariena cried.

The woman spat at her and ducked out.

Mariena lay back down, curling her legs to her chest, and gave herself over to her sorrow.

The horses stirred up a cloud of dust as the small contingency rode into town. It was still dark; the sun would not be up for another hour. But they could not wait.

Cutie pushed his horse even harder, taking the lead. He pointed the animal directly toward the jailhouse, slowing the mare only when they were within a few feet of the structure.

Jumping down, he flung the reins over a post there. He rushed up the couple of steps to the door.

And banged. Hard.

"Sheriff McAllen!"

He continued as the sounds of boots landing on the ground alerted him that the others dismounted.

"Sheriff!" he hollered.

He would wake this whole town if he had to.

The door opened, and one of the deputies stood, rubbing his eyes. Good thing the jail was under such vigilant watch.

"What's going on out here?" the man said gruffly. "You tryin' to wake the dead?"

"No," Cutie shot back. "Just you and Sheriff McAllen. Where is he?"

"What's this about?" The deputy leaned on the doorframe, hand on hip. Would he not give up the information they needed?

Cutie grabbed the man's collar. "About to get serious for you."

Brandon stepped up beside Cutie. "I'd tell him what he wants, Deputy. He's a bit...unstable right now." He grabbed for the Deputy's hand, which hovered over his pistol. "And I wouldn't turn this into a gun fight, if I were you."

The deputy let out an exasperated groan. "All right!"

Cutie did not release him.

"Sheriff McAllen is at the cafe."

"The cafe?" Brandon asked. "What's he doing there at this hour?"

"He's always there just before dawn. Likes to—"

Cutie dropped the deputy. "Let's go." He walked off the porch and toward the cafe. It sat several buildings down.

His breathing became more rapid with every step.

Brandon came up alongside him. "Maybe I should do the talking. You might be a bit too upset to—"

"I appreciate it, boss." Cutie held up a hand but didn't look at Brandon. "But this is *my* mess. I'll clean it up."

As they approached the cafe, they found that door locked as well.

"Maybe we should wait until they op—" Dan started.

Cutie knocked on their door.

"We're closed," came a masculine voice from within.

He wasn't about to be so easily put off. Cutie knocked louder.

"I said..." the voice started, but halted.

Seconds later, the door unlatched and opened. Lily appeared in the gap.

"Cutie?" Her surprise was written across her features.

"Lily?" Why did it have to be her? He had not quite settled things as he wanted to. But he had a mission. Shaking off this struggle, he said, "Sorry to disturb you. We're looking for Sheriff McAllen. His deputy told us he was here."

"Of course." She turned, opening the door further.

Cutie looked into the cafe. Sure enough, McAllen sat at one of the tables nearest the kitchen, sipping on coffee.

Lily led the group over to him. "Pa, got some folks here to see you."

"Thanks, Lily." McAllen stood, straightening his vest. "You get on back to work. I'll take care of these gentlemen."

She nodded and moved toward the back area, but halted. "Any you fellas want some coffee?"

They looked at one another and shook their heads.

"None for us," Cutie said. "But thanks."

She stepped through the door and disappeared.

McAllen remained on his feet. His eyes narrowed. "What can I do for you boys?"

"My wife has been taken by Apache," Cutie spilled out.

"Apache?" Why did the sheriff not seem so surprised?

"Yes. Her brother followed her out into the wilderness and came back telling that she was taken by a group of Apache." Brandon shouldered his way forward.

Sheriff McAllen lowered into his seat, pushing his arms out. His gaze was set on something in the distance. Was he still paying attention? "I can't imagine what you want *me* to do about it."

Cutie began to feel a bit uneasy about the sheriff's blasé attitude. "She's a citizen of Wharton City. We expect you to help us," he ground out.

Brandon interjected. "Do you know of any Apache villages near the city?"

McAllen leaned back in his seat. He seemed to be considering his next statement. And he kept his gaze on a spot far away. As if he were deep in thought.

But what was there to consider? Either he knew or he didn't. There couldn't be much question about whether or not he'd assist. Could there?

"Well?" Slim shot out.

McAllen sighed. His whole demeanor seemed to soften. "I know about a place they like to come to this time of year."

"Great! Then you won't mind taking us there." Cutie hit the table and turned to head back to the horses. They might not be too late!

Only...Sheriff McAllen didn't follow.

Why not?

He turned back to look at the man. "What are you waiting for?"

McAllen set eyes on Cutie at last. "I can tell you where the Indians are, but I don't think this is any of my affair."

Cutie crossed his arms. "Any of your affair?"

"Squabbles between the native groups are not under my jurisdiction." He seemed somewhat uncertain. Was he trying to convince himself?

"Between native groups...?" Slim's statement trailed off.

Cutie didn't understand. "You mean to tell me that a 'skirmish' between a whole village of Apache and my wife, married to a town citizen, an American citizen, is not under your purview?"

McAllen stared, but remained silent.

Brandon put a hand on Cutie's arm. "Let's take the information and go," he said low enough that the sheriff wouldn't hear. "You're not going to change his mind."

Cutie shook off Brandon and stepped forward. He leaned over the table, eyes boring into Sheriff McAllen.

The sheriff, for his part, did not flinch. Almost as if he dared Cutie to strike him.

"You're not worth it," Cutie said, shifting away.

Brandon stepped to McAllen. "Tell me what you know."

The sheriff relayed what information he had, but glared at Cutie the entire time.

As soon as Brandon had gotten enough to go on, he turned to Cutie. "Let's go."

Dan and Slim followed them out of the cafe.

Brandon spun before exiting. "The governor will hear about how well you care for the citizens of this town."

With that, the men were outside and soon on their horses. Once Cutie confirmed all were ready, they turned their mounts and headed out.

The sun had started to make its appearance over the top of the hills. Would they be too late?

CHAPTER 21

Uncertainty

Why would sleep not come? Was it her body that ached so? Or her mind that wouldn't stop?

Mariena opened her eyes and stared at the point where the tent supports met. Perhaps she could collapse the structure. What would that do? Probably only anger her captors.

Turning onto her side, she closed her eyes again. And saw Cutie's face. His brown eyes were bright and his smile was reflected there as well. Was that laughter for her? For some secret he did not wish to tell?

He reached for her, bidding her come to him. She held out her arms, longing with everything in her that he would receive her into his embrace.

Why had she pulled away from him? Why did she fight what she knew to be true?

All because of her stubbornness. Her determination to be right. To not be wounded more than she had been.

Yet he had not spoken wrongly about her.

For if she searched within, in those places that had been covered up, protected, she did believe. She always had.

How could she not? God was in the trees as the wind blew limbs to a rhythm as old as time. He was in the spring air, birds welcoming the first buds with their songs. And He was in this thing between her and Cutie.

She wanted to tell Cutie it had all been a mistake, a horrible misspeak. But as she opened her lips to say it, his visage turned and moved off.

"No, Cutie!" she cried.

He did not pause.

"Don't leave me." She shook as her body emptied itself of her grief once more.

And Cutie disappeared.

She was alone.

Would there be an end to her tears? She feared she would pour out her very soul upon this ground.

The flap opened. Two men and a woman entered. But this was not the same as the woman who tended her injuries.

The men pulled Mariena to her feet, forcing her to stand in front of the woman. But Mariena had weakened—from the emotional release or from her wounds, she did not know. Keeping her footing was difficult.

They stood her up, but her legs buckled beneath her and she fell, grinding her knees into the blankets.

Rough arms gripped her again and lifted. This time, they held her fast.

The woman stepped toward her. She looked Mariena over as one might a horse—picking up her hair and smelling it, turning Mariena's face this way and that, testing the firmness of her jaw and even pulling at her lip. Did she truly wish to see Mariena's teeth?

Mariena could not contain herself. She jerked away, tempted to spit at the woman. But she held back. That would only invite more pain upon herself.

As it was, the woman spoke in harsh words to the two men, and the one to the right jerked Mariena's face forward, his hand gripping her jaw. He squeezed the sides of her face while the woman looked at her exposed teeth.

What was this?

The woman said a word, and the man released her face.

Mariena's head dropped to her chest. How much more must she bear? When would they just finish with her so she might be at peace?

Curling a finger, the woman moved toward the flap. The men followed, pulling Mariena along.

As they stepped outside, Mariena's senses were assaulted by the sunlight.

What time of day was it? She longed to shield her eyes as she peered up. It was but midmorning.

Though they moved with some speed through the camp, she tried to take in what she could.

Many of the Apache standing around watched her pass by. Some spat in her direction. Some spoke curses at her. And not one offered any hint of kindness or sympathy. Not one.

How was that possible?

The men and woman didn't stop until they stood before the grandest of the structures in the camp. Was this the chief's home?

Dropping her to her knees, the men remained beside her as the woman entered the oversized tent.

Some moments passed before the woman emerged. And, with her, was a man great in stature and well into the prime of his life. His jaw was set, and he wore a large headdress.

He held himself well, shoulders back and chest puffed out. From all appearances, he had the authority and confidence of a great warrior.

How many of her people had he killed or seen killed? Even, perhaps, her own village?

Anger swelled within her, blossoming in her chest. But she kept it tempered. If she would take advantage of a single moment, she must choose it wisely.

The woman directed the chief's attention to where Mariena knelt.

As the chief approached, his brows rose. Was he pleased with his gift? Or appalled? Mariena could not discern.

He crouched in front of her, taking her chin in his fingers and forcing her to look at him. Letting go of her face, he ran a hand through her hair and down her braid, which couldn't have held much of her hair by now.

Standing, the chief looked to the woman. And nodded.

She pointed to the oversized tent from whence the chief had come.

The men on either side of Mariena grabbed her and dragged her within. Once inside, they threw her upon a pile of skins.

She turned to look at them. Might they help her? "Wait!" she called.

Neither hesitated. They continued until they were gone.

What would become of her?

A tear fell down the side of her face.

Lord, please spare me!

Cutie knew they had been running their horses as hard as they dared. But now, Brandon called a halt to their drive.

Why would he? They didn't have time to rest the horses. It could be too late as it was!

He turned his mount. "Can we not ride a bit farther? We are almost upon them."

Brandon leveled his gaze on Cutie. "And then have a handful dead horses."

Why must he always be right? Cutie gazed off in the direction they were headed. *I'm coming, Mariena. Just a few minutes more.*

Following Brandon's lead, he dropped to the ground and led the animal to the nearby stream. They were grateful to have found it.

"How much farther?" Cutie asked as he came alongside Brandon.

The man shook his head. "Not much. The camp should be just beyond that butte and to the left. See how this stream goes that way? The Apache likely rely on it being near their camp."

"Then why did we stop?" Cutie's urgency returned.

Brandon watched him. "I know you are eager. But we need to refresh the horses. Especially if we expect trouble. And we need a plan."

Cutie quieted. A plan? Were they not just thinking to take the Apache camp by surprise and grab Mariena?

"Do you have a plan?" Brandon's voice was softer.

Cutie kicked at a stone. "Not exactly."

Brandon nodded. "Didn't think so." Patting his horse's side, he seemed to think for a moment. "We need to know what we're dealing with. Send in a man to give us an idea of the size of the camp and the number of fighting men."

"That would be me." Cutie met his gaze.

"No, sir." Brandon shook his head. "Anyone but you."

Cutie wanted to argue, but it wouldn't do any good. The others would back Brandon up. Because he was right. Again.

But if...

"All right," he conceded. "Who do you think would go into such a situation?"

Brandon quirked a brow. Did he not trust that Cutie had truly backed off? "I thought Slim might be best."

Slim. What a choice! The man was...well, he was...probably the next best choice after Cutie.

So, he nodded. "You want to break it down for him, boss?"

Brandon handed his reins to Cutie. "Sure thing."

After Brandon walked away, Cutie's gaze followed the path of the stream. Should he? Dare he?

Making a show of walking his and Brandon's horses toward a tree, he waved back at the others. "Looks like a nice patch of grass over here."

They ignored him. Each caught in their own concerns—Brandon and Slim were now in conversation, and Dan had settled by the water to splash some on his face.

Once at the tree, Cutie wrapped Brandon's horse's reins around a branch. Then, watching the other men, he mounted without a word.

"I thought we agreed to let the horses rest," Dan called, now on his feet.

Brandon jerked his head in Cutie's direction. He seemed to know straight away what was happening. "Cutie! Don't!"

Digging his heels into the horse's flank, Cutie and his steed shot off, following upstream.

It wasn't long before he had left his compatriots behind for good and set his sights on the butte.

Moments later, he saw the tents in the distance. How was he to approach without being spotted? The Apache were numerous indeed. How, then, would he subdue them all? Even with Brandon, Slim, and Dan. Altogether, they were hopelessly outnumbered.

Perhaps he wouldn't worry with that.

Maybe one man could sneak into the camp much easier than a group. Perhaps even succeed at extracting Mariena.

Slowing as he reached the butte, he found a place to tie off his horse. There. Now he would be less conspicuous.

Creeping on foot, he approached the camp. The outskirts were easy to penetrate. Did the Apache rely on their isolated location to protect them?

Using the tents for shield, he maneuvered around them. At last, he found a woman moving through the camp. It wasn't as if he feared a man, but a fight at this point would only delay him and would likely draw undue attention.

Grabbing the maiden from behind, he held his gun to her side and his hand over her mouth.

Now who is the aggressor?

He pushed that thought from his mind.

What language did they speak? He wasn't sure. Was there any hope that this woman spoke English?

"Tohono O'odham?" he whispered in her ear.

She struggled against him, shaking her head. A lie perhaps.

Swallowing his distaste for his actions, he firmed his grip on the woman and spoke more harshly while pressing the gun deeper.

"Tohono O'odham!"

She pointed toward the center of the camp. "Chief." Was that the only word she knew in English? It was spoken well. Perhaps she did know more. But he wasn't willing to pry it out of her.

Keeping her in front of him, he moved in the direction she indicated.

A cluster of braves neared. He ducked into a tent at the last moment. The people were thicker here. This was becoming much more dangerous.

He looked at the maiden who had 'helped' him. Could he leave her here? Would she scream and give him away? It was too great a risk.

Scanning the tent, he grabbed a cord and tied her hands behind her and to her ankles. Then he used a strip of cloth to cover her mouth, careful that she could still breathe.

Peering out the flap, he stepped outside when the area seemed clear. He continued on his way, unbelieving how fortunate he was that the line to the chief's larger tent had been opened.

He looked back along his path. No, there weren't any Apache milling about anymore. Where had they all gone? It did not overly concern him. The only thing that mattered was getting to Mariena. And he had almost made it.

Stepping inside the oversized tent, he allowed his eyes to adjust to the dimness.

"Charles?" a voice, weak and hoarse, called.

"Mariena?" Was it truly his beloved?

"Charles!"

Movement in the corner drew his attention. There she was, huddled on a pallet of furs and skins.

He rushed to her, kneeling in front of her, aching to gather her in his arms. "Are you...hurt?"

She rose on her elbows, a hand reaching forth to touch his face. "Nothing that won't heal."

That was all he needed. He gathered her in his arms.

Her cries did not deter him, as he knew they were tears of happiness.

And he was overcome as well. Holding her close to his chest, he pressed kisses to her hair.

When her cries became whimpers, he grew concerned. Was she truly well? Something didn't feel right about her body.

Running hands over her back, he felt the bandage on her shoulder. "What happened?"

"Nothing to talk of now. We go." She pulled back far enough to find his eyes. "Please, let's go."

He nodded. Mariena was right. His miraculous movement through camp may not hold up. Especially not if the girl was found. Or if she freed herself.

"Can you walk?" He stood, lifting her with him.

She nodded, testing her feet as if she were unsure. "Yes."

He glanced around. What would be their best route out of here?

"You have knife?" she looked at the back of the tent.

"Yes." He handed it to her.

She held onto him and moved in that direction, stumbling along the way. But he held her upright.

Stabbing at the smooth skins, she pulled with what strength she had. They ripped, creating a slit all the way to the ground.

"Come." She gripped him and led him out of the tent.

As they stepped into the light, it became immediately apparent why his rescue had been so easy thus far.

Everywhere they looked, there were Apache braves staring at them.

Mariena gasped.

He pulled her behind himself.

She would go no further than his side.

"Get behind me," he muttered.

"No," she said through clenched teeth.

He only then saw bruises on her face and jaw. What had they done to her?

"We face them together." Her features were set, and her words determined.

He slid a hand into hers, intertwining their fingers.

The chief stepped forward, a menacing look on his face.

Thunder.

A great thunder.

And a massive cloud of dust.

Riders halted behind the line of braves.

But who? More Apache? Or had someone come to their rescue?

The Apache seemed uncertain as well. They looked around, seemingly unsure which way to turn.

As the dust settled, Cutie saw Brandon. With him were Slim and Dan. But also Sheriff McAllen and a score of deputies. Enough men to offer the Apache a good fight.

Mariena weakened, leaning heavily on him.

He lifted her into his arms.

"Chief Cocheta," Sheriff McAllen said, commanding the attention of all within earshot.

The chief faced him.

"I think we should sit down and have a chat."

"This not your place, Sheriff. This Tohono O'odham." He pointed at Mariena.

"I understand the confusion, Chief. And I apologize. This maiden," he said, indicating Mariena, "Is a citizen of Wharton City and is under my protection."

Chief Cocheta's brows furrowed.

"She is married to one of my ranch hands," Brandon offered. "That makes her part of our town. And part of my family." His eyes narrowed as he stared at the older man.

The chief glared at the line of deputies accompanying the sheriff and then at his braves. At last, he glanced at Mariena, now in Cutie's arms.

What would he decide? Would there be a great fight? Or peace?

Chief Cocheta lowered his head and crossed his arms. The braves laid down their weapons.

Then he turned to the sheriff. "Let us talk."

Cutie couldn't believe it. They were going home! He and Mariena were going home!

McAllen stood in front of the door he promised he'd not return to. Things were not as they were, though. *He* was different.

Taking in a breath and letting it out with slow, measured movement, he opened the door and stepped back through the house.

"Who is it?" the gruff voice called from within.

McAllen paused. "Walt."

Silence.

Was that an invitation? He best not wait to find out. This was his chance.

Moving to the bedroom door, he gently pushed it open.

The room was dark. Curtains had been drawn over the lone window, blocking what light could have come in. Why?

His father lay in the bed. And McAllen's heart dropped to see the once robust man but a shell of himself. Helpless. Ravaged by time and sickness.

"What do you want?" Pa's voice shook even as it was laced with anger.

"To tell you I was wrong."

"What?" The man's brows furrowed.

"I was wrong to let a wound tell me who I was. To affect the kind of father I am, the kind of husband I am, the kind of man I have been."

Pa attempted to sit up more, but his body struggled. "I don't understand what you are—"

"I would like your forgiveness, but I don't need it. I have forgiven myself. And I can live with the mistakes of my past. Let them serve as lessons, not barriers."

The older man looked at his son. His eyes glazed. "Is that so?"

"Yes." McAllen spoke with all the courage he had.

"Then maybe...you can forgive me." The man's hard exterior seemed to crumble and he fell back onto the pillows.

"Pa!" Was it the end?

A wrinkled hand rose. "I don't know that I deserve it...I certainly haven't earned it. But I, too, would like it all the same."

Now beside his father's bed, McAllen grasped the hand that had been the giver of so many things—both good and bad. "Of course, Pa. Of course."

Mariena stirred.

Please, God. Let it have been real.

She opened her eyes. Her husband's arms surrounded her from behind. The rhythm of his breathing comforted her.

Her eyes pooled.

How could she express her gratitude? They had been saved from certain demise. Who had been rescued from death more than she?

And then to be given a future alive with possibilities? It was too much.

Pressing her arms against Cutie's on her midsection, she wished for his hold to be even tighter. If only he would wake and oblige!

But even if he didn't, all was well.

Her eyes slid closed.

Cutie shifted.

Lips pressed to her neck. "Good morning, love."

"Morning." She turned to face him.

He smiled. The same smile she had seen in her vision of him. Only this version was not apt to vanish. Was it?

And she wondered, even if he did...would she be all right?

Would she survive?

In that deep place where her belief in God existed, she knew. Now it was her responsibility to let this place expand, grow, thrive.

But first, she must open up to her husband.

"Charles," she set her gaze on him.

He stilled, concerned suddenly. "Yes?"

Had she become so serious? "I must speak."

He nodded.

She took his hand and placed it over her heart. "I have found God."

His lips tipped upward.

"And He was here. Waiting for me."

He nodded then pulled her back into his embrace.

She wrapped her arms around him. "I want to find His path."

Cutie loosened his hold and set his forehead on hers. "We will. Together."

Epilogue

Cutie stepped into the house. Where could Mariena have gotten off to? Not that he had many places to look. Either she was with Cook or with Amanda.

He walked through the dining room and already could hear voices in the kitchen.

"Oh, I'm not quite sure you should be traveling!" Cook scolded.

"I am well."

"She is," Amanda insisted. "The sooner she goes, the sooner she can come back."

Cutie opened the door and popped his head into the space. "Am I interrupting?"

"We're just concerned." Cook frowned.

Coming up behind his wife, he set a hand on her swollen abdomen. "The doctor says we're fine to make the trip. We'll stop often and take breaks as Mariena needs them."

Amanda poked Cook's arm. "Did you hear that? Cutie is looking out for her." Then she turned to Cutie. "You know what a mother hen Cook can be."

Cook sniffed. "I'm not a mother hen. I'm just...well, ya'll mean an awful lot to this ole' bird."

The others laughed.

Mariena leaned in and encircled Cook in an embrace. "We will be back before you know."

"You best." She glared at Cutie.

"We'd better head out if we want to make it before dark." Cutie took Mariena's hand. "Especially with all those stops." He waggled his brows at Cook.

The older woman waved him off.

Amanda linked arms with Mariena and walked with her toward the front door. "You will write me, yes?"

"Of course. It will be good for my learn."

Cutie smiled. He and Mariena could not be more excited about what God had in store for them.

Brandon was beside their wagon before they were off the porch. "You got everything you need?" he asked, squinting in the early morning sun.

"If we don't, we've got everything but it." Cutie put his hands on his belt as he eyed the rather full cart. "We won't be gone so long."

Brandon nodded. "Don't rush back on our account. You learn all you need to about that school. You'll need it."

Mariena caught Cutie's gaze from across the side yard; her eyes gleamed.

"When do you expect to be in Tucson at the Indian School?"

Cutie barely caught Brandon's question, he had been so entranced in his wife's eyes. "Uh, tomorrow evening probably."

Brandon nodded. "It sure will be good to have you all trained up like to start an Indian School here."

Every time someone mentioned their plans to start a school for the Tohono O'odham in Wharton City, he was overcome. The reality of God's goodness and favor resting on him was amazing. How was it that God would trust him with this?

But he had learned...he did not have the credentials to judge God's choices.

"I guess you best be on your way, then." Brandon clapped Cutie on the back. "If you need anything...*anything*...you let us know."

Cutie nodded, shaking the man's hand.

Across the way, Mariena said her farewells to Nisto. She would miss her brother, but he would be well cared for at the ranch. It just didn't make sense to pull him out of school now that he had started.

Cutie gave them the space they needed. Some moments later, they moved toward him.

Nisto pulled away from Mariena and rushed to Cutie, almost knocking the wind out of him. But he embraced the boy all the same as a strange emptiness opened in his chest. He would miss Nisto.

As the moment passed, Nisto pulled back and walked toward the cart.

Cutie opened his arm for Mariena to step toward him.

They followed Nisto, speaking further final good-byes along the way.

Cutie helped Mariena into the front of the wagon before hopping up himself.

She turned to him with a smile that was for him alone. "Can you imagine this day has come?"

He shook his head. "God is good."

Taking his hand, she squeezed it.

He lifted the reins, winked and said, "Let's see where this path takes us."

Keep reading for a preview of the next book in the Convenient Risk Series!

Thank you, dear reader, for for reading along with me! If you enjoyed this story, I would sincerely appreciate if you would submit a review. It would mean so much to me!

To read more about these characters, follow along with the Convenient Risk Series. Find it at:

https://saraturnquist.com/convenient-risk-series/

Author's Note

Me again! As much as I absolutely adore my work with writing clean Historical Romance, I have quite the adventure myself with marrying my creativity with research. I make every attempt to take a real event from history and "marry" it to my fictional story, weaving the details together to an end product that has elements of both.

In *A Less Convenient Path*, we see a part of the plight of a desert Native American group, the Tohono O'odham. During the last half of the 1800s, they were found primarily in Northern Mexico and Southern Arizona.

Unfortunately, as was common during this time period, this nation, or the portion that wished to remain in the United States, was told they would need to move to a Reservation in San Xavier. So, the choice of all the Tohono O'odham tribes were either to go to the reservation or to relocate to Mexico.

What happened to Mariena's tribe (a tribe being but one segment of the whole nation of Tohono O'odham) is purely fictional. And, even as it was not my intention to write any Native American group as "vil-lianous," it is true that the Apache were the enemy of the Tohono O'odham and were known to be a warring nation. My effort here were to remain true to the history of both tribes and their interactions.

A CONVENIENT ESCAPE

Why should it be so bright and sunny on the day of a funeral? It didn't seem right. As if the world rejoiced with the sad soul's passing. Would the ground be so accepting of his remains? The thought was morbid. Even for one of Lily's darker moments.

She pushed it to the side. Not even her estranged grandfather deserved such tidings. Where was her respect for the dead? A shiver shook her body despite the sun's warmth bearing down upon her.

A quick glance at her father yielded no more certainty than she had received these last several days. The man's relationship with his own father had been a mystery. Why had she never known her grandfather? What kind of man was he? Her uncle spoke of the man rather well. But her father's features betrayed his feelings beyond a shadow of doubt—somewhat of a blessing, as he would not utter one word on the subject. At least, not to her.

Perhaps he had spoken to Joseph. Wouldn't her brother have told her? They shared everything. Or so she thought. Peering to her other side, she spied Joe. Though he was three years her junior, he stood a solid foot taller. Not that she minded. He had become her confidant and protector over these last few years when Ma's antics had...had become more difficult to bear.

She would have been lost without Joe. Somehow, he kept on smiling through it all. How did he do that?

He shot her a look. His gaze deepened and his hand covered hers.

She squeezed it.

A cough to the other side of Joe drew his attention.

Ma.

It became a coughing fit.

No. Not today.

Lily closed her eyes. *Dear Lord in heaven, not today.*

Joe released Lily's hand and drew Ma closer to his side as he pulled out his handkerchief. Perhaps no one would think any more on it. And Joe would keep her contained.

At least Lily could hope.

She chanced a glance at Pa.

He glared across his small family, as if daring any of them to step out of line and embarrass him. Tarnish the great image of Sheriff McAllen.

Lily shook, unable to control her body's reaction. She pulled her arms around herself and sniffled.

Pa's handkerchief appeared before her.

Without turning in his direction, she slid out a shaking hand to retrieve it.

How much longer must they remain here—a spectacle before the whole town? On display? Every movement, every sound scrutinized? It became more than her nerves could manage. A familiar unease pierced her beneath her ribs.

She tasted bile.

It would not happen. She would not let it.

Clenching her teeth, she swallowed against the pressure in her throat.

At last, the preacher finished speaking and stepped to the side.

What remained? The prayer? Had he prayed?

Not yet.

What was he waiting for?

Reverend Jones looked to them expectantly. To her.

There was something she was meant to do.

She sensed Pa's eyes boring into her.

God, if You have any mercy, enlighten me.

Joe laid a hand on her shoulder, rubbing his fingers there and pressing her forward.

Forward?

She stepped out from the line. Toward the grave.

Oh, yes. Her flower. She was to place it upon the coffin. Ma, too.

Glancing back over her shoulder, she reached for Ma's hand. Threading her trembling fingers through Ma's, she led the unsteady woman toward the pine box.

Ma's footfalls were not even. Lily prayed others wouldn't notice.

As they drew up to the coffin, Lily gulped. She had never been so close to a dead body. Nor had she ever wished to be.

Thankfully, the box had been closed and sealed. Not that she would have even recognized the man within had he been lain out as if in sleep. She had not known him in life.

It seemed wrong to playact this way—this pretense of sorrow, of grief. She forced her guilt to the side...as usual. And laid the rose upon the pine box's lid.

Ma followed suit.

Lily turned to step back into line, but Ma would not budge. Lily's stomach sank. They were so close.

If only she could beseech Joe. He would help her. But if she peered at him, everyone would see.

What was she to do?

Her whole body seemed to shake. She leaned closer to Ma. "It's time for us to step back," she whispered.

Ma continued to glare at the casket. Her eyes glazed, uncomprehending.

Lily closed her eyes and licked her lips. Then she tugged at her mother's arm again.

The woman would not move.

And then Lily was being pressed. Ma was pushing her.

Lily held tightly to her arm.

"No, Ma," she pled. "Not here."

Pa was behind them in a second. His arm around Ma, pulling her away from Lily.

But that didn't deter her from continuing to reach for her daughter, intent on inflicting some sort of harm.

Lily froze, aware that she had become the object of everyone's attention as Pa led Ma into the anonymity of the crowd.

But Joe's calming presence was there a moment later. He took her arm and led her back to their place.

Lily's aunt and cousins placed their flowers without incident. Then Reverend Jones stepped forward and spoke some closing words that Lily didn't hear. The pounding of her heartbeat in her ears was too loud.

Everyone around her bowed their heads. But Lily could not. Would not. She did not wish to speak to God on this or any other day.

Joe tugged at her sleeve. Had he noticed? But she refused to oblige him, continuing to stare straight ahead.

The prayer ended and the crowd dispersed.

Time to find Ma and Pa. Or was it?

Must they?

For nothing good awaited her there.

A handful of well-wishers approached her uncle and aunt, and all but ignored her and Joseph.

It stung, but she tried not to let it. There truly wasn't a relationship lost between her and the man buried this day.

As the churchyard emptied and the preacher said his personal farewells to the family, Joseph offered an arm to Lily.

She took it and let him lead her toward the small town streets. Would they seek out Pa? He had most likely taken Ma to the jail—the best and quickest place to get her out of view.

Lily did not wish to face either of them.

But Joseph was more the dutiful child than she.

As they walked, she tried not to slow their steps too noticeably. Still, she needed some extra moments to still her racing heart. How could it be so erratic?

But as they neared the main stretch, Joseph turned them toward the school.

Relief released some of the tension in her shoulders. And she fell into an easier pace with him.

Only then could she concentrate on his words.

He spoke of nothing of consequence—the weather, the happenings of the town. Benign topics that any passer-by would be able to overhear without concern.

As they neared the big tree beyond the school, he stopped. "Want to swing?"

She furrowed her brows. Swing? A woman her age didn't partake in such a girlish pastime.

"I'll push." He smiled.

She crossed her arms. "I don't know if that's entirely appropriate."

He laughed. "For a brother to push his sister?"

"For a grown woman to swing," she countered. Was he crazy?

Turning his head this way and that, he leaned toward her and lowered his voice. "Who's gonna know?"

She rolled her eyes.

"Come on, Lil. I know how much you used to love it." He grasped the rope on one side of the swing. "You know you want to."

He was right. She did. And there wasn't anyone around to wag their tongues about it. Maybe she could...

"All right." She threw up her hands.

His lips spread across his face. He maneuvered behind the wooden seat and held the ropes.

She turned and sat, clasping the ropes just above his handholds.

He lowered his hold and pulled the swing back. Then released it and sent her soaring.

And she left the earth. Everything...her troubles, her problems...all of it fell away, and it was just her. In the sky, the gentle breeze surrounding her as she moved back and forth in a steady rhythm.

She wasn't sure how long Joseph indulged her, but when she slowed, it was too soon. As he allowed her momentum to still, she was breathless from laughter.

"You don't smile enough." He held out a hand to help her up.

Grinning, she held onto the moment for every last sweet piece of joy it could give her. "I could say the same for you."

He ducked his head, looking to the ground.

"What?"

Shaking his head, he avoided her gaze.

"Joe." She pushed at his shoulder. "What are you hiding?" Though the mood was playful, dread crowded at the edge of her mind.

His smile fell. Things became more serious.

"Joseph?" What was wrong? Couldn't they share everything? Since they were young they'd often only had each other to lean on. What was this?

"It's probably time we head back." He tugged her hand onto his arm as he moved off in the direction they had come.

She pulled her hand from him. "Something's not right. Tell me."

He paused, looking at the ground and then at the horizon. Then at her. His one brow pressed down and the other lifted. Almost as if he were pained.

The trepidation from earlier returned. Her heartbeat thudded in her ears.

"I...um...took a job as a ranch hand at the Miller ranch."

The ground disappeared from beneath her. Or at least her knees wouldn't hold her anymore.

She gripped for his arms.

He steadied her.

They had always been there for one another. And now he was leaving her? To face them alone?

"What...?" The word sounded weak to her ears. Had it even been audible?

He eased her back onto the swing. And pushed a hand through his hair. "I'm sorry, Lil. I just...I can't do it anymore. I gotta get out and live my life."

Why couldn't she feel anything? Sad? Angry? Anything? All that existed was this numbness.

"I need you to understand that. Please, understand that."

"W-When will you go?" Somehow, she had made a full thought and formed a cogent question. Somehow.

"Monday." He let out a breath.

"Three days?" That wasn't much time. No time at all for her to get used to the idea. Much less prepare. Or…find a way out. No, that was impossible.

She was stuck in this nightmare.

And he was leaving her to face them…alone.

To read more, find *A Convenient Escape* here:

https://saraturnquist.com/a-convenient-escape/

A Less Convenient Path (Book 3)

She is in a hopeless situation. He doesn't have a chance.

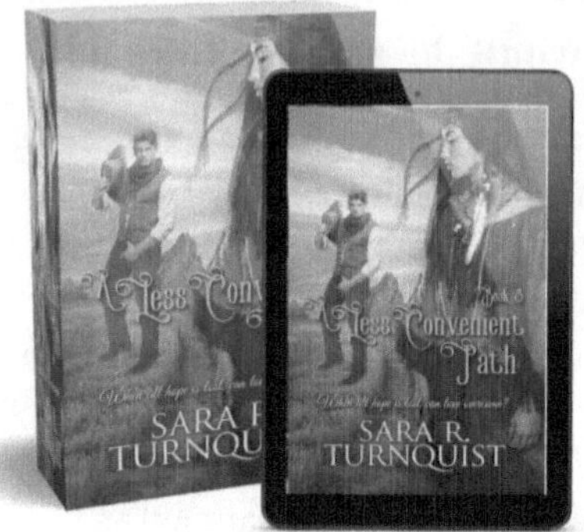

Mariena's native nation has been ordered to a Reservation but her tribe was attacked en route. She and her young brother wander in a wilderness filled with dangerous animals. Until...

Cutie happens upon them as he flees his own demons. Can Mariena awaken something he never expected? Even bring him to believe in himself once more?

A story of two people without peace. Will they find in each other the very things they are missing?

A Convenient Escape (Book 4)

She has nowhere to go. He has nothing to lose.

Lily has known hardship and rejection. Her brother takes a job at the Miller ranch. Now with no ally, she becomes desperate to get away...by any means necessary.

Dan is prepared to do whatever it takes to ensure Lily is cared for... even if that means proposing marriage.

Will they make it to the church? Or find themselves victims of lies, disillusionment, or the ire of an Apache rebel?

An Inconvenient Acquaintance (Book 5)

She wants adventure. He needs a place to belong.

Ada the new schoolteacher in Tombstone. Her desire for independence stems from tales of the west. But she never expected to find herself torn between two men—one who promises safety and security, the other's future is uncertain and offers excitement.

Slim is determined that he will not become involved with a woman of privilege, Ada's fiery personality intrigues him. And soon he is vying for her heart with a man he'd rather not trifle with.

Will they find what they seek in each other? Or will they become caught up in a shootout at the O.K. Corral?

These Golden Years (Book 6)

A collection of short stories through the year.

Dorothy "Cook" Miller and "Uncle" Owen Miller are living their best life and marriage. Though it is not without bumps along the way. Join them as they walk through the year together with its measure of mishaps and laughs. This collection of short stories shows that marriage can be fraught with misunderstanding. But also has its share of lighter moments.

An Less Convenient Arrangement (Book 7)

She has lost all hope. He has little desire to stay by her side.

Sadie finds herself in dire straits after her father absconds with everyone's money. Her mother's failing mental stability also becomes a trial she is not certain she can overcome. Is there anywhere she can turn?

Though his one goal is to return to Richmond and a partnership in his father's law firm, David is drawn to Sadie and softens to her plight. He offers what help he can, but resists being pulled into the mess that has become her life. Until he starts to care beyond that initial attraction.

Can she stand strong against the challenges facing her?
Will David risk following his heart regardless of the cost?
Or take the first out offered to him?

Ranch Hands Collection

Four Stories from the Miller Ranch

Acknowledgments

Why is it that something so important could be so hard to write? My journey is filled with people who have encouraged, supported, prayed for, and cheered me on. Without them, I wouldn't be who I am and I wouldn't be here for certain!

For everyone who has touched my life, I thank you for your influence. I wish I could thank each of you by name, but there just aren't enough pages.

For my ARC (Advanced Reader Copies) Team and my Launch Team, you are so good to let me try things out on you and bounce ideas off of you. I appreciate each of you!

Mary, who read this book and hounded me for more chapters, you are probably the reason I kept on schedule.

My editor, Julie Sherwood, you keep me in step, novel after novel. How you do it, I'll never know.

Cora Graphics, your artistry poured into the cover is nothing short of astounding! Thanks for sharing your talent.

VerBull Photography, thanks for getting my "good side" :-)

Word Weavers Page 13, my online critique group, you have helped me hone my pages and kept me challenged. I so enjoy sharing the craft of writing with you all!

My husband and number one fan, Greg Turnquist, thanks for making my writing time possible in a crazy house with so much going on. You are my best. Always.

For my sister, you make me want to be better. For my dad, you make me feel so good to have achieved this dream of writing. For my mom, I will love you forever. And for my kids, you give me every reason to smile.

Last, but certainly not least, my readers, you give me a reason to keep writing.

About the Author

Sara is a coffee lovin', word slinging, Historical Romance author whose super power is converting caffeine into novels. She loves those odd little tidbits of history that are stranger than fiction. That's what inspires her. Well, that and a good love story.

But of all the love stories she knows, hers is her favorite. She lives happily with her own Prince Charming and their gaggle of minions. Three to be exact. They sure know how to distract a writer! But, alas, the stories must be written, even if it must happen in the wee hours of the morning.

Sara is an avid reader and enjoys reading and writing clean Historical Romance when she's not traveling.

Please follow along with her journey through her newsletter at: http://saraturnquist.com/list

Happy Reading!

facebook.com/AuthorSaraRTurnquist

instagram.com/sararturnquist

x.com/sararturnquist

youtube.com/@SaraRTurnquist

pinterest.com/sararturnquist

Also by Sara R. Turnquist

CONVENIENT RISK SERIES

A Convenient Risk

An Inconvenient Christmas

A Less Convenient Path

A Convenient Escape

An Inconvenient Acquaintance

These Golden Years

A Less Convenient Arrangement

Ranch Hands Collection (ebook only)

CRIPPLE CREEK SERIES

Hope in Cripple Creek

Christmas in Cripple Creek

Faith in Cripple Creek

Love in Cripple Creek

~Prequels~

Leaving Waverly

Leaving Stoneybrook

LADY OF BOHEMIA SERIES

The Lady Bornekova

The Lady and the Hussites

The Lady and Her Champion

The Lady and Her Secret

RAILWAY ROMANCE SERIES

Laura, The Tycoon's Daughter